I0789022

Feargus

Judith Elliot McDonald

Aurora Books, an imprint of Eco-Justice Press, L.L.C.

Aurora Books
P.O. Box 5409 Eugene, OR 97405
www.ecojusticepress.com

Feargus
by Judith Elliot McDonald

Library of Congress Control Number: 2019938526
ISBN: 978-1-945432-31-6

— 8-2019 —

Feargus

Judith Elliot McDonald

Aurora
BOOKS

Aurora Books, an imprint of Eco-Justice Press, L.L.C.

Aurora Books
P.O. Box 5409 Eugene, OR 97405
www.ecojusticepress.com

Feargus
by Judith Elliot McDonald

Library of Congress Control Number: 2019938526
ISBN: 978-1-945432-31-6

— 8-2019 —

This is a work of fiction. Names, characters, businesses, animals, places, events, locales and incidents are either the products of the author's imagination or used in a fictitious manner. Any resemblance to actual persons, living or dead, or actual events is purely coincidental.

Acknowledgements

Many friends and professional associates contributed their knowledge, time, personal anecdotes, and tales of beloved dogs during the writing of this book. Thank you to the following:

Debbie Eversole, Sylvia and Larry Mangan for many personal stories of animal husbandry; Steve Allender, who put the first gun in my hand; Audrey Duke, FNP, for advice; and librarians at Oregon State University School of Veterinary Medicine.

My principal cheerleaders and readers Johnna Hickox, Kathy Walsh, Toni Kirkeby, Lowell Kobrin, Judy Brown, J. Cook, Larry Watson and Nikki Agee.

Much appreciation to my early development editors Aviva Layton of Los Angeles, and Sheila Ashdown of Portland. Line Editor Megan Willis of Los Angeles was also a great help on numerous occasions.

And to my lovely daughters Elissa and Lara, son-in-law Nate and light of my life granddaughter Elliot.

And thanks to Anthony Trollope who inspires my writing world.

This book is dedicated to the memory of
Johnna May Antonette Kahuaokalani Hickox
Booklover, dog lover, faithful reader, cheerleader, friend.
Aloha

Long ago, the Lenape' who lived in the east were many. Then, the old people would say,

"A person should not question or abuse dogs. Before a person comes to where Kishela'ma'kang the Creator lives, they will first have to cross a huge bridge.

"The bridge is at a fork in the road on the Milky Way in the sky. All the departed dogs guard this bridge. The Lenape' who live well walk the road beyond the bridge guarded by dogs. Those who live badly walk the other road, never stopping. That is why it is trodden down.

"No one who has done harm to a dog will be allowed to cross over to the other side."

The Grandfathers Speak: Native American
Folk Tales of the Lenape' People

Hitakonanu'laxk
Interlink Books, New York, 2012

1
Catalyst - 2004

I should have said no, that's all. No, I can't go to the humane society to look for a dog today, Ian. No. I'm not ready.

Not today, maybe not ever.

I have a history with dogs. Not a good one. The idea of a new dog terrifies me, fills me with an anxiety that presses in on my sternum. It shortens my breath and hisses in my ears like a hognose snake.

The subject of an adoption had come up between us, two or three times before now in the brief year and a half we had been together, but I hadn't been able to make my own personal point of view understood for a number of reasons. The whole subject caused me disquiet, and the thought of explaining so many long-repressed feelings always made me want to flee the room screaming.

Ian was a lifelong dog owner, and he had the sweet but, in my case at least, overly simplistic idea that any negative experiences in dog husbandry could be expunged by the love of the right dog. And perhaps he was right. But my dark history with dogs is anything but simple, and any kind of solution to my anxiety would need to be clever and forbearing.

Feargus

Right before I moved in, Ian had lost a very beloved pet in an unfortunate accident, a real pal is how he described him. He had been looking forward to this hunt for the perfect replacement rescue dog once he began to recover from that loss.

I was in the studio very early that sunny Saturday morning. I estimated that I had two or three hours of editing to do. I'm a writer and I was on a deadline, hoping to finish an edit and hit the 'send' button before noon.

I'd been at work for about a half hour when my kind, considerate partner came into the room with a large royal blue hand-thrown ceramic mug. It was one of the set of four he bought for me as a birthday surprise from my favorite potter at Saturday Market.

The mug was filled with some steaming fruity, robust Kenya Peaberry coffee.

"Maybe this will help. It's the Peaberry."

I held the large vessel carefully in both hands and sniffed.

"Oh, how special. I'm sure it will keep me going nicely. Thanks."

Ian loved this coffee, a rare bean which has a special unique flavor because it has not yet split in two at harvest, or perhaps it has split, I don't remember. I just know it was something complicated. He ordered it once a year from an importer in San Francisco, and drank it rarely and usually with some amount of ceremony.

We had been chatting for a few minutes, about my project, about the weather, and what we were having for dinner. Then he very innocently ventured a step into this worrisome subject.

"I thought maybe we could make the rounds of the animal shelters this afternoon, Tracy. I've been collecting all the things we'll need for a new dog, and we have just about everything, except the collar, of course. I'd like to start looking."

Ah, new relationships. We are both adult professionals, we've both been married before, and we both bring significant amounts of baggage into this house.

Sometimes the merger seems a little bit tentative, as if we're not quite sure how the other person will react to an idea or a question, so we back into it with humor or obvious caution. It feels at times like the air is just a little bit thin between us.

Perhaps most new relationships go through times like this, I'm not sure. We're each so highly conscious of the other person, their wants and needs, known likes and dislikes, that we fail the spontaneity test. I think we'd both like to be freer, more intrinsically joyful and lighthearted.

I thoroughly believed that this time would arrive. I could feel our trust deepening day by day, but it had not yet shown itself in its fullness, not quite yet.

There is no doubt at all, however, that I loved Ian with all my heart. Absolutely. I would hope that nothing would come between us. So I agreed to the hunt for the hound, unable to find any rational reason to say 'no.'

"Okay. Of course. I'll try to be finished here by noon. Are you running with John this morning?"

"Right, John and a couple of his graduate students. The River paths, I think. He and I are going to stop by Home Depot after. I can't stand that drip in the guest bath and John just likes to hang out there and compare all the barbecues and smokers. Then you and I can stop by the shelter if you're up to it."

My experienced fingers found my wicker coaster on the overcrowded desk and placed the coffee mug down with the knotty feelings of defeat and resignation deep in my heart. Come on, girl, I scolded my anxious self, put a smile on your face and do it.

This man had become my faithful partner. He shared my life. He needed to look for a dog, that was all there was to it. There had been a moment to equivocate, to say please, please, please I'm not ready, but there had been straw in my throat and the moment quickly passed. Of course I would go. Of course I would. I put my hand on his cheek.

"Sure."

"See you in a couple of hours."

He kissed my forehead, looked into my eyes for a second, and smiled his warm wonderful crinkly-eyed and charming smile. Then off he went.

When I heard the garage door close and the engine fade away, I got up from the desk and moved to the double doors which opened onto the little private patio off the studio. I sat down on the wide top step with an unstoppable sigh. It was clear to me that there were going to be highs and lows in this otherwise innocent endeavor, surely.

The studio, my writing room actually but that sounds so industrial and cell-like, was on the west side of the house which lay just at the edge of a patch of semi-urban Oregon forest. The small private patio which nestled adjacent to this room was laid with red brick in a crisp herringbone pattern.

Feargus

Chartreuse Irish moss filled in all the joints and junctures. Simple dense escalonia ringed the perimeter of the space. Three blooming magenta rhododendrons clustered against the east fence behind a couple of white Adirondack chairs. It was a small sliver of heaven, a brilliant extension of the room, and, as a rule, served as a peaceful haven for me. A place for contemplation and quiet.

The bricks were still damp from the previous night's rainfall, and they steamed their collected moisture up into the shafts of bright morning sunlight. The air was heavy with the rich earthy scent of fir and ferns and fungi that grow in abundance just beyond the fence.

I had been sitting there for quite some time, almost paralyzed, arms wrapped around my knees, cup of precious coffee gone cold, deadline surely missed, when I turned my gaze back into the room and my squinting eyes met those of the big brown dog in the green metal-framed photograph on the top shelf of my wall of bookcases.

Feargus.

The iron gates were being breached, I could feel their edges beginning to fracture. Bits and shards of memories, the joy, guilt, pain and sadness that I had buried for so long, they would all come gushing out like acidic chunks of projectile vomit spewing from my unprotected heart. They could not be ignored any longer.

I should have said "no."

2
Family - Fifteen Years Earlier

Everywhere there was moisture. The previous night's rains seeped, oozed off the moss-laced branches of the Alder and Red Cedar and Douglas-fir, like constant sweat from some giant, universal soaker hose.

The sun had now finally begun to peek its first scattershot rays over the high ridge, piercing and stabbing the hissing branches. It came blazing down, if just for a few hours, onto the fecund mid-summer subsistence garden, turning the vapor rising off the nearby East Fork into enveloping plumes of dense snaky mist.

Here, at the small homestead up the river, younger daughter Jennifer and son Matthew, along with Rob, the paterfamilias, were getting ready to go to town for the weekly roundup of bulk groceries and other non-subsistence necessities.

Five or six multi-colored push-pins had been stuck in a map of the Northwest when they made their decision, five years before this time, to settle here alongside this river, a good distance from the town. The push pins indicated a number of remote locations with basic services, good cheap land and a reasonably temperate climate.

There had previously been multiple attempts to find a niche, a homestead, a harmonious life – with different religious groups and in various states, but those situations always wound up betraying or disappointing this family in some way.

Feargus

They liked the location of this property on first sight and plunked down their small all-in nest egg to start anew. But all was not to be peace and dirt-under-the-fingernails serenity.

Earlier on this very morning, as their shopping lists were being prepared, there had been yet another domestic row. These sparring sessions, about one thing or another, were common. It didn't take much for the parents to put the gloves on.

This time it was a maternal warning about the possibility of giving in to spontaneity. Don't spend too much money, stick to the list of staples, no extras. Stick to the budget. Shop the sales. No Extras!

There were always attractive 'extras' at the big box store, and the mother, Nancy, understood the tantalizing pull of new toys of all kinds for each member of this shopping party. Her mission was to keep everybody in control and under budget. But she often despaired in her efforts. She just plain despaired on a fairly regular basis for any number of reasons. Each family member had learned to deal with it in his or her own way.

Thus, with requisite admonishment, the gatherers set off to town. Chastised by the strident lecture, the three headed off, playing word games and complicated numbers games to make the eighteen mile journey pass. Over the green Chandler vertical-lift bridge, and down the river to the Isthmus Slough Bridge and into the town they went.

Nobody who'd ever seen a pretty town could ever identify this town as such.

It was a square block town, hardscrabble and bramble-edged, a working town with all that suggests. Even in its long-past heyday as a finished lumber port, it still wasn't a pretty town.

Bars and brothels had dotted the block and stucco waterfront then. Unfortunately, the water itself was cut off from the society of the town by the single line of standard gauge four foot eight and a half inch width railroad tracks.

Since this little family of gatherers did not care that much for the style of the town or its architectural cohesiveness, the not very pretty town served its function.

But they would have agreed that it always seemed that the town had no 'there.' It was amorphous and uncentered. It was neither fish nor fowl, neither town nor mill. It was near the coast, but not on the coast. It neither prospered nor failed. It just was. And it suffered the fate of almost every other small mill town. Boom and bust. Cause and effect. Repeat.

It was bust time now, and almost all those buildings in the not very pretty town had had their original first floor facades ripped off and re-imagined multiple times over the years. The upper two or three floors of these buildings, however, were left to fend for themselves against the ravages of storm and wind and rain and deferred maintenance.

Those same vacant and windowless upper floors too often served as temporary homes for the seasonal transient and homeless men and women of the region, sheltering their bodies, if just for an hour or two, against the very same personal ravages of storm and wind and rain and deferred maintenance.

For this family's own reasons, and for better or worse, the pin in the map signaled that this was the place they had chosen to create a home. They were taking a huge chance on this little homestead up the east branch of a little river on the edge of the world.

In the town, there was a substantial middle level of commercial construction, interspersed between the flippant and cheeky fast food chain stores. These were the solid, cinder block, boring, square, and metal-clad or metal-roofed structures which provided commercial spaces of unrelieved and suffocating monotony.

Through such square block buildings on the south end of the town, our homesteading pilgrims wove their way until their errands were almost complete. There were just a few bulk items left to procure.

At last they arrived at the big-box grocery mart whereupon they parked their truck nose-in and came eye to eye with a man and a woman hovering over a pale blue laundry basket full of five or six squirming brown and black puppies presided over by a large rust and black exotic-looking mother dog, and where one particular puppy caught Jennifer's attention.

Feargus looked up from his wriggling or sleeping siblings.

Jennifer squealed Oh Dad, look! He's so cute, can we get him, please? Look at him. He's the most adorable puppy I've ever seen.

And adorable he was at nine or ten weeks. He was a brown fat thirteen-pound fur ball, more than adorable. But, and this was a large but, he was still an 'extra,' a canine adoption, still a commitment for the next twelve or fifteen years, a daily obligation for most of family, still a perceived unnecessary burden on the shoulders of the lady of the house. And, perhaps worst of all, he would be an unbudgeted expense!

The boy, the man and the girl looked at each other. They knew there would be hell to pay when they arrived at the homestead up the river. Nancy had already been ranting about even just a theoretical new expense before they left on their excursion. These three were definitely renegades and more impulse driven, so might this be the very sort of thing that she anticipated?

Even though the threat of domestic ire and ice was in the air, photographs of Feargus' disparate and unlikely set of parents and grandparents were cheerfully produced by the seller, and then reproduced on the color copy machine in the big box store, along with his veterinary records.

Rob and the woman negotiated a price, then a cardboard banana box was secured from the grocery side of the mega-mart. Puppy food, flea collar, flea shampoo, leash, and tons of sturdy new chew toys were all purchased.

Then, almost as an afterthought, the other things of a more immediate nature – those things which formed the purpose of the erstwhile shopping excursion, those things like large size containers of bleach and olive oil and toilet paper - were hurriedly procured, and the group headed, with a new family member, back out the east side of the less than pretty town toward home. The kids were excited and nervous, but ready to face whatever consequences were to be encountered there. Rob kept his thoughts to himself.

Feargus had, up to the moment of this adoption, spent very little time outside the confines of a laundry basket, a small back yard, and the vet's office so this trip to a new home was way more than he bargained for. He wanted out of the cardboard box that did not contain other warm napping or squiggling pups, and he didn't really quite understand the movement of the noisy vehicle.

The trip wasn't so bad in the beginning, out of the parking lot and back over the Isthmus Heights Bridge, around a few corners and then up straight and fast along the water's edge, headed toward the green Chandler Vertical Lift Bridge and over the South Fork of the river. Not so bad at all.

But then, after the nice straight stretch, the road sidles along the snaky Millicoma River, swerving left, then right, and then left again and again. Feargus' tummy didn't really feel quite right, and he was unfortunately sick all over himself in the back of the truck in between an excited Matthew and Jennifer, just an inch off the terry cloth towel that was supposed to keep him dry.

Eventually, after mucking about in his own little bit of throw-up, he braced himself as best he could and settled down for the rest of the ride.

The river bifurcates at the tiny hamlet of Allegany, and our destination homestead's branch heads to the northeast along the east fork of the Millicoma River. The road at first skirts the edges and then dives right into the lush and wondrous Elliott State Forest where the Standing Nation of Western Hemlock, Western Red Cedar, Big leaf Maple, Red Alder and Douglas-fir hold reign, dense and tall, connecting earth to sky in strength and rich diversity.

All the rest of us are interlopers in this ancient moss covered cathedral, and we should lay our footfall softly. This secondary road was deeply rutted and full of basketball size potholes, with treacherous muddy curves, soaked through and through with the late spring rains, and it had to be taken a little slower.

Amid thick, lush trunks of fir, with the rivulet frothing and cascading and galloping off the rocks, and overlooked by stands of great old growth trees, it was a tourist's and photographer's dream. But Feargus was queasy, anxious, and not planning a photo album of the trip. So, when he wondered, will it end?

While the children argued over a potential puppy name, vied for whose bed he would sleep in, and generally squealed with fear over how their mother would scream and rage, as all this was going on in the back seat, Rob spent the long slow drive along the beautiful river thinking deeply of another beloved dog.

That last family dog had been with them for many years. A shepherd mix, which means shepherd and part who knows what else, she had been brought into the family years ago by Rob when he married Nancy and came to live with her and her two older children. That animal became a trusted and reliable friend to the entire family for the ensuing twelve or thirteen years of her life.

As a gray muzzled fifteen-year-old living in a complicated family setting, she had equally contrary and mixed loyalties. She had gotten too old to herd, too tired to guard, and too exhausted to continue to be a peacemaker.

So, one late starry mid-July night, she laid her tired arthritic, body down, in a relatively comfortable rut on the furrowed road in the dark, where the maniacs driving pick-ups could not see her, and where she could sweetly rest her bones. And the maniacs did not see her or even sense her on that particular night.

Feargus

One maniac in particular, having finished off a six-pack with a friend, was driving up his road in his heavily financed midnight blue automatic 1989 Ford F150 diesel. It was a four wheel drive truck with custom 8" shackles and 49" military tires and with 2.5 ton Rockwell axles, and a triple rifle rack, two-thirds full.

He didn't see or even sense the old dog resting in the rutted road. He was driving at twice any sane accepted speed for a deeply pot-holed tertiary road. The truck's two right oversized tires hit her and she was gone in a second. She was home at last.

Rob pushed hard back at the rest of that memory. This was a new dog, a new day.

3

A Crack in the Armor

Fortunately, our first outing to visit to the Humane Society was unsuccessful. Fortunately for me, that is, but not for Ian. As we turned onto the long driveway and proceeded up the hill to the neat and compact shelter building, I thought that it felt odd that I had never been here before. I had made annual contributions, attended fund raising events, and drove by it a hundred times, but never actually got out of the car and went in to the facility.

The weekend volunteer who greeted us was a colleague of Ian's and they immediately began to chat about some administrative situation at the university.

A nice young woman staffer asked me if I wanted to wait in the cattery. The cattery. I learned that the dogs were in the kennels and the cats were in the cattery. This was a large open room with every imaginable cat toy and device, cube, hammock, and probably fifteen colorful, slinky, elegant cats playing and snoozing in all imaginable positions.

Along two sides of the room ran a series of tiny four foot by four foot glass-front rooms containing just two or three animals in each. These little quiet rooms were to house animals who are having difficulty adjusting to their altered situations. The whole place was so clean and soft, my first reaction was that it seemed like there was a cloud of estrogen in the room, even though there were equally male and female animals in the cattery that day.

Cats in groups give off an extremely female aura.

Ian popped his head in to apologize for keeping me waiting. Then the nice young woman took us out the back door to meet some dogs. The kennel had a very different sense and feel. It was much more masculine over there. First of all it was open to the air for about a foot where the walls met the roof.

On either side of a straight concrete slab were long rows of large clean metal cages, each with its own dog house toward the back outfitted with blanket and chew toys. Ian was disappointed that there were only a few dogs in the front cages, the ones closest to the entry door.

The staffer told us that a lot of lucky dogs went to new forever homes on Friday, yesterday. Fridays in general are popular days for adoptions, apparently.

Walking down the center path, I looked at the five dogs and was struck with a phrase, the origin of which I could not identify: We do not like to consider animals whom we have made our slaves as our equals.

I had no idea in the world where that idea came from or why it came into my head at that moment, but there it was. I asked to meet a blond Lab mix. He seemed to be about three years old. A dog this age and size would have made an excellent rescue for us, but it was clear he was not ready for rescuing. He resisted coming out of the cage, and he was skittish and eas-ily frightened when he was finally coerced out onto the concrete walkway. Neither Ian nor I could make a connection with him. He started to shake uncontrollably when Ian came near him. Hopefully this dog will soon meet the person who will recognize his particular pain and be open to dealing with it. And hopefully the dog will respond.

Next door to the Lab, Ian saw a funny young little bulldog that he liked, but he didn't think she was the dog for us. His one criterion was to have a dog that could go running with him, and those little legs would not be able to do that.

On this day the dogs that were available to adopt were all too big, too small, too old, or too young, too something, for our wants and needs.

There were some other dogs huddled at the back of the kennel. When I asked about them, I was told that these three were feral dogs that had been brought in early that morning. They had been trapped by the staff at dif-ferent locations around the county and they were now being quarantined.

I got just a bit closer and noticed that they sulked and snarled quite a lot, but, to me it seemed like it was just bravado, just posturing without any real menacing intent. The staff thought that all three of them had been 'on the road' for quite some time.

The staff planned to leave them together in the same cage for a few days. If they don't harm one another or act out too aggressively, then they would separate the little group into individual cages and do some testing to see if any of them could be rehabilitated and offered for open adoption.

The thing I remember most about them is their stony cold eyes. I was pretty sure there was no dog for us among that group. On the drive home, Ian finally, hesitatingly asked a question about my dog anxiety.

"I sense it's a kind of mysterious love/hate relationship. And possibly much more than that, but I don't know. Do you want to share some of it?

I sighed.

He smiled.

"You don't have to, Tracy. Don't let me push you."

"I will. Of course. It's time."

And so I would have to make myself ready, at last, to tell him some, at least, of my complicated history with dogs. I was a little, I mean a lot hesitant. I had no idea how far open the doors to this history were able to swing and if, given the necessity, that they could be closed up once again.

I don't know if it was funny or ironic, but there was a great brilliant mockery of implausibility in this attempt at a detailed confession. My anxiety reactions had been described by a number of friends, to some extent correctly, by saying that I simply did not 'care for' dogs. I did not care for dogs. They make me nervous. That could be right in a multitude of ways. I cannot deny that, but it is so much more.

I was never comfortable with dogs. Never liked the drooling the barking, the shedding, the expectations placed upon me by a dog's devotion, the necessary training, or the possibility of having my favorite Pikolino special-occasion boots destroyed while they were being turned into slimy chew toys.

Never liked the idea of the cold wet surprise discovered on the polished oak living room floor in the early morning semidarkness when I reached my hand down for the ironically named yoga posture 'downward facing dog.'

Then there is the odd licking of various parts of private anatomy, not just of a dog's own self, but of other dog beings as well at any time and in any company. Oh now, must you, dog? Here? Can you not see that I'm having a dinner party?!

Feargus

Before I met Feargus I thought that dogs were just a terrible complicated nuisance. My relationships with dogs were never these grand, loving, stick-tossing best friend situations.

They were far, very far from it.

Ian changed position in his seat and half-smiled.

"Do you know why you have these feelings?"

"Oh my goodness, yes."

"Let's have it."

I took a breath. Could any of this lifetime of complicated experience be explained? How much should I tell him? I took another deep breath. Would he over-analyze it, or would he toss it off as silly nonsense. We would just have to see. Another deep breath and I began.

I had inherited a completely irrational fear of dogs from my frequently irrational mother, bless her cynophobic heart, who would cross to the other side of the street if a dog was half a block away, and who would absolutely turn into an ashen inanimate gargoyle if a dog was loose and off-leash anywhere in her vicinity. That was my earliest introduction to canine interaction.

Mother hated cats as well, house cats, alley cats, Manx cats, leopards in the zoo, all cats, but not in the same way that she hated and exhibited her fear, her sphincter-clenching, molar grinding, fingernails-in-the-bloody-palms fear of dogs.

My six-years-older-than-I brother kinda, sorta liked cats, after his own dark, peculiar, primitive fashion. He would bring home unsuspecting neighborhood cats after school and chase them around the house with the big loud silver Hoover vacuum cleaner until one got so caught up in the blue and gold damask dining room draperies that our mother was sure to ask questions. He shut off the vacuum and let the cat go, laughing as it raced out the front door with fur standing on end, with a tail as rigid as the bell tower at Saint Mary's Church just down the alley and around the corner. It was probably time for big brother to graduate to some other amusements.

Over time there were other pets in my early childhood household. They were all hard won, and none terribly successful in this cold gray atmosphere of animal contempt. In our side yard once resided a stunted, decidedly handicapped yet gregarious white duck named Hopalong who was somehow perpetually undergrown and rakishly crooked as a result. There was also an obese white rabbit named Pinkerton who had occasional seizures and who would knock herself out in the narrow corridor between the storage bins and the brick outside wall of the kitchen.

The occasional garden snake was admitted to the home as well, but we didn't tell Mother about the snakes. We often lost track of them after a little while. I don't remember why that did not bother me.

As far as anyone who might be interested could tell, the cause of my mother's terrifying dog phobia was a well-kept secret. Any kind of light being shed on the subject might have helped mitigate the outright inheritance of the trait.

But no, Mother did not reveal her weaknesses to others, including family members, in understandable language. She veiled and secreted her heart. She spoke in parables and allegories. Yet, she still expected, even anticipated, comprehension and understanding.

It may be that I have inherited some of that behavior. I sometimes find that I am just a little bit out of myself, watching myself behave thus.

Unfortunately, I did not excel at exploring the dark depths of Mother's especially opaque and deliberately illucent mind, so I was cowed into silence, deluded by ignorance and left with the suspicion that all dogs were to be feared and reviled. This is how my life with dogs began.

Feargus

16

4
Trials

My admitted canine neurosis does not mean that I never personally owned a dog. I had, twice before the time of this telling. Neither situation turned out well. Even so, I must do my best to tell these stories as I remember them.

When I was a little girl of about eight or nine, there was Buffy.

Buffy was eight pounds of adorable, a darling little beige something, probably a Lab. My father proudly purchased him from a chain pet shop in the nearby shopping mall. We were urban Philadelphians. We didn't go out to the country or to other cities to some breeder. We got a nice clean puppy, who we tap tap-tapped at for attention through the solid pane window of the pet shop at the mall, and who came with all the right papers as well as a spurious 'guarantee' of satisfaction.

Money was exchanged, a cardboard carrier was purchased, and the precious cargo was driven home and placed on the living room floor where this new canine friend instantly went pee the second his feet touched the worn dark varnished oak. This was not an auspicious beginning, but nevertheless my father was excited.

We have a dog!

The rest of us looked at his excited and amazed face, and then we looked at the dog, then back at him.

Feargus

What were we supposed to do now? He certainly didn't have a clue.

As it turned out, we mostly just stared at the little guy, wanting him to be some sort of live action avatar to meld and coalesce this emotion-starved family. What an enormous burden for a sweet six-week-old puppy. Only then did we begin to sort out the chores and a feeding schedule and walking responsibilities. I don't remember that the concept of training, a training philosophy, or even a training routine were ever introduced.

In a couple of weeks, however, despite our highest hopes, best efforts and dearest desires, he died a horrible, lingering and completely avoidable death, with my Dad and I, hopeless and helpless in our horror and dismay.

My mother, however, remained upstairs for the worst of it, enjoying yet another good reason why she prayed the rosary on a daily basis to the unseen and unknown God Almighty, Son Jesus, and Holy Ghost. Piety would have its reward.

The veterinarian my father consulted, for more money than our GP would have charged for ten visits, said it was canine encephalitis and he did a spinal tap to confirm it. Too far gone was the verdict. We'll have to put him down.

What?? What are you saying?

My father, obviously not much of a pet expert, could just not quite fathom this idea. Put him down? What do you mean? We just got him, we just found out how to love him. No I can't do that to him. I can't kill him. Surely there must be another way?

The vet said that he was sorry as hell, but there was no choice. My poor tormented father said he still had to think about it, at least overnight. He just had to think, somewhere away from this office, somewhere private where he could weep, call on God for help, process the brutal reality of it, and try to move on. So the only advice we could get from the vet was to take him home and just keep him as comfortable as possible.

Distraught, meek and vulnerable as we were, we naturally got an absolute, unequivocal counter-slamming denial of culpability from the lying apron-wearing, pet shop franchisee.

We confused and lost new canine parents just threw up our hands in ignorance and dismay and hoped, prayed for the best, or for some miracle which would make the situation less horrifying than it so obviously was.

So, at home, little Buffy lay on his side, quite uncomfortably, for another day and a half, on a cotton blanket on the old dark red brick floor in the covered shed of the back yard while his spinal cord disintegrated into jelly and his hind legs no longer worked and the flies buzzed around his uncontrolled anus and his wet pathetic please-make-it-stop eyes.

Eventually my father couldn't tolerate the pain any longer, his own or the dog's, and tearfully decided that this would be the day he would take the badly damaged puppy in to be 'put down' by the vet.

I went off to school that last day with those profound visceral images of the suffering puppy pressed into my brain's pre-frontal lobe. I tried to sit in class, on the far left side of the room, against the giant windows of the old building, hopefully out of harm's way, and tried to be a good little Catholic school student.

Sister Mary Stephen, apparently holding some long-standing grudge against god and parents and the school administration, knew I was distressed and in tears, although she never asked why, and locked me in the coat closet while she lectured the other fourth graders, within my hearing, about the depravity of admitting certain precocious and privileged children to first grade at age five, even if they can read at a second grade level, and can add however many numbers, because they are just not emotionally ready for the rigors of academia and my God, it will show at some point, maybe years later, but it will show, as God is my witness.

My puppy's dying.

Did anyone care? Other than my father, I don't think anyone did care.

That was my first experience with dogs. And for better or for worse, it is laid down like a guide track in the soundtrack of my existence.

The memory is crystal clear and the impact from that memory has left a bruised and aching indentation where the joyful first puppy experience should have been.

Ian and I had reached home and were now sitting at the kitchen island with a glass of chardonnay. Ian touched my hand.

"It's good, Tracy, its good. Keep going."

"Spoken like a psychologist."

"Yes, of course, but your history is telling me how I might be able to help make this next dog experience an easier one. Just one question, though. When is the last time you told someone this story, a friend or a therapist?"

"This is the first time I have shared it with anyone, I believe."

"Oh. Interesting, because that's enough unaddressed early childhood trauma for several lifetimes. Please go ahead if you want to."

I did continue, because I had one more dog ownership story to unload on this unsuspecting man.

Feargus

Growing into adulthood, I never even considered another attempt at dog ownership until almost two decades later. Life by then was considerably different. There were so many high hopes, so much investment, so much naiveté, so much trust involved with this next dog.

By this time I was no longer a child but an adult with children of my own, living on a high dusty wind-blown military base in the New Mexico desert.

In this second relationship was with a live-in canine named Torbjorn. I had been well acquainted with Torbjorn's father, who was the steadfast companion to a flight surgeon colleague and he was a prince of a dog, really. Actually I think if I remember correctly, his name was Prince.

Regal and restrained, Prince seemed to make every move an exercise in studied composure. We admired this dog. We got to know him well and the time we spent with him was quite remarkable. He was truly an exceptional dog.

After much pleading and cajoling, his owner, our friend, was finally convinced that we should become the proud owners of one of Prince's pups. Unfortunately, there is no accounting for the vagaries of genetic predisposition.

Torbjorn was trouble from the beginning. He wasn't at all like his father, like Prince. He was sly and sneaky and cold, always one step ahead of you, ready and able to show you as much disdain as the canine world can offer. He had ice in his Nordic veins, much to our great surprise and sadness.

Being in the same room with Torbjorn was as close to training and I was going to get. I not only had no idea how to go about training a large willful dog, but I also had this grand disinclination to do so. Without an alpha in the house because of our crazy and unpredictable work schedules, he made it quite clear that he was the boss.

I would go to the front door and call him as he sat auditing the neighborhood from the bit of lawn in front of the circular driveway. He would get up from his sitting position, stare directly at me for about five seconds, and then he would turn his back to me and sit down again in the opposite direction. Yes, this is the pet I want.

This behavior went on for some months, even after we moved to the Pacific Northwest and a whole new environment.

Torbjorn got pissed one night, for no apparent reason, and decided to swat my then eighteen-month-old baby across the face as she sat in her high chair, probably because she wouldn't relinquish a piece of her slobbery toast.

Punishment seemed the likeliest reaction to this frightening event. So punished he was.

Hit, if I remember correctly, and screamed at definitely.

The very next night, same time, and again with no provocation, he jumped at the face of my four-year-old and punctured her right upper lip with his right canine. By this time the dog weighed a good fifty-five pounds and the image of his big face and huge jaw lunging at her face was horrifying to child and parent alike.

Hysteria and furor reigned down upon the unsuspecting dog, like a fiery tempest from Hades. He was hurtled down the stairs to be chained in a cold dark back room in the basement until some disposition, any disposition could be made. On the next day he would be gone and dogs would be banished from that household forever.

That next misty gray morning he was roughly, and with extreme prejudice, I must confess, handed over to a local hobby rancher who lived out of town, and banished to the far corners of the county where he would eventually learn to work for a living among hard-working humans, a flock of giddy errant sheep, and a half dozen brown cows. He hardly waved a surly bye-bye as he departed.

I swore in my heart to remain dogless for eternity at this point. My short unhappy history with animals in general and dogs in particular did not necessarily bode well for the future.

I paused in my story of Torbjorn and exhaled a long sigh. We'd been sitting for quite some time. Some ethereal spigot had been opened, but I felt like I had to close it down right now. I couldn't go on. I shouldn't go on.

"I need to stop."

"That's fine. But so far you haven't told me anything about your relationship with Feargus."

"We'll have to save Feargus for another time."

"That's fine. How do you feel about going back to the shelter next weekend?"

"Do you think all the malignant spirits have been freed? Am I cured?"

"Oh not quite yet, I'm pretty sure of that. What do you think?"

Ian teaches Psychology. We try not to let it get in our way.

"Next weekend. Of course we can go back."

In some place deep in my hardwiring, possibly somewhere in the center of my amygdala, I was already starting to anticipate our next trip to the shelter with anxiety.

But today, today I went. I went to the shelter and looked at dogs. I thought that was a good beginning.

5

Who is this Feargus?

Feargus understood absolutely nothing about the basic idea of a 'new home.' He could not conceive that this idea might be fraught with questions and unseen dangers. He was on a road to who knows where. 'Curved, muddy, deeply rutted and treacherous' feels like an ominous beginning for an arrival at a new home and a new commitment, but Feargus had a big, brave heart and could face anything that came his way.

He also had a cool temper and unsullied memories of the few kindly humans he had known. This left him open and unguarded as he stepped, or rather was carried, into this next phase of his life. He wagged a slow, half-mast tail, which, despite his normally rambunctious optimism, showed his unusual tentativeness and insecurity.

He was quickly cleaned up and surreptitiously whispered into the house, then into the family room, in the arms of a human on tiptoe, who was herself not immune to trembling trepidation at this moment.

The house was quiet.

In a few minutes, the wood-frame back porch screen door squeaked open and the tight newly-installed replacement metal spring snapped it shut with a slam, at which sound Feargus gave out two startled involuntary high-pitched puppy yelps.

Silence once again.

Feargus

Matthew grabbed the puppy's muzzle, pleading with silent eyes, no, please, be quiet, oh please. But it was too late. The yelp had been carried on the air like an evacuation siren in the murky darkness.

The mother, Nancy, raised her chin to listening level, cocked her head slightly to the side, then quietly and methodically placed a handful of dirt-covered carrots and a head of butter lettuce on the counter.

She slowly and very deliberately took off the sun hat, untied and folded the red, white and green striped apron and placed it carefully next to the hat, rinsed off and deliberately dried her hands, set her stainless steel water bottle in the sink, then took three carefully measured steps around the kitchen wall divider where she came upon two guilty-looking and uncomfortable adolescents and one gloating and smirking adult. She also found herself staring into the huge shining black eyes of one adorable round brown and black puppy.

The ensuing rant was unpleasant to be sure, with flailing arms and red cheeks and not so very veiled threats. Nancy wagged her finger in the faces of the children and stomped her feet. There was some screaming involved, mostly about another mouth to feed, the lack of order already in the house, the plain stupidity of another wild creature to train, for god's sake. It was partially a replay of the lecture given before the trip began, but in a higher tone and a more fevered pitch and dramatic attitude, and offered up, this time, to three sets of guilty but deafened and defiant ears. Most of this latter part seemed to be obliquely directed at Rob, who sat back in his recliner and continued to smirk without a verbal reaction.

Feargus would never be fond of these new high-pitched screaming sounds and, when they started he would sit in the far corner of his box with his head and his tail tucked under him. The big gruff man seemed a little bit like the big man in his first home. He would have to wait and see if there were other similarities. The young girl seemed nice but very excitable. The young boy was more solid, and Feargus liked his energy. He didn't know what to think about this new family.

Nancy would always be willing to let it be known that she neither wanted nor cared for Feargus, probably because she had no say in his purchase. On many occasions, she would make him the brunt, the scapegoat for any and all of the myriad problems that faced the family. He did this, he did that, he was evil incarnate. At this moment, however, the dad and the two younger kids had already bonded with the brown bundle and it was too late to do anything about it.

Bit by bit, as he grew and learned things, Feargus was allowed to experience his surroundings. Rob kept a tight rein on the training, and nobody in this rigid family constellation dared to cross him, even though his 'training methods' quite often seemed harsh and maybe even cruel, especially with a dog that obviously wanted so very much to please, and who had enough able and plastic intelligence to make him capable of meeting almost any human demands.

Feargus recognized that this human was the one whose ideas mattered most.

As a very young dog he would be told to sit and be still as different plates of food morsels were placed quite close to him. He was not allowed to react to the food until he was given the sign to eat.

This kind of training might be fine, it might actually be beneficial, in a group or pack situation, or with incorrigibly bad-tempered dogs, but it seemed a bit much for such a nice, respectful family dog, who never gave any other indication than that he just wanted to please and be accepted, and who had enough innate grace not to need such heavy-handed, abusive treatment. Animals often have more grace than their human overseers. A dog with the size, strength and canny intelligence of an adult Feargus had the capacity to rule the household, but instead he chose to do what was asked of him and to do it with a kind of manly grace.

This gangly puppy would grow up to be a very handsome dog – handsome, strong, healthy, stately, aloof, wary and devoted. With an interesting genetic mix of previously purebred material, he might have just been called a mutt in this current incarnation. But that was only if you didn't know him. You would not, could not, even think to call him a mutt to his face. Later, as an adult, he was regal, composed and majestic, and those descriptions would fall easily from your mouth.

Perhaps we should take a careful look at his intriguing background.

On Feargus' mother's side, his genes were a study in contrasts. Chow and Doberman.

His full thick rich rust-colored coat, his blue-dotted tongue, his powerful and sturdy chest, his dignity, his strong, sound legs, and his independence and stubbornness were inherited from his round, emphatic Chow grandmother, along with his loyalty, his aloof snobbishness and self-governing nature.

Feargus

His proud neck, long limbs, gracefully pointed black tipped feet, his energy and eagerness to learn new things, his intense bonding, loyalty and fearlessness could all be attributed to the elegant Doberman other half of that maternal liaison.

Feargus' father's side was a genetic extravagance. Labrador and Timber Wolf.

Patience and stability, along with occasional goofiness, abundant energy, a wide jaw, large nostrils and a sweet predictable immaturity came from his Labrador grandfather. That happy slightly goofy and otherwise unremarkable grandsire Labrador had been mated with a silvered semi-domesticated Timber Wolf.

From his Timber Wolf grandmother of ancient genetic soup came a quiet, regal, intelligent, almost stoic and calculating reticence. She also passed on a slim torso, large teeth, high stamina, a keen and watchful intellect, and a perfectly symmetrical and beautiful face.

Like Feargus' other grandmother the Chow, this grand dame was not and never would be a pet, but would always be an equal. She did not make easy friendships and she did not suffer fools. These particular characteristics were most definitely inherited by our Feargus. He would be devoted and watchful but he would always be slow to consider you a friend, wary of the obligation of friendship and forever his own man. Once he allowed you into his heart, however, you would be there for all time.

He was a product of this exotic genetic mélange, Chow, Doberman, Labrador and Timber Wolf, and he did his best to be true to it all.

Once in a while, although rarely, Feargus could be quick to accept new people. It was probably just something in their aura, their vibe, their smell that made him an immediate friend, at least until he was proven wrong.

With people in general, he was cool, observing and aloof. He had this intrinsic ability to weed out the chaff of humanity and home in on those characteristics that meant something to him personally. He had some basic awareness of human traits like honesty, kindness, selflessness and understanding. Beyond that, his awareness was limited to sensing passivity and aggression, and he chose between humans with those traits on a very basic level.

In people, Feargus looked for a kind of cross-species accord, and he found it frequently throughout his life, not always in the form of his owner, but often in the immediate vicinity of the owner. Those relationships that he considered permanent were just that, 'till death do us part.' He picked and chose among those relationships warily, but remained open to all possibilities.

His soul was as old as forever. You could never doubt that. You might often find him, over his lifetime and in various locations, sitting quiet and alone outside on a clear moon-filled evening, on some deck or some far-flung lawn, just placidly listening to the many sounds of his world and staring up knowingly at the twinkling unknowable stars.

Feargus

28

6

Friends

A pair of milking goats would play a significant role in his life. Feargus was soon allowed access to the back yard and other areas beyond, specifically to the shed in which dwelt three lovely and friendly goats. One of this trio was a sweet mild-mannered pure white, straight-faced kindly Saanen, who nuzzled and licked the little guy as if he were her own child.

This sweet girl was our dear Bernadette, big, gentle, calm, and a great milker. She had been with this family for two years, a gift from a neighbor family moving away to the city. Goats belong to the family in toto, not just to their mates. Bernadette and her open heart felt strongly for this new canine family member, and she was willing to welcome him to the best of her ability. This was a strange household, and this sensitive goat knew he would have to weather some unpredictable human behavior if he was to survive and be even reasonably happy. Goats can be this wise and thoughtful, it is said. She smiled on Feargus, and he responded with a knowing canine smile, and by presenting his elongated neck close to her pure white face for licking. They formed an immediate bond that would remain unbreakable to the end.

Bernadette's steadfast caprine companion was a large, sleek, and graceful Nubian dairy goat named Annie who was a great, fleshy girl with long, pendulous ears, a slightly Roman face, a secure butterfat content of twelve percent, and the most flavorful milk to be had anywhere in the county. She had some gray shading under her eyes and down her face as if her mascara had run in the rain.

Annie had been purchased from a breeder at the local county fair. She was chatty and curious and most definitely not meant to be sheltered in an unsecured enclosure. An escape artist at heart, she could find her way out of almost any pen. Multiple alterations had to be made in fencing and gates for her protection.

There was also a stocky, short-legged quiet and gentle South African Boer, a chunky pleasant meat goat on whom we will not bestow a name, or describe in any kind of detail, or imbue with any sort of anthropomorphic attributes because we know that her fate is not that of the happy long-lived dairy goat, but rather that fate which is the result of expedience and a freshly stropped cold-steel knife which would keenly slit her jugular just behind her beard while her trusting head rested unaware on Rob's knee, as he crooned sweet and loving nothings in her ear and stroked her innocent and unsuspecting flank.

Feargus was a happy if cautious lad. He quietly grew into this new world of family and goats and chickens and cats, of vegetable gardens, swift rushing water, slick mossy fallen tree trunks, strange little forest animals, and other perils and pleasures of the world which lay here, so very far beyond his mother's musky milky smell, his snoring siblings and a blue plastic mesh laundry basket.

Always cautious and reticent, always watching, he was easily and eagerly trained, and he did not dare to tempt the forces at play in the human world. There had been times, like the one when he chased a mouse through the middle of the flower garden, prized dahlia stems cracking and toppling like dominoes, peonies and pansies and primroses uprooted and crushed, when all was not peace and love, but those times were rare, and he learned quickly what mattered to the lady of the house, and to the others, and how to best maneuver through the various minefields in his complicated life.

Feargus was not without friends in his environment. Argyle was a slinky, sly five-year-old shorthaired white and flame-tipped part Siamese, and he was forever good-naturedly pouncing on Feargus from bookshelves or tree stumps or rafters in the hen house. He did little damage to the dog because his front and rear claws had been removed three years before at Rob's insistence as a condition of any kind of cat presence in the house.

Rob hated cats. With venom. Heather, the older girl, dearly wanted a cat.

After much negotiation, and with promises by all the kids to do extra chores and to pay vet bills with their own hard-earned money, an agreement was encompassed and a cat procured and declawed against the recommendation of the vet, the neighbors, and all other rational individuals who understood that 'declawing' meant the equivalent of taking off the end of every finger up to the first joint in a human and rendering the animal unable to defend itself. But Rob insisted. No claws or no cat.

Feargus sat and watched Argyle. Had Feargus the ability to abide in a state of consciousness even just a tiny bit higher than that which he was given, he might have been awestruck at the remarkable adaptive plasticity exhibited by this nimble cat. As it was, he just looked on with curiosity and wonder as he watched the cat bring down any number of brown-backed juncos with his clawless feet, in a highly choreographed aerial ballet worthy of a feline Bolshoi Ballet.

Argyle would sit very, very still for a long period of time. He had to exert great effort to have mastery over his active tail. The flocklet of juncos hardly noticed him. Then he would inch forward and hold again. Finally he would single out one bird and, dispensing with the standard feline rear-end wiggle before an attack which might have attracted attention, he would spring six, seven, ten feet into the air in a four-legged grand jete', clasp the designated bird firmly between his two clawless front paws and bring it down to earth in his mouth.

Feargus liked this cat with the orange ears, and he liked the goats. He even liked the chickens. He could be seen quite often on the back porch afternoons in the late summer sun with four or five happy Rhode Island Red hens walking up and down on his chest and abdomen, using him for hill-climbing exercise, with the other chickens generally aflock about him. At these times he lay immobile with his eyes closed and his ears twitching. Four new California White chickens were purchased from the grange and introduced to the farmlet when our subject dog was about ten or eleven months old. Two of the four were obviously dog-averse and hopped and fluttered and bawked a throaty squawk every time Feargus came near the hen house. There was something in that bawk and that flutter which spoke directly to some ancestral brain cells in Feargus' head, brain cells which might have come from any or all of his progenitors.

On a misty Sunday morning when the dutiful if affected and sanctimonious family members were away at church in the town, said family became the possessors of one less plump California White pullet.

Feargus

This interesting fact was conveyed to them wordlessly as they disembarked at the driveway, where they were greeted by a happy, proud, excited and white feather-covered guard dog, animated, elated and ready for more play. They also encountered a nasty mess in the coop and some very skittish birds.

Gates would now have to be closed and chickens would need to be secured. Feargus had shown a new, surprising side of himself, and the complexion of the relationship of pet to family had changed.

Reactions ranged from horror to awareness. A new respect for this thoroughly true to himself canine was engendered in this family. As much as he was willing and able to obey and follow the lead of his humans, so was he, on occasion, equally responsive to and at peace with his true and basic nature.

He was finding his place, his time, his home. Unlike the poor bony perpetually feral cur that has no home, that forages and frets his days in shadows and sleeps his nights in fear and disquiet, that finds his way warily, alone and without ease, Feargus, on the other hand, in one year's time, had got a place, and a family. He was secure. He was welcome. He was home.

Not all canines were so fortunate. At this very moment, not far away, maybe fifteen miles or so as the crow flies, from the warm, soft and dry spot where Feargus lay his head this night, several abused and malcontented domesticated dogs were considering what might be their fate on the other side of their respective fences or enclosures.

7
Mischief

They were just thugs, really, a discrepant band of misfits and malcontents, awash in their own discord and alive to the possibility of mischief. They were common, ordinary delinquents, who recently discovered each other less than twenty miles or so to the west of the cozy farmlet where Feargus was busy chasing butterflies in the sun.

Perhaps it might be more correct to say that these five dogs dissolved into each other rather than discovered each other.

It was an odd coming together at a grunge-encrusted dumpster behind the grange just south of town. After hours this poor dumpster became a magnet for all the detritus from the neglected neighborhood which included the nearby trailer encampment and sundry vacant and decrepit buildings.

The first to arrive was Nacho.

Nacho was most recently living in her third 'forever' home. She'd struck out twice before with two hopelessly good-hearted but equally ill equipped and unprepared families. Both had good intentions to be sure, but they lacked the will and imagination, or just plain good sense, to manage such a spirited dog.

She had spent the six months before that third adoption in foster care, behaving herself and waiting. Then she was offered this new opportunity for the possibility of her next 'forever' home.

Feargus

On the look of it, Nacho thought this would be a seemingly comfortable existence with regular high quality meals, a clean soft bed for sleep, a mountain of chew toys, and two humans available for interaction for an hour or two a day and a few more hours on weekends.

Poor girl, her uncontrolled terrier-herding mix impulses made her almost unfit for a calm family life with two working adults who didn't understand what "appropriate for your lifestyle" in the humane society booklet meant, and with a yard that was way too small for her incessant circling.

Nacho had one and only one objective in her life. She wanted work, good solid work. She was not attracted to the lazy life of a lap dog, especially not for two perpetually stressed out and chronically exhausted humans who supposed that she would be the perfect companion for the one hour a day they had in their schedules for nuzzling with a fur-covered warm blooded dependent.

This was expecting too much of her. She wanted to manage a family and other pets and the neighbors' pets and the neighbors' kids, and get them all organized and straight, with her as the leader, in command, the good little maestro.

Every day, as she circled her little enclosure, she thought about that other world, the one outside. She would love to be able to follow the enticing and diverse smells she picked up with her refined and capable nose, those smells that came at her from every direction and that would waft temptingly on the double-time late-summer coastal winds into her little square patch of yard.

She would often stand perfectly still with her eyes closed and her nose just aquiver, imagining what was on the other end of that thread of scent that had just reached her. She wanted to make use of her rambunctious curiosity, chase those smells down and deal with them, understand them and make them fit into her world.

It was so hard for her to have absolutely nothing to do, and to have absolutely nothing expected of her, every long day, day after day. Left to her own devices, and without an objective or an ambition, she would surely get into some sort of mischief.

She finally discovered an opportunity for freedom from this boring yet anxiety-provoking existence.

After she had dug her way around most of the perimeter of the tiny yard, and tried to jump the fence, slamming into it so often that her ribs ached and her body was bruised and sore, she finally hit pay dirt at a cracked board in the ancient silvered cedar wall.

She chewed and clawed at this potential opening until her paws and her muzzle both bled. When she finally broke through a small space through which she could squeeze her battered body, she didn't wait for further bonding opportunities with this couple, but opted out for greener pastures, see yah, sayonara, I'm outta here. I'll lick my wounds later. She never looked back. Not for solace or companionship, or any of the other amenities that living with humans could possibly provide.

Nacho was a quick smart girl. She would have no trouble finding food and a modicum of shelter while she sorted out what was to come next. Her trusted and talented nose brought her, in a blissfully brief two hours' time, to a full over-stuffed dumpster just a few blocks away. This would be an excellent spot for her to make a modest camp for a night or two.

She would not be alone for long.

Bjorn was an almost purebred Norwegian elkhound; there was a sneaky German shepherd in there a couple of generations back, but otherwise he had all purebred elkhound parentage. He had been sold as a pup to a local family who had dutifully read every word of the AKC information on elkhounds and just knew he would be their forever dog. But, so very sad for these nice folks, because Bjorn, unfortunately took in many ways after his paternal sullen and self-possessed namesake grandsire Torbjorn, who had come to this farmer/breeder's family under extreme circumstances more than a decade before.

Bjorn had proved on several occasions that he was just a tad too aggressive with children. Then, when he wasn't otherwise sulking, he frequently reduced the family to tears of frustration with one of his snotty refusals at communication.

Trainers helped, and he was such a good boy in front of them, but the moment they turned their backs, that sideways smirk reappeared, and he did exactly as he pleased as he stared right into your eyes.

There was no established return policy attached to this local, casual hand-shake of a transaction between the previous breeder and the new family, so one day, after about three months of difficult and patient ownership, the dad just showed up at the breeder's doorstep with Bjorn on a tell-tale short leash. Just not gonna work for us, pal, sorry. Keep the money. Find him a better home. We failed with him. Sorry.

Then Bjorn was offered another opportunity. He was purchased again, as a gift this time, for an older disabled man who lived by himself, used a wheelchair most of the time, and wanted a companion and a little protection from a guard dog. Nothing much was expected of Bjorn in this configuration, so nothing much was tendered. There were always regular meals, a good amount of table scraps, and a fair-sized and well fenced yard with a cat to chase, so he managed to make himself acceptable, if not particularly lovable. He barked just enough at the mailman to show that he was able to recognize an intruder.

But, one day the man had a first-time female visitor and the dog would absolutely have none of it. From the first ring of the doorbell, he was all over her. He snarled and barked and bared his teeth until the poor woman dropped her basket of homemade goodies on the kitchen table and bolted for the back door with barely a fare-thee-well to the poor lonely-again but hopeful homeowner.

Without ceremony, back he went once again to the original owner. Like some mechanical revolving canine he returned to the less than delighted farmer who was running out of options for disposal of this dog. He would have to keep him, he supposed, and train him to herd his small flock of sheep, a fate exactly as that of Bjorn's grandsire Torbjorn. So he was put to work in the fields. He adapted fairly well once all the parameters were established and agreed upon.

Sometime later, after a couple of years of dutiful if churlish and occasionally mean-spirited aggressive herding and fitful guarding, and even though his meals were pretty good and pretty bountiful, he got a wild hair and snarled kiss my shiny sterling-silver slightly overweight Norwegian ass to the farmer and took off for parts unknown, on this early August night during the first of this year's two blue moons.

An hour of free trotting on a 'who-cares-where' trajectory brought Bjorn just a sniff from the heavily aromatized dumpster at the grange south of town. He soon realized that he wasn't alone.

He got one little peek at Nacho's steely black-eyed, ears-up, stiff legged stare-down, the slightly raised hackles, and the covetous guarding of what in the dog world would pass for as food, and his toadying alter-ego, with its sly submissive posturing, quickly kicked in with averted eyes, tucked tail, a lick of her muzzle, and an awkward roll which would endear him sufficiently and without event, even though it was pure drama.

There was enough food for both, no need for confrontation or altercation. Overt obeisance was always his back-up plan around other dogs, and that would do for now.

After a few reticent but quietly compatible and uneventful days, during which Nacho made it quite clear, with a growl and a stare, that she would have the better sleeping niche and the best of the food that was available, our dumpster divers were joined, still in the south town badlands not far from Coalbank Slough, by an unlikely vagrant number three.

Here came Cotton, an odd little mix of whatever breeds the sellers thought you would like her to be, maybe some Pom, some Rat Terrier, and perhaps a little Lhasa? Anybody's guess. Her father was not available for inspection or questioning. And her mother was a mixed breed white dame.

Cotton was quite simply a yapper, a perpetual yapper. Her human family, from way over the tall green bridge north of town, got tired of her initial cuteness real fast when they realized that Cotton was going to yap her head off day and night regardless of their efforts to train her to ride silently and smile her cutest and very best doggie smile while being carried along in an oversized handbag, and perform like a stuffed little doggie for all their friends.

As she grew and her weight headed toward twelve plus pounds, her legs grew long and spindly and her nose pointed sharply. The adopting family also realized around this time that Cotton was not going to resemble her mother, and she would never again be the tiny black-eyed puff ball faux canine they were sold, and so they made other plans for her future without consultation or remorse.

This family had no real commitment to the animal. They were merely in search of a few fashion points that would lend them a certain amount of trendiness or chichi swank. For some reason that could be known only to the mercurial gods of fashion, carrying a little dog around in your purse had become chic for a short period of time. Unfortunately, Cotton was too gawky and goofy looking to qualify as chichi, swank or trendy, so she had to go. It was an unceremonious decision. These folks would discard an unfashionable pair of shoes the same way. Oh really, they are so last year. Cotton didn't suit, so out she would have to go.

It is a great responsibility for any human to agree to maintain a domesticated state for the life of an animal. It takes commitment, follow-through and dedication. We pet owners do not all perform this task well, and our failures present a conundrum for the animal. We simply cannot throw a pet out like an unwanted or outdated dress.

On her family's mission to take Cotton to the pound, she 'accidentally' bolted from the gigantic black SUV somewhere along the five mile stretch of Libby Road, which in those years was an infamous dumping ground for semi-domesticated pets, former 'big ticket' household appliances leeching toxins, miscellaneous rusted car segments, and an assortment of local humans shooting off weapons of mass destruction.

After a period of disorientation on a barren stretch, during which no humans were available to react to her incessant yapping, Cotton headed for what smelled like town. Her excellent olfactory senses were in prime shape, and she happened upon our first two outcasts as they basked in the afternoon sun. She fell comfortably in with this group. After quickly sizing up the situation and giving Nacho a submissive crouch, a tucked tail, and a lick of her muzzle, she merged, in a moment of noiseless gratitude. Now they were a trio.

Several reasonably uneventful nights went by, and the trio began to fall into a tentative pattern.

A week or so later, in the early dark hours, there was a commotion. A loud, growling, barrel-chested, posturing, rear-end sniffing, seemingly endless but really only ten-minute standoff erupted out of nowhere.

This clamor announced the appearance of Buster. Because of the noise, several neighbors made repeated calls to the Sorry We're Closed—You're On Your Own Animal Control Department at the county. As a result, numerous perfectly good greased-over steak bones and half of a still-warm hamburger were left behind in the canine hormonal frenzy cum stand-off of the moment.

Begrudgingly, the Gang of Three, with Nacho's guttural blessing, cautiously admitted Buster, its fourth member who strutted up front almost, but not quite even with and well to the side of Nacho. She made it plain with a side-mouthed growl that she didn't like her prime position challenged, didn't like it one little bit. But Nacho was smart, and she had to admit that she kind of liked the idea of this new dog's equal terms and his lack of toadying. She thought she would bear with it, though, at least for the moment. She could take him down, if necessary, at any time.

Buster was a lab/pit bull cross, but the lab part was recessive and he looked more like a strong and sturdy pit. He was what some would call a periodical, or a secondary feral.

He had a home, albeit, a little rough around the edges, but he would often take off from this ragged domicile for weeks at a time, just to see how the other half was living. During these away times, he usually went south, and one time found himself riding out a storm in a dilapidated feed shed luxuriously furnished with the back seat of an old mini-van. Pretty good digs. He was more than likely not the first adventurer to pass this way in the recent past by the canid scent that enveloped the area.

If the local bounty of trash-can scavenging got scarce, or if he was threatened, he'd go on home and see if anybody there still wanted him.

Perhaps, in that surly world of stinking pots of stove-top crystal meth, someone who was reasonably unstrung might remember to throw him a bone or a bowl of the molding bargain dry dog food from the twenty-five-pound bag that had been left outside since before the rains came. Perhaps somebody would notice that he was hungry. Buster never knew for sure what to expect.

When he was home, if you could call this dubious drug-ridden filthy, angry dwelling a home, Buster was always a little high from fumes, but hey, he still had all his teeth and, at least for the moment, a mossed-over corrugated tumbledown roof next to the peeling kitchen door to keep him out of the worst of the weather. Now, right this minute, and in these next few moments, he was about to make a somewhat more abiding choice.

He thought, even though he was pretty much a loner, that he just might ride along with this new bunch of cast-offs for a while, might give it a try, just to see what happened. Allegiance was not an emotion that had yet factored into his experience or home life. Allegiance, or loyalty, was a come and go, never-to-be trusted emotion. His would eventually come to an understanding of the word, but that would come later.

Mischief, however, although it wasn't always the first thing on his mind, was close to follow.

Buster already knew the extremes of poverty and he didn't think he would have much to lose in this new configuration. He would try hard to let the dominant old bitch have her way. He would try to keep his fight-first attitude under control and not get into any kind of battle, especially with the big silver hound, then he would make the effort to be the beta and steer clear of the mischief that seemed to perpetually hover near him.

The Lab part of Buster was pretty happy with going beta. Even the Pit part of him knew that beta was not a bad place to be when you're on the road. He would do his best to be content and see what happened.

There was one fifth and final joiner to this homely group. A dog named Jack wandered into the group a week or so after Buster.

He was accepted, or rather acquiesced to by the pack, and took up his place on the periphery, toward the back of the pack, with neither fur-flying arguments nor silly submissive shenanigans, as they moved along the sandy shoals at Englewood.

The other four knew him by his attitude and his rather strong and pungent scent. They also knew that, although he was yet another mouth that needed feeding, he posed no real threat to the members of the group, merely an occasional but probably perpetual petty annoyance.

Good natured and naturally submissive, Jack had the habit of humping anything in sight. Castration for him was just a bump in the road. He thought he was the king of the hill, top dog, perpetually walking with his hind legs just a little bow-legged to accommodate the larger-than-life balls that he imagined were still there. The fact that he nuzzled and licked an empty scrotum just to kill time, and with absolutely no sense of loss, mattered to him not at all. It was to him as if nothing had happened. In his head, he would muse, I am Mister Ready, if you please. And I will always be Mister Ready.

If Jack had owned a black beret, or even knew such a thing existed, he would have worn it with pride and a kind of jaunty dignity as he made his neighborhood rounds.

One bright sunny late July day Jack was let out of the yard for his usual morning neighborhood ramble, glad to escape the noisy and stressful house where he had lived for four or five years. He was glad to get away from the screaming, crying, and punching, the threats and the police sirens which regularly erupted after the fight which followed the most basic discussions.

After he'd ambled along, made sure that he anointed all of his customary stops, gave a little chase to the old orange tom cat at the True Value hardware store, and dallied at the fence of the neighbor's house, where a new female puppy howled out to him from the pen inside the gate, he returned home a few hours later to an astonishingly quiet, mostly empty rental house.

He was left - along with a mountain of overfull black plastic trash bags, two charcoal gray long-haired ten-week old kittens mewling for food, a pile of stained and stinking mattresses, a rusting barbeque, various bits of crippled lawn furniture, bags and bags of reeking garbage, a heavy old worthless TV set, and a screaming, stomping, apoplectic, cursing landlord - to find his own way in the outside world.

It would take less than twenty-four hours, as he rambled south and down the west side of the Slough, for him to catch the earthy scent of the other four rag tags and escapees, and find a new and equally dysfunctional family.

But a family it was, nevertheless, these five feckless dogs, a family in which abandonment and desertion were known quantities and where trust needed to be earned.

That idea of mischief arises here once again, from the Old French meschever - to come out badly. It is a deep and complicated thought, good for musing on wandering walks, or while doing laps in the swimming pool. To come to mischief. To meet with calamity. Ominous perhaps, but it fits the situation.

All these ferals are complicit in some kind of mischief, intentional and calculated, or as the clumsy result of ignorance and uncertainty.

So what do we call this pack of motley canines? What is this thing that we turn over in our hands and consider and examine, like a Christmas snow globe on crack?

What we see, as we look at the plastic snow finally settling within the globe, is a tableau of five scruffy dogs surrounding a great golden dumpster. And this feral arrangement is a coalition of the scrappy, the misconceived, and the unfortunate, the dregs of canidae, bent on some sort of karmic mischief.

These dogs had nothing. They also meant nothing to any of their previous human owners. Why is that, we wonder in our innocence? The answer is because they were victims - of human caprice and ignorance, and sometimes bold-faced intentional cruelty. Most of their owners were content, relieved in fact, that their dogs had gone missing. They felt neither remorse nor regret.

But this pack of dogs deserved this new attempt at some kind of redefined freedom, with its iffy societal camaraderie and its inherent potential for complete peril. They would take the plunge, the chance, and see what happened. Regret was not in their canine vocabulary.

Together they would have something that could almost, but not quite, replace the vitality, the life force that had been surgically removed from each of them in the early days of their lives.

The normally expected fights over females and mating were off the table for this particular group, but opportunities for new kinds of devilry would soon present themselves.

They were a small band of bullies and troublemakers, taking strength from each other, with their communal minds bent on whatever might be waiting for them over the next ridge, or in the next yard, down the river a bit, or behind another of the ubiquitous, strewn about, rusting tire-less abandoned trucks, on the next cloudy and moonless night on this cusp between late summer and forever.

It would not be long before the first casually obtained taste of blood stopped them in their tracks, and changed them all further and forever.

42

8
Family II

Here, at his home up the river, Feargus had an active and varied life. The older daughter, Heather, was staying pretty quiet, out of the line of fire, so he saw much less of her. She had her schoolwork and her part-time job, but she found the time to toss a stick on occasion. The two younger children were his real pals.

Feargus learned to stay on the sidelines and watch during 'learning circles' which is what home-schooling parents call what other educators would call time-outs. These time-outs, however, came with the occasional child (most often the boy Matthew) being pinned to the carpet by a wailing parent in a test of wills as to which could recite from memory the entire whatever-seemed-important on that individual day. You will know all the vice-presidents backwards! You will recite the alphabet in Cyrillic! You will do whatever I deem you need to do at this moment, goddamn it!!!

It was perhaps the timber wolf quarter of Feargus that spoke through his genes to his observant psyche and instructed him to choose his battles. That regal ancestor may have been whispering 'don't get involved in someone else's fight. Watch and wait. Be still. Avoid confrontation. Circle quietly around to the other side of the meadow. Fade into the trees where you can't be seen and be patient. Stay aware. Dissolve into the graying evening and disappear.'

So Feargus watched and learned. He, who was being pinned to the ground at this moment, was the friend who would take him on long, oh so long treks into the wilderness over the old logging roads of the Elliott State Forest.

He had a special bond with this young lad, this warrior, this young god who would in a short two years' time go from an angry, beleaguered teenager to become an accomplished young man. This young human could run him, poor dog, into the ground until Feargus, being beyond exhaustion, would need to be picked up by the human who would carry him over his shoulders for the last five miles of the journey. There was much in this young man for Feargus to trust and admire. He could feel the strength of the warrior in the boy and related to it on a primitive and elemental level.

Feargus was more wary of, and downright uncomfortable around small children. He didn't have a lot of exposure to these little humans, but there was something in their oblique energy that spooked him, made him feel watchful and just a little bit on edge.

Occasionally Nancy would care-take the neighbor's two very young children when normal childcare fell through for the woman. Feargus seemed to be in awe of these small creatures and he was confused by their noise, their intensity, and the different kind of attention they received from the adult humans in the household. His brow would knot up and his ears would go all atwitch. His tail would stay at half-mast in a cautious undecided semi-wag off to the right, a sure sign of some discomfiture.

On those days he would trot down toward the river or spend the day with the goats, or become scarce in some other way. One time, when he was still just a big puppy, he spent the entire day on a pile of camping blankets on the floor of the linen closet off the main bathroom. He never came when he was called for this entire day, he held his bladder, and just slept in a nice clean warm dark place until his world was quiet once more and it was safe to roam about freely.

Rob and Nancy had crafted this homestead to provide almost everything this family of six would need. The two younger children were home-schooled, kept to a tight schedule and they were also kept on a short leash. Social time was severely limited. Volunteering at the nursing home in town was encouraged instead of social time with friends.

The little subsistence garden was designed to deliver much of the produce needed, given the limited sunshine, and the chickens provided eggs and the occasional meat for a potpie. The goats gave up their milk and fresh goat milk was frequently sold to a young family from Shinglehouse Slough who had a young son with a cow's milk allergy. Occasionally one goat would be raised just to harvest its rich lean high protein flesh. Very little was needed from the resources in the not very pretty town.

Here on the homestead, beets, greens, broccoli, cauliflower, and onions were grown in profusion. At harvest time they were eaten fresh, pickled, canned or dried.

Tomatoes, which would not grow in the tiny garden because of the lack of sufficient hours of full sunlight, were bought by the bushel from the neighbor on the other side of the road, on the other side of the hill, who had the benefit of almost full southwest exposure. These lovely large dark red tomatoes were canned and dried and frozen and sauced.

An occasional trout was caught in the fast shallow waters of the East fork, just outside the back door and around the neighbor's fence. It was a homemade and homegrown world all the way, and for four teenagers it was complete isolation and utter boredom, a long way from any sort of teen social life.

There was also the nit-picking, internecine, eternal squabble game between the parents to deal with. And it was a nasty mind-game of point tallies and guilt and gotcha.

Right now there was the ongoing battle over whether or not the academically precocious fourteen-year-old, Jennifer, could be allowed to take some advanced placement classes at the community college. Rob was against it, so Nancy made sure it happened, driving hours out of her way every day to get the girl to school even though Rob worked less than a mile from the school's main gate.

Rob, the primary earner, was strict, demanding and intolerant of dissent. No fast food, nothing fried. Just plain simple food. Eat what you are given and be grateful for it. That was his motto.

One sunny mid-week afternoon Nancy and the two younger children, along with Feargus, were coming home from an unscheduled group project visit to another home-school household. She had left a stew of goat meat and potatoes with garlic and turnips in the crock-pot and freshly made bread, so there would be dinner.

Just as they turned the corner from East Bay Road to head up the river, they saw what looked like the Rob's black Nissan half-ton truck pulled over on the siding of the road heading east just under the green Chandler Vertical Lift Bridge. They crossed the highway and took the turn-around under the bridge and came out behind the truck.

Lies, deceit, inconstancy, arrogance and gall! Behold the dictatorial parent sitting in the front seat halfway through the inhalation of a giant all-beef bacon double cheeseburger with a walloping double order of fries from the last fast food stop on the way out of the south end of town toward home. Caught in the act! It was obvious that the righteous disciplinarian could be a liar.

How many times had these double dinners taken place? Everybody was mad. Everybody had their own side and their own anger and their own particular view of this blatant breach of family trust. Each member had their own scar from the rigid food culture of this family.

The story flew like a hummingbird around the hamlet-sized community. Years later, and at different times, the story was repeated by various neighbors to the amusement of all.

The same bullying double standard was employed when Rob was offered a large mature black cat by a co-worker. This cat was brought into the home one night after work with claws intact. He never gave a second thought to the angst and disquiet caused to the family by his absolute edict on the declawing of the first cat.

This second cat, who bore the name Mister, was a big, take no prisoners, back alley kind of Tom who terrorized chickens, hissed at Argyle incessantly, and tried to take chunks out of Feargus' moist black nose. Feargus had not yet learned about claws. But he would not be fooled twice.

Rob thought Mister was just about right and would not listen to a single word against him. And that was, indeed, that.

From time to time, some particular friends would come to visit for the day, and they would bring Sammy, their big, square-jawed docile yellow Lab who was always a joy to be around. These were good times for Feargus. Sammy was a sweet, affectionate dog who liked to play and run and cuddle with everybody. He had his decidedly goofy side, and the two dogs were like friendly old souls, like aging teenagers, together in a flash, romping off to the river's edge, in search of their own kind of sport, which had mostly to do with chasing sticks, play fighting, ganging up on Mister, splashing on tumbled rocks, and snoozing through sweet sunlit naps.

Rob agreed to board Sammy for a week while his human family went out of state for a wedding. It would be a grand week for Feargus with the minor exception of the encounter with the nutria.

The nutria is a homely and roundly despised creature with luxurious fairly stiff fur, a rat-like tail, and a foolish face with thick coarse whiskers and very bright orange, very sharp buckteeth. This rodent loves to burrow into riverbanks and slough sidings and ponds. It causes problems for people, mostly, people who depend on roadbeds, or stream banks, or dikes that can be weakened by the gnawing of these large nuisance creatures.

Nutria were brought here to the northwest part of the country to be farmed for their fur back in the 1930's when it became obvious that the natural fur market of beaver and sea otter had been depleted.

A new market for rodent fur was, however, understandably overestimated in the subsequent post-war era and these non-native rascals were irresponsibly unleashed upon the Pacific Northwest to be fruitful and multiply, a call which they were most happy to heed, dutifully reproducing as often as three times per year. Not only do the devilish things erode stream banks and roadbeds, but their average size of sixteen pounds embodies a voracious herbivore who enjoys all the fruits of the subsistence gardener's bounty. Crops like beets, melons, and virtually all vegetables fall prey.

In addition, they absolutely love the sweet precious shoots of sod grasses, which serve to hold banks and prevent erosion. So the Nutria thereby became the all-around pest that virtually everyone can hate with ease and equal satisfaction. Conscientious citizens should feel free to shoot one, should one be seen in their backyard. They will be applauded and hailed. Medals may be pinned.

Nutria have sharp flat chisel-like intensely orange front teeth. There is an iron-containing pigment in the enamel of their teeth, and they show up as bright orange beacons of potential nastiness. These teeth grow constantly, so the animal must have its share of gnawing and grinding on semi-solid surfaces or the teeth will start to cause problems in the animal's mouth. So the nutria chooses to chew and gnaw incessantly and indiscriminately. One morning during Sammy's stay, Rob, with Feargus and Sammy in tow, headed down to the gushing fork to check the stability of a small log dam placed recently in a side channel to encourage fish habitat.

It was a bright and cheery mid-summer day when they came upon a large adult nutria eating grass shoots on the bank. The dogs surprised the rodent, one on each side, their tails high and rigid, coming closer and, growling with closed mouths, bodies tense as coiled springs.

Feargus

Rob made his best effort to verbally restrain the dogs, but they were freely off-leash and beyond listening. They came at the nutria from both sides, closing in on it from left and right, cornering it with apparent mayhem in mind.

All animals, when they are cornered, will attack, and this nutria was no different. Eyeing his options, the rodent laid his eyes upon the unprotected ample shin of the human which loomed at the center of his field of vision. He took a leap toward it with his sharp bright orange teeth protruding from the center of his cheeks.

Feargus saw the intent, and with the rodent just inches away from the man's leg, lunged at the creature and took the full force of the sharp orange incisors that ripped through his upper lip. Incensed and bleeding, Feargus chomped down on the thing's neck, shook it violently three or four times and flung it with force downstream into the rocky roiling water, not be seen again.

A visit to the vet, a few stitches, hugs all around from the humans; our dear Feargus was a hero once again, with his dear friend Sammy as co-growler and back-up protector.

Feargus proved again that he was a solid member of this family, and that he was very much at home.

9
Payback

A home, a family, is a microcosm. It is a place of shelter and growth, of learning and preparation for its inhabitants to perform as adults in the great outer world. We have all been variously prepared.

My early life, for example, was sheltered, sheltered by apathy and neglect, not necessarily by intention. I found I was unprepared for the world when I came upon it. These four siblings in Feargus' home would also find themselves unprepared for the world, confused and often at odds with efforts to establish normal relationships.

I have felt for a long time that home is a place that is spawned by necessity not by reason, by chance and not by design. We can look back on it and dwell in its thick choking mists, or we can lift our faces into the wind and leave it all behind.

The older girl just wanted out. She wanted some fun, wanted a life without so much argument and control, and she got most of what she was seeking. She got out and started a new life for herself far off in another, bigger town. Although she liked Feargus and thought he was a smart, attentive dog, her interests and likes were more involved with cats.

She had to protect cats and kittens from her father who perpetually threatened the pillowcase in the rushing rocky stream as the remedy for too many neighborhood kittens. Three kittens in a pillowcase with a big old rock and toss it in the swift-moving East Fork and problem solved. This was reported to have happened more than once, though it is a hard thing to prove. She was happy to be away.

The parental sniping and aggressive banter continued, but now took a slight detour.

Now it would be the time for payback for Jennifer going off to take college courses at fourteen.

Matthew had recently decided he would be happy to join the military and try to become a specialist. His mother screamed and stomped and said no, no, no. She railed and fumed and sputtered. And a day or two later her husband drove the boy to the recruiter and signed the enlistment papers. He held an ace-high full house, a checked mate, an eight ball in the corner pocket and a giant smirk.

Off the boy was packed to basic training. As time went on and he proved himself to be a warrior on every occasion, they were all very proud of him and bragged about every amazing achievement.

Upon every subsequent embarkation of one of the young humans, the homestead was made less and less of a home. It became more like a boarding house with everyone busy with their own lives and own hours and own needs, and with clever bits of avoidance behavior thrown into the mix.

The seasons marched ahead with cold inevitability. This time the berries were left on the vine. The garden had been planted late and a little carelessly and it did not produce the yield of former years. Chickens were not replaced with new stock; eggs were left a day or two on the roosts. It had to, was bound to, eventually come to this decisive moment.

She was done, she said, in a moment of exquisite self-regard. Over and over she said it with various pithy shakes of the head and meaningful rolls of the eyes. Done - whispered through clenched teeth or shrieked pointlessly with only numb and exhausted ears as audience. Done with it all, the unintegrated marriage, the children, the animals, just plain done, done, done.

She had a beautiful brand-new house of her dreams, perilously carted up the narrow rutted tertiary road to her feet in precarious stages and then assembled on a Tuesday morning less than a year ago.

And now, the last of her brood was soon to leave. This action would give her all the time in the world for all the goofy projects and home-based business schemes, and as many loaves of her favorite soggy lifeless zucchini bread as she could imagine baking. But the idea of being alone as a couple, and facing life in a marriage in which there only remained sludge and sham, in which both parties were mercurial, hateful, volatile, angry and unfulfilled, was just too much to bear.

So she kept to her word and took off. Literally. She put on her Tibetan multicolor dream coat, her sturdy built Rockport's and off she went. On foot.

Down the gravel driveway, past the railroad-tied once thriving victory garden, off onto the pitted road, a lone black over-stuffed soft-side suitcase in hand and a couple of totes over her shoulder, intending to walk, we can only guess, the eighteen miles to the not very pretty town and who knows what, until the incredulous daughter, despite her youth, seemingly the only real adult in this lovely family portrait, finally got into the truck and picked her up as she was reaching the second mile marker in the dusty gravel road and delivered her safely to the women's shelter in the town.

So the screaming stopped, but the hatred remained.

And that will be the last we will see or hear of Nancy, another of the humans, albeit not our Fergus' favorite, vanished from his life forever.

In only one months' time it would be late August and preparations would be finalized for Jennifer to go away as well, to finish college a couple of hours away.

Some furious changes were to take place at the homestead when the family was totally gone. Furniture and tools were sold and given away. Chickens were adopted by neighbors. The farmlet, now fallow in the soon-coming fall, was turned over.

And then, on a bright late summer afternoon, Rob gently led Bernadette and Annie up the ramp at the back of the black half-ton truck. The couple was secured, and then the tailgate was firmly closed. They would be going to their third home.

There was a family who used to get Annie's milk for their allergic young son. They had said they would take both girls. They had a lovely sprawling property just at the confluence of Isthmus Slough and Shinglehouse Slough, where the tidal flow turns like a sharp elbow grinding the banks at the turn. They had a cat, chickens, an active inquisitive eight year old boy, and a fine, intelligent, aging Border collie mix to keep them all in line.

It was a perfect place for the girls. The mother did some kind of programming and worked at home a lot of the time. The father worked in the nearby town, but also travelled a lot of the time, so it would be a grand home for the sweet girl goats.

Feargus

Back up the river, the homestead was further diminished by the absence of the friendly goats, and the gift of Argyle and Mister to another nearby neighbor.

Rob worked long hours in the town. Feargus did his best to amuse himself on those long dreary days alone. He chased the squirrels down the slippery bank that was beginning to become overgrown, unchecked without the foraging goats. Salal, blackberry bramble, and pesky twirling Morning Glories thrived in their new freedom.

He caught some kind of fish – was it a trout? Did he care? It was his first, caught off a sandy shoal along the river.

Feargus further amused himself by lying in wait behind the goat shed and frightening two sweet unwary does who were in the habit of using the property as a path to the water, chasing them in their big lopey strides back up the hilly side of the road and into the trees. He also good-naturedly chased the neighbor's cat across their yard and up onto the roof of the shed where she sat, out of his reach, and hissed and snarled most ineffectively.

But mostly, he sat in patient and stoic solitude and watched the birds, listened to the sweet refrain of a Swainson's thrush, slept unmolested, without any chickens to march along his ribcage, and chased butterflies in the late summer sun. He tried to make the best of his situation. He was lonely. Very lonely. So much had changed. At bottom, he was a family dog without a family.

As I continue to reflect, I am struck by some similarities between Feargus' life and my own. That sounds strange, perhaps, but I believe it bears itself out.

Four things of note happened when I was five: first, we moved to a larger house in the same neighborhood; next, my maternal grandmother, who was very kind to me, passed away quietly in her sleep; third, already reading, I started first grade without the benefit of kindergarten; and last, my mother breathed a sigh of relief and happily and hurriedly returned to the work force.

This meant that for the next several years, my after-school home was with my ancient paternal Irish grand aunt who was seriously em-brogued, and whose husband lay upstairs in the long, extended, final phases of his earthly travail.

This child, who was seen and not heard as requested, or actually as expected, was also too often unseen as well. I have little or no memory of home for the next five years of my life.

Life also pitched and yawed for Feargus.

The solitary dog poked around, alone in the goat shed, unseen and unheard. He sniffed the stanchion where Rob used to trim the goat's hooves. He nosed around and rubbed their remaining scent all over his face. He missed his goats. He had loved those goats. They were his family, much more like a family than the humans, any day. He missed their nuzzles - their sweet female warm nurturing nuzzles. He missed eavesdropping on the rhythm of their complicated conversations.

Every so often he would let out a stifled cry of longing but there was nobody there to acknowledge his sadness. It may have just been a huge sigh of boredom rather than of loneliness, but it was more likely that his episodic memories of the goats caused him sadness. Poor dear Feargus.

They were all gone now, the baby kittens in the pillowcases, the bigger children, the mother, the boy who was his friend, the goats, the girl with the squeaky voice, the cats, and at last, the man.

Even Rob was gone as well for most of the day and early evening, and sometimes longer than that.

Because, for some completely inexplicable reason that now, so many years later, defies all rational argument or credible excuse, the large moody man with the big brown dog moved in with me.

◆◆

I continue to muse over the idea of home. What exactly is a home? Is it smells, sounds, or possibly companions? I don't know for certain. I think home is a vague, elusive and ambiguous thing. It is ineffable and abstract to the romantics among us, stony, cold and vacant perhaps for the realists.

The idea of home changes for us throughout our lives. Our memories of home are liquid and uncorroborated. They twist and morph, from the real into the unreal. We reach, stretching and extending to the limit of our capacity, for this picture we are straining to see, and it becomes vapor and disappears before our eyes.

Creatures that manage to live without the benefit of homes, without the enveloping care of loving families, creatures that strike out or are cruelly left alone, those creatures have very different stories to tell.

Feargus

54

10

Entente

I came to understand that the feral pack had been cautiously edging toward a kind of mutual entente at about this time.

Each dog had his own reservations and suspicions, but as a group they seemed to be trying to come to some kind of organizational agreement.

Agreement. It isn't always a hard thing to reach. It can be so at times, I suspect, but not always. Often it is a harder thing to explain than to achieve. Try to explain an orange, or stardust, or maybe childbirth.

A handshake, a nod, a silent exchange of rings, a hand held over the heart, a raised glass or hand, a bowed head, a tucked tail, each one of these actions may signal an agreement of some kind, a pact, an entente.

I think these very simple symbols, often unspoken, are capable of enormous consequence. Yet they are performed with varying degrees of intelligence, information or forethought. That has been my experience.

Who hasn't come to an agreement and then thought better of it? Before the words And Now I Pronounce You are out of the joiner's mouth, before the last curl of your signature is down on the Just Sign Right Here on the dotted line, before that last second of freedom, before that door is closed and locked, there is that last thought: Damn … maybe … I wonder … what if.

I watched this happen not very long ago at the coast. I attended an afternoon engagement party out on the point and I saw 'I Wonder If' happen right there in front of my eyes.

Feargus

The scene spoke for itself fairly eloquently. On a perfectly mottled sun-lit patio over the ocean, where perfect climbing pink roses clung to the trellised walls, there was a lovely party celebrating the engagement of a handsome young couple.

There was perfect fresh food with mountains of steamed clams, newly caught cracked Dungeness crab, and several huge wild-caught cedar-planked salmon. Someone had brought a case of perfectly crisp peachy Willamette Valley Chardonnay. Soft live classical guitar was being played unobtrusively in the background on a raised deck, and casually well-dressed people wearing Patagonia and Arc'teryx, were hugging and shaking hands and laughing with the wildly enthusiastic groom-to-be. All was perfect. Absolutely perfect.

Except.

Then the brother of the bride-to-be raised his glass and proposed a toast to the couple. That was when I saw it. In her eyes. The tiniest glimmer of hesitation, a tweak of the cheek, a barely perceptible flutter that went across her face in a flash, like a shadow from a fast-moving cloud on a windy coastal day. I was standing right across from her and I saw it.

I don't think we often face up to these doubts and back away in honesty and openness; at least that has been my observation. Rarely do we jilt, or flee at that last moment. But, and this is a significant but, we often carry that finite kernel of doubt deep within us throughout the relationship, throughout the life of the accord.

We can come to agreement, to our desired entente, and live almost happily ever after, but we still hold onto that nagging, disagreeable, vexing shred of an idea, of a doubt, that plays incessantly in the background of our thoughts, like the drone instrument in an Indian raga that provides the constant repetitive bed of background to spotlight astounding sitar virtuosity. But this drone also cushions and muffles, to some extent, the highs and the lows of our listening experience.

What matters most is that agreement has been made, heads have nodded, and understanding has been reached. Entente has been accepted.

Entente within a feral pack of dogs is equally complex and intensely interesting.

———◆◆———

Jack, who was the last to join the loosely configured feral alliance, arrived with a mature and taciturn perspective and only the smallest of questions or doubts.

He made his satisfactorily accepted nod to the group, with a hunched body, lowered head and tucked tail. He then trotted cautiously and quietly into this new undefined society. He was hoping to make some sense of it, but without a care if he did not. He might wind up the perpetually tardy member of the group, but that didn't bother him one little bit. He would keep his eyes open and his head screwed on straight and see what came along.

Jack was cautious and reticent. He was wary of bonds, of superficial relationships, of the idea of kinship or anything resembling a family. The scars from his rocky life lessons were not far from the surface, and both his associative memory and his infantile episodic memory were awake to the possibilities of pain and disappointment as a potential outcome. These two last conditions seemed to be the accepted characteristics of his existence.

Most of the ills in his life were brought about by relationships with humans. But opportunities were few without the shelter and predictability of a human home. So at this particular moment he set his wariness aside and was ready to accept this opportunity. He would accommodate to the extent he was able. He was braced for entente with these members of his own species, and he was willing to be bound to that decision.

————◆●◆————

This whole idea of bonds is complicated for humans as well as for dogs. I am thinking of matrimonial bonds, of filial bonds, societal bonds, ancestral bonds, of compacts and settlements and understandings. Are they real or are they merely imagined?

I am bound to tell this story. It has sung in my heart like a sullen siren for many years, and like a deep jab from the barbed quill of a porcupine, I have only one choice now, it must come out, regardless of the damage in the process.

Yet I am merely a chronicler who picks strings of words out of the ether and assembles them into mounds of binary coded data for others to decipher. I do not depend on compassion or understanding, I am simply bound to finish my tale.

Feargus

The ferals feel bound to each other at this moment also, but in a very different way.

—•••—

Jack took a good hard, objective look at the infantile awkward tribe he had just agreed to join. Democracy did not exist in his dog world, and his main desire was to determine exactly where he stood on this ladder of canine hierarchy. So he observed, and made his assessments.

That silly sly submissive silver gray one would probably steal food and, though he was powerfully built, he was a little too overweight to be very fast, so he would not likely cause much trouble in the pack, even with his perky ears and his stupid tight curl of a tail that never wagged enough to reveal his true feelings. Sneaky. Pure-breds were usually sneaky. He might be a fine companion, a powerful and alert watchdog, but he might also be dangerous and subversive. This one could be sixty-five tightly packed pounds of trouble. In a few days, Jack would have a good idea which one it was to be.

It was pretty clear to Jack that the gray one knew how to work the other dogs, too. Noodge a little, then back off. Steal a stick somebody was playing with, and then roll over on his back with his stomach and neck exposed. I was just kidding; I didn't mean anything, see? I was just playing around.

The silver one gave off a big-chested growl to protect his hoard of food scraps, yet he was always after the other guy's food as well. He was content to be the sly old fool, but what self-respecting dog volunteers to be the omega? What's his game?

Surely he's got one. Sooner or later they would all know what it was. He was a big blinking red caution sign, and Jack knew a lot about caution.

Who, Jack wondered, was crazy enough to invite this little white yapping thing to the party? She wasn't even worth humping.

It's true. Cotton was twenty-some pounds of noise, and not much else. Why can't she ever give it a rest? Every once in a while the Elkhound would have to go over and try to sit on her to keep her quiet for a time. That is until Nacho growled him off, with her teeth bared and her tail straight. Then Nacho would roll little Cotton, before she could even struggle. After rolling her, she would place one paw firmly on the fluff ball's much littler chest, or she might stand directly over her with all four legs on the ground around her, and those black piercing eyes staring down at her.

Sometimes Nacho would have to hover over her and watch her for another few minutes to see if Cotton let out even the tiniest of yelps. And then, if Cotton absolutely positively could not control her noisy self and erupted in a hailstorm of yapping, Nacho would repeat the process of roll and glare, until Cotton got tired, and that was usually enough to make her give it up for a while.

The poor thing, she was such a caricature, with her big round starburst fluffy off-white Pomeranian head, looking very much like an exploded cotton ball, her pointy face, her beady little narrow-set black eyes, her longish spindly terrier legs, her goofy excitability and her skinny tail with the huge white pompom on the end. She wouldn't eat much they all knew, so that wasn't so bad. But she spooked at every little thing, and nagged them all, which simply made the rest of them agitated and anxious.

She'd never experienced an alpha human, so living in this new hierarchical arrangement was her first experience with any kind of discipline.

She also loved to nip and bite, often just a tad too hard. Her small mouth could open surprisingly wide and it housed some exceedingly sharp little teeth. When playing with Buster, she would often draw blood, which got her a snap and a growl from several pack members. Her needle sharp teeth and small but strong jaw may have been the only tools with which she could compensate for her size among these much larger dogs, but it was definitely annoying to her mates.

Cotton was another canine that needed a job to do - a job she was good at and for which, at long last, she would gain some approval from this new family. That job she would soon find, perhaps not the career we would wish for her, but her skills would indeed be used.

Jack had pegged Nacho for a classic bitch. It wasn't hard to see she was in charge. Jack watched her take down the yapper and then, in a spectacular display of alpha maturity, just a little later, take down the Pit mix who was picking an argument with Bjorn.

Faster than your eyes could follow it she had him down, even though the Pit was twice her size. Down and with her foot on his big broad chest, staring down into his eyes until the pain of her glare made him look away. She had years on him, and the pit had to respect that, so he took it and rolled. Buster was no match for her, especially given her age, and he knew it.

But Jack was taking notes. If she could take down the Pit, watch out.

Nacho was brown and black and wiry, with the decided look, from the rear or the side, of a blooded Airedale, plus a little salt and pepper around the neck resulting from her nine or ten years on the planet. But Nacho turned around to reveal a shocking and comic snub-nosed dark brown/black jowly pug face. What a mess of thirty-five pounds of feistiness.

Nacho was never allowed to whelp. Her 'townie' first owners were sure that there was no discussion on the matter. Consequently, Nacho thought estrus was a messy joke played on other females and she wasn't even curious. Thankfully, she escaped the whole thing.

But her neutered alpha self knew she was facing another kind of maternal challenge in this new game, and it might be time to call on some of those skills which are hard to deny regardless of actual motherhood.

She clearly believed in her ability to ascend the social dominance hierarchy in this motley family, she had done it before, and she was fairly satisfied thus far with the other dogs' submissive interactions. She innately knew that if she ever showed that she did not feel secure in her position as alpha that she would have to exaggerate her station immediately and show aggression rather than competence, which could be a problem at best, and deadly at worst for a dog of her size.

On the other hand, it would be an equally risky test to stay on the road alone. That was the decision she made the moment she shot through the hole in that broken fence. She knew that she would need some companions. But she wasn't about to play second best to any other dog. That was her dilemma. So here she was, alpha to a motley bunch of unknown and unpredictable cast-offs and rejects who might at any time call her on her status.

It has been observed that rovers generally won't attack a female unless there is food involved. Most rovers on the road, that is. But what about these previously domesticated wimps, what about them? There was no way to tell.

Most dogs in general won't go after a dog older than they, and goodness knows, they could all see that she had some years on all of them. Jack, of course, might be older, but you couldn't really tell, and he is not in the running for a leadership position in the pack. But being the leader also meant that Nacho could never let down her guard. Ever. Being in charge was going to be a full time job.

It was important to all of them that she stay the alpha. If they were to remain a pack, they needed her wisdom and abilities.

Their alternative choices were not good. Buster, the Pit mix, was one of the leading contenders, but his one-on-one aggression pattern and his short temper ruled him out.

Bjorn's laziness and general lethargy and churlishness made him less than leader material.

Certainly Cotton and Jack were not even candidates. So it was, in the greater scheme of things, Nacho's calling, and she knew it, embraced it.

As the days went by and he took it all in, Jack was developing a deep sense of admiration for Nacho, and was generally in agreement with the calls she was making. He was feeling glad to be a part of this interesting family, and looking cautiously forward to what might happen next.

The big question mark in Jack's wary, suspicious mind was Buster. He'd give him a wide berth for sure because any one in this infantile society could be a victim in an instant with a forty pound Pit in the group.

Jack could see in Buster's eyes that he was constantly calculating, watching the other dogs, gauging their weight and strength, as well as their weaknesses, stifling his innate aggression, but always on the prowl, always prepared.

Buster was a hefty block of high-energy Pit attitude and the only thing keeping him on the nice side of mean was the part of him that was Lab. A handsome, trim, short haired mocha brown, Buster had the characteristic lashless eyes of the Pit that seemed to be devoid of any kind of emotion, regardless of any other physical clues. He had a thickly muscled neck and a broad well-sprung chest and was clearly the athlete in the group.

Pretty good lookin' dog.

That big red flashing caution light went off again in Jack's head. Wariness flashed across his consciousness. This one could be unpredictable.

If he was to bond himself to this group, he would have his eyes wide open.

◆●◆

I personally shudder slightly at the thought of any and all kinds of personal bonds. I am not quite in a state of peace or understanding with any semblance of shackles or chains, real or imagined.

I see filial and matrimonial and societal ties as if they were being displayed in a three-dimensional chess game, full of illusion, variation and triagonal movement. Nothing in this context is exactly as it seems. All previously considered linear conclusions must be negated and destroyed. Something else, something obscure, must be inserted into my understanding.

This is my own, my personal predicament at this moment in time, with my heart open and unprotected. I must struggle through it, make the effort to find sense in it, dissolve my fears and make peace with the idea of trust.

Dogs are simpler.

They ask less. They are mostly content with awkward kinship, camaraderie and an understanding of the communal needs. Unlike the well-protected human, they care less about the shields or armor which they may have to drop in order to coexist, or the accommodations they may have to make, the compromises which will be demanded, and the truces that will have to be extracted, in order to survive to the future.

They just accept.

They accept and try to adapt to the best of their ability.

That is the point where the dogs and I diverge.

11

The Road

This newly formed group of ferals spent a few more uneasy nights somewhat rudely congregated in the region of the dumpster on the south end of this plain town. But, as they grew in numbers, it was clear that they could not stay there forever.

The hulking blue metal dumping bin was regularly picked up and emptied, then noisily slammed back down onto the concrete corner of the lot while the vehicle digested its contents.

The property on which it sat was surrounded by native weedy cover, represented in this location by a rich diversity of roadside and field plants, nature's cast-offs - Shepherd's purse, hemp-nettle, willowherb, the ubiquitous blackberry bramble, goats beard, yarrow and relentless alder saplings, to name a few.

Nobody ever slept very well at this location. There was a constant and seemingly endless glut of new surreptitious dumpster donations, emptied from the back seats and trunks of beat-up old cars owned by various locals.

Not one of the dogs moved during these drop-offs, but stayed still and invisible in the taller weeds. This was especially hard on Cotton, but she held on to the understanding of the needs of the group and did her best to accommodate her new tribe.

Hunger was at bay for the moment and the pickings, right here at their feet, were more than sufficient for the entire ensemble. Right now it was probably best to lay low and not attract attention.

There was a great big brown tool shed behind an equally brown one-story house that sat forlorn, faded and in foreclosure, on the bank-side of the slough road, not far from where they stood. This property abutted a small neighborhood grocery with its own characteristically disgusting dumpster.

This abandoned shed structure was nestled neatly among homes with cars in the garages and overflowing trashcans in the driveways. It was toe-nailed against the backside of the house and protected on one side by a half-wall protrusion off the garage that also provided privacy from the street.

A small cracked and broken gray-painted concrete pad from what was once a patio led off to the left. Here a tired dog could take a nap in the sun, unseen from the street. The roof of the shed, ancient sun-cracked corrugated plastic, would keep out most of the rain, and there was a pile of several rolls of formerly orange old shag wall-to-wall carpeting that had been torn out of the house and left there to survive the elements. This otherwise useless packet would provide some bedding up and off the soon-to-be-cold ground.

Nacho did not understand the concept of 'foreclosure' but nevertheless had scoped out this spot on one of her early morning pre-dawn forays into the neighborhood, and felt its vacancy. This new fresh morning she barked her flock awake and shepherded them in the direction of the shed and tried to settle them in. It was a good temporary location, and they each found a spot they liked with very little rift or argument. This might be their home for the next little while.

The coming night was to be the first formal night of this grand convocation, this canine ecclesia.

Jack got as comfortably nestled as possible for a restless sleep. A lot wearied and a little worried, he was interested in seeing what would happen to the group when it came time to look for food in the morning. But for now, the group was at a troubled rest.

Cotton was so exhausted from excitement that she was the first to drift off to a twitching dream-filled sleep.

Bjorn appeared to sleep, but you were never sure if he was pretending, just lying there with his big chest heaving, awake and listening.

Buster slept the sleep of the just with a loud bit of snoring from his big barrel chest.

Nacho was active in her role as the great Mothering One, and slept with one eye open. Entente or no entente, she felt some disquiet and would keep watch on this mongrel crew. Anything could happen.

Jack was restless.

Disquiet and uneasiness can be terrifying. Sometimes that moment of questioning happens within seconds after you've signed the form, or taken the plunge, or gotten all the way into the car, sometimes it is just some casual comment from an unconnected third party: Did you know about (fill in the blank)? So you say to yourself, because you can't tell anyone else: Can that be true? Could that really be true of him, of them, of life?

But you know, in that layer of understanding that resides just under the skin of your back at the nape of your neck, the part of your skin in which cold shivers reside, that it could be true. As hard as you try to deny it, you're sure enough of the signs to know it could be, might be true. Just then you feel a cold heavy weight in the upper end of your small intestines.

Jack had this same sense of uneasiness.

He was probably Cocker and Springer, but oddly taciturn for either of those breeds. Over his lifetime he had been smart, fearless and painfully loyal, even when it was grossly undeserved.

The humping proclivity, which he seemed unable to master, was from no particular breed or genetic trait, more like a racial memory of some sort, with no excuses and no explanations.

He had a questioning, melancholy gaze with under a furrowed brow. His coat appeared to be mostly black, except when the sun hit it from a particular direction. Then it turned a brown full of highlights of brass, gold, copper and bronze. That was when you could see the Cocker shine through.

He was quite clearly overweight, particularly in the region of the abdomen, which protruded well beyond his rib cage, and he was more than a little slow in his reactions for his age.

Jack didn't deserve some of what life had thrown at him. At nine years old, he certainly didn't deserve the vacant trashy yard he returned to after his recent morning meander; he didn't deserve the constant uproar of that last household.

He didn't deserve the situation that was just previous either. In that case, his owner of almost three years, an adequate provider and kindly, if less than an energetic master, refused to wake up one morning, even with Jack's best whining and repeated efforts at face-licking.

The body was then eight hours cold, and Jack was very agitated, had to relieve himself multiple times in a far corner of the room, and finally started to whimper a bit before a neighbor heard an unusual noise and called the local police and thus began the series of events that made Jack a ward of the court, put him into foster care and then up for adoption once again at which time he was adopted by the feuding, screaming, brutalizing young couple.

He was just a darn good dog. A good boy, Jack was, a really good boy. Unfortunately, in his lifetime, very few humans had ever said those words to him. Good boy. It's a simple thing to say, with a scratch on the chest, or a stroke behind the ears, it would have meant so much to him. Good boy, Jack. That's my boy.

He had that funny, endearing way of cocking his head on the rare occasion when he was scratched behind the ears. He was thoughtful and cautious and intelligent. He might have found a better home had he not had this damned humping propensity which earned him various forms of punishment including more than one frustrated beating from more than one owner over time. He never did seem to get the connection between the action and the beatings.

This time, he knew that there was nowhere else for him to go. Relying on humans for anything at all was pretty sketchy, so he was looking forward to a new life in this pack, in this artificial family. All his hopes and dreams were evident, splayed out in fact in front of him right here, the day that he stopped at this south town dumpster - a curious place for such enormous hopes and dreams.

In ten weeks' time, however, our dear humping, faithful Jack would be dead of Canine Autoimmune Hemolytic Anemia, a gift from his Cocker Spaniel ancestors.

At this moment, his immune system had already begun to attack and destroy his own red blood cells. He was well into the disease, well past the point of medical intervention.

He was a good boy as he progressed in his illness. In the not very distant future his liver and kidneys would give up the effort. He never complained, never whined. What a good boy. His sickness, and both the pack's group and individual responses to it, would be just one more architectural element that would delineate and describe the members of this contorted canine family.

For tonight at least, there would be a tentative, tacit, informal agreement for the mutual good.

This entente is frail and flimsy, like a large fine crystalline ice formation susceptible to the slightest affront or change of temperature.

Not every agreement can withstand this state of fragility and imperma-nence without consequence. The structure will hold just as long as it has meaning and as long as it has substance.

Or until it no longer has either.

67

Feargus

12
Background

I needed to snap out of this crippling mood and get to work.

There was an inquiry from my agent sitting in my inbox. For some grotesque reason, the project dealt with my least favorite subject of the moment – dogs. How could this be? I seemed to be surrounded with dealings about the one creature on the planet which I would have happily avoided.

The computer screen sat blank at the corner of my desk like some unsparing AI overlord, waiting for me to construct a reply to the inquiry. Procrastination is a delicious retreat from reality, but I knew I would have to try to concentrate and get started. There was yet another deadline involved, and I surely didn't want to piss off my agent.

It is through the quirky and subjective prism of words and narrative that I view the world. I am an adaptor. My agent connects me with people or institutions with ideas or concepts and I explore the subject and express the ideas in some fashion for the general public.

In other words, I take other peoples' basic research or manuscript, or possibly a memoir, and adapt it for a wider audience. That end product could be a film or a television series, a classroom, boardroom or perhaps some international granting agency.

I have been doing this work for many years, and I have found a comfortable market for this kind of writing. It's good solid useful employment for me. I have even been fortunate to have won the occasional award for a couple of projects.

I love language enough to be happy that writing has become my work and that I am told that I am reasonably good at it. I also minored in History and that training has made me a steady and thorough researcher, which is a great asset for a documentarian.

At the time I am describing, I had a deadline to make an initial reply to the proposal on this new topic related to dogs. I didn't yet know very much about the project, I just had to tell them if I was interested. There would be a big box of materials arriving by FedEx in the next day. Then I would have the opportunity to make a more careful decision.

Would I be interested? It's about dogs. Am I interested or do I want to run, wild-eyed and screaming, in the opposite direction, out, across the brick patio and out into the woods?

Maybe I could postpone the reply to the next day. I thought that seemed like a good idea. My mind was a little too foggy to make any serious decisions. Times like this I miss my old friend Maggie.

Maggie was Ian's wife. She and I had been best friends since college. A little over two years ago she was diagnosed with pancreatic cancer.

This dreadful news came with almost no warning. There were a few weeks of diminished appetite accompanied by some surprisingly rapid weight loss. Even now, in retrospect, there were very few clues.

Maggie and I were constant friends, so she asked me to be with her whenever possible during this difficult process.

We, Maggie, Ian and I, sat across from four serious white-coated professionals. The primary on the team sat calmly with his hands crossed on the desk. One colleague stood behind him, looking stolid but defeated. Another, a young woman intern or fellow, clenched her jaw so hard it twitched.

The lead physician fussed a bit with the silver-colored paper clip holding the pages of the reports in front of him. He asked the intern for something additional which she produced, and in just another few seconds Maggie was given the coldly accurate prognostication of 'very little time.'

A few questions were asked and answered, but nothing that was said would be remembered. The white hot hiss of those three words seared the insides of our heads like branding irons and blinded us to any other understanding.

That assessment had been chillingly correct. Maggie left this earth a blistering, head-spinning, body-ravaging two months later.

Every attribute of life as we had known it just one day before that awful verdict, just seconds before, had changed. Everything we thought we knew was replaced by this other harsh, impossibly ugly new reality.

Ian was instantly ready to resign his post to be with her every second, but Maggie would not hear of it and their daughter Astrid agreed. She knew, I am sure, that research and teaching comprise the fortress of his life.

Looking back I can see that the stimulation and exchange in his graduate courses sustained and grounded him during that awful time.

He and I had known each other for almost twenty years. But when Maggie got sick, we became unquestionably interdependent.

I spent the last week of Maggie's life living in the guest room of their house, doing whatever I could, emptying trashcans, assembling bits of food, keeping things clean, answering well-meaning but ill-timed phone calls, accepting food. I placed each lovingly cooked casserole in the fridge, which was now crowded with other neatly-wrapped examples of love and concern, then returned the Corning Ware dishes washed clean of the generous but uneaten casseroles. Yes, yes, it was delicious, thank you for caring.

Ian had nodded off. Just for a minute, he thought. Sitting in the living room in his recliner at the side of the rented hospital bed with the tubes and the drip, and the annoying intermittent clack and hiss of the machinery. He just nodded off, at three am, just for a second he thought. He awoke with a start, and she was gone.

Our shared grief and raw dumbfounded horror over Maggie's sudden passing were overwhelming. But now, for just these few minutes, there was just the quiet.

Before the noise, and the ambulance, and the EMTs lifting her onto the gurney and taking her away, before the signatures and the final instructions, all the necessary to-do and the efficient clatter of the bed being taken apart, the room stripped down again to a living room, a room once again for the living, before all that there were these few brief minutes of intense and absolute silence.

There would so much work to do. There had been no time to prepare, to think it through. Everything now had to be done in a hurry.

There were dispositions to be made of her personal belongings like her beautiful clothes and pieces of hand-made jewelry, many of which had been bought for her by Ian over the years. Then there were her books, so many books, beautiful books on art philosophy and art history, some of them signed editions by several of her well-known friends and colleagues.

Then of course there was her own artwork as well as the work she had collected over a lifetime in the field. It was overwhelming. Each piece required a decision of some sort. We offered many of her things to those people whom we thought would appreciate them, we put aside all of the pieces that their daughter Astrid had requested, and sold a few things at those galleries which routinely carried her work. Finally we gave away quite a lot to her favorite charities.

The toughest choices came when he had to pick the paintings and other artwork which would remain in the house as a representative sample of her body of work. When the volume of that sampling seemed like it was tipping the house over into a museum, or a memorial to her, some of the choices had to be reevaluated. It was a hard line to walk, but Ian was clear and level-headed about the decisions.

He had spent months and done a valiant amount of work in downsizing their huge 'together' house and he was just about ready to put it on the market. He took a short weekend in the mountains with some friends, for a breath of air away from the chaos.

Then in the midst of all these choices there occurred another meaningless and untimely twist of the roadway of life, Argo, Ian's nine year-old Lab was exposed to some sort of undetermined neurotoxin while being boarded at a neighbor's home over the weekend. He had a massive seizure and died on the spot.

This was just plain cruel. You could see the weight of this new sadness on Ian's body as his shoulders rounded and his face adopted two permanent lines between his eyes.

At that point, when he was simply exhausted from so many months of effort, he asked me to help him sort through a couple of boxes of photos which had been sitting, stern and unwavering, in a corner of the living room for over a year.

Most of the pictures were old vacation or business trip shots and didn't have much meaning. But there were a few shots of Ian's and Maggie's baby grandson, and some good pictures of old Argo, and they needed preserving.

As we dug into this latest task, he talked for a moment about his love for his daughter. When his first and only grandchild was born, he realized how much a person's heart is able to expand to meet every new addition, how love has that unique and wonderful capacity to expand to infinity. More love begets more love and it can roll perpetually on and on.

We were almost through with the photo chore at hand. We had been laughing at some ancient Halloween photos of Maggie and me as ridiculous red-cheeked can-can girls being silly and loud at a university party.

Ian put down a photograph and sat back in his chair for a moment, looking out the window. Then he leaned forward and looked at me with those piercing gray eyes.

"Tracy, I've got something to say to you."

"What is it, Ian?"

"I didn't think it was possible, I mean after Maggie died, I didn't think at all for a while, you know that."

He paused. I nodded. I knew how hard he had been hit.

"But I have to tell you that I have grown to love you."

That definitely got my attention and I dropped the photograph in my hand.

"I understand that I can love you and it can be alright. That is if it could be alright with you, of course. This is taking such a chance, because you may not feel anything at all like that for me."

The lower half of my face broke into a gentle smile while the upper half contorted into a frown of sorts, a look that says in combination, 'I love what you just said but I also feel the pain you've had in saying it'. He became momentarily uncomfortable at that reaction.

"Sorry. Really. So sorry."

"Oh please, Ian, don't be sorry."

I put my hand on his arm and looked into his happy, sad, questioning eyes. I did not remove my hand for a long moment. I found myself forcing down the rising hot moist urge to cry. I squeezed his arm.

"Ian, I have a meeting downtown in twenty minutes."

"Go, go. Don't let me make you late."

We awkwardly pulled ourselves together. At the front door I took his face in my hands and kissed him. I don't think he kissed me, I definitely think I kissed him.

"I feel like it's too soon, Ian. We need to talk a bit." "Of course, we can talk, but I know its right."

We never really talked any more about it, never brought it up. We have simply been together almost every day since.

For the most part they have been wonderful days and months.

The truth is, however, that we have had our moments.

Feargus

We have had tearful, beautiful, wonderful moments of intimacy, moments when we clung to each other in the intensity of deeply satisfied longing and the need for solace and fulfillment.

We also had less satisfying moments. The awkward moments are always about small things, inconsequential things, like the darkness of the toast, or cream not soy in the coffee, or leaving the other's car parked on the street, or I don't know what else.

We have been negotiating a cautious new path over well-worn and deeply rutted roads. We have each had to step back for a second and regain our ground, then begin again.

I would like to say that every new moment was fresh and precious to us both, but I believe we were both very much alive to the inherent complications of this newly morphed relationship. And now, this idea of adopting a dog has suddenly further complicated things for me. At times, however, and quite often, we have been also very close to feelings of complete joy and contentment.

Their house, Maggie's and Ian's, which had been placed on the market, sold quickly - in just a few weeks. Quite a surprise given the economic conditions at that time. It was located well and priced right, still the two real estate hallmarks even in a tight economy.

As that house was closing, Ian found this lovely slightly smaller house which he bought for two reasons. It had a spectacular and dramatic cook's kitchen with a skylight and a wet bar, and, it had enough space that we could bring together my extensive cooking gear with Maggie's equally fine collection of epicurean gadgets. Even better, it was a kitchen so large that we would be able to cook and bake together.

The second reason he bought it was because it had this most delightful cozy, fireplaced den, which would become my writing room. This special room leads out to the laid brick patio which so often absorbs my attention for long periods of time.

The writing room is also often a reading room for us both.

It houses part of his library and some of Maggie's rarer books neatly placed along one long wall. It also hosts what remains of my own reference library, slimmed down considerably since the advent of Google.

The room accommodates a lovely large simple oak table where I can spread out if I need to, or where I can occasionally meet with a colleague or two.

It is a quiet room always. A haven. Acquaintances are rarely invited into this room, and strangers almost never. It is our lair.

It took no convincing at all for me to move here from the stagnant and not very pretty coastal town where I was living, in fact this move was very exciting. A move to the valley had been on my radar for some time. I was delighted to make the change, and leave behind the grip of the past and all its murky and disquiet associations.

We wanted to create our home here. A house is different from a home. We spent an intense and somewhat revealing deal of time trying to define what a home meant to each of us.

But this thing, this entity, this set of vague parameters and questionable virtues which we call 'home' is an elusive and curious creature.

Sometimes, for me at least, home is just a particular voice on the phone, perhaps the timbre of that voice will give me a certain awareness of home. Other times the stimulus is just a sound - like the metal-on-metal squeal of the wheels of an elevated train as it negotiates a tight turn in a densely populated urban setting. Perhaps it might be the lugubrious wail of a loon across a glassy lake at dusk, lonely, alone and seeking some kind of harmony with the world.

Each of us holds in our memory or at least in our imagination some picture of home, blurred, distorted, and idealized perhaps, but a picture nevertheless.

Some of us spend our lives in a desperate struggle to re-attain or to rec-reate or to re-imagine that elusive impression, that ideal.

And then a few of us exhaust ourselves, trying to extricate our psyches from the emotional and histrionic pull of home, trying to dislodge ourselves from it, trying to escape it.

Ian and I wanted to thoughtfully create a home that was peaceful and neutral, a safe haven for ourselves, our families, our friends. We also wanted it to be a place where those who knew and loved Maggie would also feel welcome and comfortable. It was a big order, but we would each try to find our way.

But here, inside this cocoon of my cozy writing room, with its efficient well-equipped computer desk, its big broad work table and comfortable overstuffed sofa and chairs, with a little late era Miles Davis playing on the sound system, all was calm and quiet. I was at home.

The winds had come up just a tiny bit, rustling through the escalonia, and I noticed that the clouds were making increasingly rapid progress on their trek to oblivion.

And with no particular idea to force it away, my mind returned to this one persistent thought - that my dear Ian needed a dog to complete the process of making our house a home. It's a fact which I had to face, regardless of my personal narrative.

We were having drinks with a group of friends recently and the topic of our efforts to formulate, to intellectualize and verbalize a definition for 'home' came up in the conversation. We were all laughing and throwing out both sensible and silly ideas, when Ian calmly said – "A home is good hot food and a sleeping dog."

We all laughed, most of us able to relate to the statement on some level. Ian got a small round of applause and a couple of pats on the back, but the look on his face went deeper than amusement. So there it was, once again. That phrase was his truth and I was going to have to acquiesce to it, trust it, and believe in it.

And then the image of Feargus throws a shadow across my mind. Several years before this time I had lost Feargus, the very special, very handsome dog in the photograph. I was uncomfortable revisiting that story and the events which surrounded it. It caused me anxiety and sadness. Ian was respectful, perhaps overly respectful toward my feelings. He knew that I had not touched on that subject in the first stages of my canine unburdenings.

I thought, in his avoidance of the subject, that he was making a kind of sacrifice without knowing all the details of the story. I was just a little uncomfortable that he thought he should make such a sacrifice. I was not completely sure we needed to talk this thing out to its end, but since the opportunity had not presented itself, I left it alone.

That is one very significant difference between us. I hold on to the hurts, the pain. I keep them close to my heart and have never been able to share those feelings beyond a certain layer of exposure without extreme anxiety.

Ian, on the other hand is an open book. Thoughts, ideas enter his process, get washed through his impressive intellect and are then flushed away or catalogued, except for his experience with Maggie. That memory remains just under the surface, tender and sore and reactive. But even though these negative thoughts exist at the surface, he doesn't allow them to claw and dig their way into a deeper more permanent emotional level. They will not cause a block or a logjam, as in my case, of undealt-with passions.

For Ian, Argo had been a good old dog, but he was now long gone, and the time had come for him to be replaced. These were just simple facts devoid of embellishment.

I, on the other hand, was simply neurotic on this subject. These two perspectives were going to have to merge.

In this relationship we tread softly and respectfully. We are each keenly aware of the other's strengths and fragilities. We are also equally aware that this relationship is different from any other that we have ever experienced, and that it is a great gift if we can make it work.

So it seemed to me that my neurosis might be ripe for a purge. I could begin to allow that here was a tiny little bit of sunlight poking a little finger into my consciousness on this idea of a new dog.

I lectured to myself that this was the here and now, not the creepy shadow of my past experience. Yet, I would have to prepare myself to tell Ian the whole story, so that this new relationship could proceed unimpeded by regret and self-reproach, justified or not.

My eyes fell on a little pile of books on dog care and dog training which I had picked up from the library a few days before this time. I picked up the top one and leafed through its cheerful pages, brimming with helpful and encouraging ideas and photos of happy dogs and happy owners. Again, I felt just a little bit nauseated, and the anxiety returned.

I picked up the dishes from my lunch. I was getting nothing done standing once again at the door to the patio looking at the sky.

Somewhere up in those capricious clouds there might have been a solution of sorts to my disquiet, but at that moment, memory and reminiscence collided. I was helplessly at the mercy of the history of a special dog who . . . well I was going to say changed my life, but that phrase seems so very moth-eaten and over-wrought.

No, I can't truly say that Feargus changed my life, because I believe the trajectory of our lives is infinitely malleable, affected by many influences, not just one.

I can say, however, with complete assurance and honesty that Feargus, and the band of five feral dogs who played a significant part in his life and death, changed my understanding, awareness and attitude about dogs. Once and forever.

I walked around the desk and picked up the green picture frame. The metal was smooth and cool, my fingers touched that slightly rough artificial velvety backing on the frame and my left thumb rubbed over the sweet black muzzle of the big rusty brown dog in the picture.

Thoughts of Feargus, and his happy, sad, ordinary, remarkable life often gnaw at and seep around the edges of my consciousness. Those memories have become once again crisp and real.

13
Neglect

I was prepared to tell Ian a great deal of the story of my relationship with Rob, and by extension with Feargus, but not all of it. Some of it just might not need to ever be shared. He knew a little, because of my long term friendship with Maggie. She knew all about Rob, from the beginning to the bitter end. But all of this mutual history was crisscrossed with sharp-edged metal bands of pain.

Down deep inside, I think I preferred to keep some of the story to myself. But I wanted to at least try to communicate some of the more significant points which I felt Ian was quietly dying to know. I knew it would all zero back in to my dog phobia, so I let it rip.

We had just finished a nice leisurely weekend breakfast. I was clearing plates as Ian poured another round of coffee.

"So, Feargus lived with you and Rob?"

"Yes, for well over a year."

"Oh, for that long? I hadn't realized. How did that come about?"

I took a deep breath. I was going to have to go there.

It had been with considerable fear and disquiet on my part that, one early-winter day, this new friend Rob and his big elegant rust-brown dog, were introduced as permanent residents into my home.

Feargus

I've been asked by many people to explain what in the world brought us together, we were such odd fellows, and although it looked like a strange combination, it is probably not too hard to explain.

I was asked to join the board of a non-profit charitable organization. Rob was already a board member, and we were thrown together on many occasions when our various skills and creativity and drive seemed to sync and blossom.

I had been alone for a while, and I found the companionship pleasant and hopeful. The ink was not yet dry on his divorce, but Rob wasn't a man who was very long without a woman, so we fell into a routine that seemed familiar and automatic. There were working dinners, then drinks, then once he just stayed at my house after a long meeting.

"Stay."

That was all I said after the last straggling board member finally bid us adieu.

I never expected one little, one simple four-letter word to carry so much resonance. Before I could consider the consequences, and they were right there in front of me to acknowledge, we were living a kind of 'who cares what anybody thinks' existence, being defiant and careless and initially, I think, for a while, at least, pretty happy. I think so.

Superficially at least.

It would never be an easy relationship, never completely satisfying to either of us I think, but it took us a while to figure that out, because on the surface we seemed to be having a great deal of fun. There was a ton of creativity and collaboration, and there were amazing results. We were able to boast of wonderful achievements, seemingly with no effort.

Alongside and concurrent with the productivity, there was also obfuscation and manipulation, some not very veiled anger wrapped up in a history of erratic behavior.

Now, as I uncomfortably look back, while trying to hold on to some innocence and objectivity, it becomes apparent to me now that our relationship was a clicking, ticking time bomb.

How I wish that fact had been evident to me at the time.

I didn't listen with sufficient attention, I suppose, to the casually tossed-out stories about a history of run-ins with police and street corner brawls and a short stay in the locked ward of a hospital in another state. I thought a lot of it was colorfully embellished bravado. And people change, do they not?

I was in awe of his high intelligence and did not acknowledge that there were other feelings, like fear, uncertainty, enabling, and the constant undercurrent of violence that were involved in the relationship. And then there was alcohol, lots of alcohol, and the uncontrollable effects of its guile.

Proper attention was apparently not paid by me when his older daughter Heather pulled my daughter aside at a family event and told her that I should be careful, that down deep, he wasn't a nice man at all.

It was not an idea with which I felt particularly comfortable, I believe understandably. We planned to be married a couple of months after this time. And for the most part, I was happy and productive. And selfish, I suppose. To be honest, I had witnessed the occasional flashes of a kind of Mr. Hyde persona lurking not very far from the surface, in the glint of an eye or the slam of a door.

I pushed those thoughts away, far away into that place of denial and disbelief that carries us often into the open and welcoming arms of disaster.

In my pragmatic and nurturing mind, I was vain enough to think that a comfortable nourishing environment and intelligent stimulating discourse would somehow eventually mitigate any and all pathology. And perhaps I was not yet ready to think of his behavior as pathology at all. I didn't want it to be so.

I did not yet realize that, in addition to Mr. Hyde, I also might have to watch out for the Messers Smith and Parker, who were the more subtle yet equally terrifying fellows in the quadrangle. Those two absolutely loved taking on the façade of the person I knew as Rob. They were subtle, sophisticated, silently menacing.

I really don't remember much of the courtship all that well, it was a whirlwind, not a courtship exactly, just a blur during which we lived just for ourselves.

This new relationship was very public because we both had our community positions and associations. It was also peculiar because of our widely dissimilar backgrounds, religions, friends and tastes.

The relationship created a trap for Feargus and he was an early casualty of the union.

He was the one who was always patiently waiting at the door, proving over and over what a good dog he was, and how accommodating he tried to be. He was quiet and uncomplaining, despite our long absences and overt neglect.

He was patient and he waited without comment, even though he fretted about the sounds emitting from his owner's bedroom. It seemed that both 'parents' were taken away from him at these times and transported elsewhere, somewhere far away from him. He could have eaten the end off of the living room sofa with impunity, not that he ever would do, but he could have done - during these times.

Here we were, Rob and I, enjoying the heck out of this new intense adult relationship. And then there was this pet, who had previously played an active and pre-eminent role in the life of a good-sized family, with a variety of other animal companions, and who was suddenly found to be extraneous, more like an adornment, an accessory, rather than a partner in a family.

In this new life we humans had our work, we had our civic and social obligations, and at home we had the new adventure of getting to know each other.

We never, I never, thought of the dog as a third family member. We never thought of the dog very much at all, I am ashamed to say. At home we spent most of our emotional capital trying to erase for each other the many years of neglect, loneliness and denial in a purely physical way.

There were no longer any children at home to be considered, so we were free, and we lived free with great regularity and abandon. Such behavior takes time, time away from Feargus which meant that once again, his needs were neglected.

We worked all day, spent a few hours on one of our projects, made it home, locked the door, and in two minutes, coats off, sweaters off, piles of clothes on the floor, slammed up against a wall in a fierce vein-opening of need, pounding, crushing out every living thought or thing in its path. Cold calculated raging sex on any given dark rainy night.

And still the poor, faithful dog sat by himself inside the unheated canopy in the back of the pick-up, cold, alone, quiet, waiting until one of us reached to turn out the porch light and remembered that he was still outside.

Or perhaps we forgot him altogether.

Ah yes, hubris.

I had no background or education to question, or to say that this situation was wrong, although I felt a nagging, gnawing discomfort. I left the dog to his owner and never saw myself as a co-owner even though the dog was living in my house.

I plead ignorance.

Yes, I know that ignorance is no excuse. But it is all I have to offer.

How aware was Feargus? How much was he suffering or confused or bored into mindlessness? I really had no idea, but I think that it was right around this time that I may have become aware, at least to some small degree, that I was participating in this good kind animal's abuse.

How could this possibly work? Feargus went from truck to garage, back to the truck, out for a brief walk, or the occasional trip down to the boat to play with some other waterfront dogs, then back to start the cycle once again. It was no life.

How could I not have understood, or cared, that this dog was suffering? The answer to that sounds like a bad excuse, but it is the truth. I was clueless. Up to that point I had never heard the term 'sentient beings' when describing dogs, never heard those words. And if perhaps I had heard the expression, it had no reason to resonate with me.

Rob certainly never treated Feargus as such. I know. I know.

Ignorance is no excuse. I'm not excusing myself, I am saying that

I was ignorant. Mea culpa.

No matter what is said by professorial talking heads about the dog's memory being limited to associations, being stuck in an eternal present if you will, I am sure down to my toes, that Feargus mourned the loss of his former life of freedom and sunny, fresh-air canine prerogative. I am certain that he missed his goats, and the talented clawless cat.

Humans have a strange history of attitudes toward animal awareness. We spend countless hours dressing, filming, overdubbing, and training our pets to behave like humans.

We also constantly affix anthropomorphic attributes to our pets, constructing his thoughts for him and captioning those invented thoughts onto photographs to share with the world. Poor thing, he is unable to communicate those encaptioned thoughts with any kind of understanding that we currently recognize, so we must voice him like a cotton sock puppet.

Yet, at the same time, as much as we want our pets to be human, we also display enormous arrogance in that we deny these same animals even a modicum of grief, when their partner, child, human family or a cage mate is killed or dies of natural causes, or just disappears. We put that animal back to work, as a herder, as a companion, as a foot warmer, and never consider that creature's feelings.

We mourn our animal friends when they pass. Why should we deny this complexity of feelings to them when they have a similar life experience?

Feargus

A former neighbor friend, Charles, whom I had known for a number of years, and who is undeniably an animal-loving fellow by his easy self-description, consistently displays a kind of scorn for his otherwise adored canine companion because that animal is thought by him to be able to live only in 'the current moment.'

His dog had recently ingested a non-food object which was lodged in his intestines and had to have immediate surgery to have the object removed. All went well in the surgery, but upon arriving at home for recovery, the dog was understandably uncomfortable and huddled forlornly in a corner of his crate, whining.

Charles was not ready to accept his pet as a patient, and he was very careless about giving the poor animal his pain pills at the proper times.

"He won't remember this, so he doesn't need all these meds."

Charles' wife made strong objections with pleas of logic and kindness, but she did not get through. I think some of us still assume, from what we have been previously told in our boxy black and white Cartesian way of thinking, that the animal has no lasting memory.

Scientists used to tell us that dogs have a memory of mere seconds. Yet, many normal, everyday, otherwise unremarkable dogs that you and I have known are able to memorize hand commands and names of objects and people for a lifetime.

I reminded Charles that he was quite fond of showing off the dog's hand command memory at every opportunity, and wouldn't that countermand his 'no significant memory' theory.

It is amusing to me that many of us spend our lives in counseling, practicing meditation, struggling with our stress, following strict religious dicta, all in order to attain the higher consciousness needed to allow us to simply 'live in the moment.' Yet we denigrate the animal that we imagine thinks thus, in the moment.

Ah, yes, there is hubris, once again.

Ian put down his coffee mug and took my hand.

During the time that Feargus lived with me, there were always big Thanksgiving dinners. I loved having a house full of people and cooking a great meal with no agenda other than to give thanks for the abundance we enjoy. This particular Thanksgiving was the first with Rob and the dog living under my roof. We hadn't as yet told anyone that we were all one big happy family in my house. Feargus was generally a sociable and appropriate fellow, and I was not worried about his ability to charm my guests.

So it came as a surprise to a few people when there was some commotion outside as the doorbell rang and Feargus gave an inquisitive bark or two. A couple of forever friends who were keenly aware of my dog owning history were chortling: No, a dog? This can't be the right house! We're in the wrong place for sure; there can't be a dog here!

Much laughter ensued and the new family member was welcomed warmly on that Thanksgiving Day. It did seem odd, especially to me, to have a dog in the house. But, soon, by that Christmas, in fact, it would begin to seem perfectly normal.

What is more than odd about the situation was my continued absence of understanding of this or any dog, even one living under my roof.

In the summer I had a friend visiting from Boston. We all went to the little downtown marina to fiddle about on our boat and possibly go out on the bay if the wind stayed down. There was some problem with the engine that Rob was addressing so I thought my friend Bill and I could take Feargus and go for a walk south along the waterfront.

The whole walk, the dog was stubbornly trying to get in between me and my friend. It became very annoying and I felt myself getting a little irritated. I would correct him with a little yank and move him to my left and he would immediately scoot around to my right.

We reached the end of the walkway and turned around to head back. I was now on the right and the dog on my right. Feargus trotted along happy as life itself.

"How was your first formal dog walking?"

"Fine, except that on the way down he was very annoying and kept trying to come around behind me."

Rob just looked at me like there was a tiny Martian protruding from between my eyebrows. He cocked his head slightly to the side.

"He's trained to walk on the right. He thinks he's being a bad boy if he doesn't stay on that side."

Rob rolled his eyes at me and shook his head. I don't know if my hand actually came up and slapped me on my forehead or if I just thought I made that I Am So Stupid gesture. How embarrassing.

"He's trained that way?"

"Yes, to walk on the person's right side."

I had no idea. Really, I did not have any idea of his training.

Things were pretty loose in our house, and other than what seemed to be a few mean little tricks played on the dog, I did not know that there were such expectations. I knew he was a pleasant, well-behaved dog.

Ian had shifted uncomfortably in his chair.

"May I interject?"

"Of course."

"Maybe it's my background, but wasn't that a little passive aggressive simply not to tell you and then watch you make a fool of yourself?"

"The easy answer to that question is a resounding yes."

"And, to further confuse the dog?"

"He loved the gotcha game."

Ian washed and dried our empty blue ceramic coffee cups, placed them back on the open shelf, and stood with his back to the sink as I continued the scene on the dock.

Rob and Bill immediately started talking in boatspeak so I sat down on the bench and looked into Feargus' big black eyes. I profusely apologized to the dog. He looked back at me as if to say It's OK, I knew you would figure it out eventually. And I'm still your friend.

My naiveté was astonishing. I supposed, like my father before me, that you brought a dog home and he or she became part of the family, in some kind of magical interspecies melding of shared aspirations, by sheer will and good intensions alone.

I would take nothing regarding Feargus, or any other dog for that matter, for granted ever again.

Later on in that first year of our relationship Rob started to develop some peculiar ways of 'playing' with the dog. He would call him, and then without warning, slap him flat-handed right across the side of the muzzle, claiming that the dog liked it, that it was fun, that they were 'playing.'

Feargus would let out a little whine and walk away. The parts of him that were Chow and Timber Wolf were screaming Hey, I Expect to be Treated with Dignity and Respect – the kind of respect that I will return to you if you show me that you are worthy of it!

My mind was screaming. How can you abuse him like that? But I was not able, not willing, to take a side in this war of possession and domination.

Downright peculiar kind of fun, that. But it was just one of the many exhibitions of the undercurrent of violence and control which were emerging as explicit in Rob's behavior.

So there it was. A warning. Yes, I think it was my warning. Even those Rob purported to love still might expect a hard slap upside the head from time to time. They might also like it.

Fergus was not free. I knew that and the dog knew that. But he was patient. He watched, and listened. Early one morning, I opened my eyes and they fell directly into the black, bottomless eyes of Fergus as he sat on the chair opposite the bed, his rear section seated but his chest and legs in an agitated left-right pace.

An almost indiscernible grrr rose from his chest. It was easy to see that the thoracic growl was directed at Rob. He had apparently awakened before me and had been sitting at the foot of the bed just staring down at me for I don't know how long. Feargus apparently did not like the quality of the stare, or the feeling of unease.

When I was sufficiently awake, Rob removed his gaze, got up and walked away without a word. I scratched the dog's chest and he got up from the chair, stood looking at me for a moment or two and then loped silently and moodily off.

I felt a chill at the back of my neck. He was protecting me. The dog was protecting me. This dog had, perhaps, some deeper more primitive understanding to which a human was not privy, that a human could not quite fathom. At least I could not envision that understanding in my naiveté at this time. He understood the danger better than I could at that time.

I had a champion, and it was not a matter of dominance or strength, it had more to do with kindness and affection. I was left with a definite unfamiliar sort of dis-ease associated with this thought-provoking scene.

As I look back on it now, which I do most reluctantly, I realize that, at that moment, when that cold shiver ran through my body, that I became the new owner of this lovely animal's patient, undying loyalty, and that if I needed him, the dog would always be my friend.

Rob was the one who had changed, whose ardor had chilled, who now jailed and hit and hurt, whose very presence had begun to feel disquieting and threatening.

On the other hand, I was the one who cooed and soothed, and on those most basic of emotions, and possibly with some finer instinct, the dog made his choice. We can't know, we can only imagine.

88

Feargus

14
Epiphany

Sadly for Feargus and me, this awkward triangulated relationship came to a climax on one particular chilly day.

I wanted to go for a walk, just a simple walk, no more than that. God knows how I preached exercise to so-often-deaf ears. But this was a gorgeous bright, blue, crisp, cold coastal day and we felt like a bit of a ramble. Flat, even surfaces were the best for Rob's chronic bad back so we drove a short distance to a spot off the bay where, in those days, a nice paved road led out to the marshes.

Here in this estuary, a great rich conflagration of migratory and resident wildfowl - Brown Pelicans, Great Egrets, Sandpipers, Grebes, Red-Tailed Hawks, Great Blue Herons, Swallows, American Kestrels, Pintails, Mallards, Widgeon, Green-winged Teal, Red-shouldered Hawks, Loons, and a dozen species of duck - congregated in annual succession.

This litany of birds fed upon the sumptuous low tide buffet of clams, Dungeness crab, insects, worms, immature fish and baby mice which scurried through the wetland eel grass, and hard-stemmed bulrushes.

We were going for a good easy walk, in this paradise of a place, about a mile each way I estimated, maybe a little longer. So I parked the mini-van at the beginning of the trail and got out of the vehicle. Rob was slightly ahead of me. He had recently stopped waiting for me, even crossing a busy street I was always on my own. There was no longer any gentlemanly grace about the man. He continued on, with his gnarled Madrone walking stick and his water bottle in hand. As I locked the car I stopped and glared wide-eyed at Rob.

Feargus had heard the sliding door to the vehicle roll shut. He looked around the empty garage. He smelled the kibble and the fresh water in a full bowl, and knew he would be here for a while.

He heaved his resignation sigh – three short inhalations and one long exhalation, usually accompanied by a plop down onto a soft surface of some sort. There were no soft surfaces in the garage today. His bed, which was usually brought down for long stays, had been forgotten.

He looked around the garage. There were a couple of big machines which were usually noisy and rattling, some hard plastic storage bins, and some big containers of really bad smelling stuff. Not a lot for a dog's amusement.

The little windows at the back of the room were too high to let in any serious light, or to see to the outside.

He paced the room, around and around, his pointed paws measuring the space. Round and round. No herding to be done here.

No cats to chase. Nothing.

He sat down on the cold floor, got up, paced the space and did the same thing again. Round and round.

Up at the front of the garage there was the big wooden garage door which sat just a little wonky on the concrete and did not quite meet the surface. Either the door was warped or the house was a little off square or both.

Under the door, for about a foot's width along the right side, there was a small shaft of sunlight. These precious rays ran under the door and shot into the space for about six inches. The air, right there, was fresh from the outside. So much better than the smell of motor oil, or detergent or weed killer.

Three sniffs, a huff, and he plopped down in front of this shaft of light, his right front paw toying with the finishing strip of wood which ran along the bottom. The adhesive had come slightly loose from the dampness, and the thin piece of lath curled off the door like a wayward cowlick.

The strip came loose with a little toying, and then Feargus' big white canine teeth got interested in the piece of wood. Time went by. Soon a good sized piece of the strip, and some of the surrounding wood, was torn off the inside of the door and gnawed down to splinters.

The sun had left the spot. He put his head down on his paws and went to sleep.

I locked the van with a start and looked at Rob.

"Do we own a dog?" Grunt.

"If we do, where is he??"

"I guess we forgot to bring him."

We just stared at each other for a long moment.

"Should I go back for him?"(Of course I should).

"Whatever you think."

I love questions. Answers are so much more elusive and chromatic.

But questions such as "Do we own a dog?" questions like that are hard and solid and black and white – and always reveal, even without an answer.

Do we own a dog?

Was he even still a dog, that sad creature that we left sitting on cold concrete, gnawing away in boredom and frustration at the splinters of veneer on the inside corner of the garage door? Who was he? He was a country dog, and we could never force him to be a townie. How could we show such inexcusable arrogance?

How lame is we 'forgot' him. No, damn it, we left him. We left him incarcerated once again, in a cold drafty concrete and cinder-block garage, while we took a lovely two-mile stroll on a lovely brisk chilly sunny day, with lovely fresh clean air off the ocean, down a perfectly lovely path along a beautiful causeway out to the bird-infested estuary with nothing else in mind but a walk AND WE DIDN'T BRING THE FUCKING DOG!!

How absolutely far out of our personal realm of consciousness had he gone, oh, he of the perfectly pointed paws, he of the loving gentle limpid black eyes, he of the dutiful obedience, of the devoted loyalty, of the bound-up loneliness, of the unmitigated sadness and regal patience? How far out of our consciousness had he gone?

We went for a lovely walk out in the fresh cold clean air, and we never thought of him, never even considered him. When we would finally go home and allow him out of his cold concrete prison, our persons would smell of all those wonderful fresh natural things that were carried on the winds, things like salt air, sea creatures, grasses, all those things that left their scents on our faces, in our hair and in the fabric of our jeans and thick sweaters. He will know that he should have been with us. He will know that we left him behind. He will just know it, dammit! Dammit!

I was just too completely mad to scream!

Feargus

Witness my humiliation. Judge me for my actions. I am still so very ashamed of this that I could cry, because this is a very basic, very intrinsic flaw in my character. Despite and regardless of my quixotic and ill-fated history with animal husbandry, I had accepted that Fergus would become a part of my life in some way, part of my set of human responsibilities, and I failed him, failed him so many times, in so many ways. Feel free to judge. Heap what you will upon me. I deserve it.

We walked out to the end of the spit in stunning silence, barely greeted a cheery passerby with his inquisitive and friendly Cocker Spaniel, took a few deep breaths at the end of the paved walkway, and headed back to the parking lot.

"He has to go. This is cruel."

"I know. I'll see if the goat guy wants him."

I was shamed like I have never felt shame before. It hurt then. It still does as I think about it now, like the loose flap of a nasty oblique paper cut that gets caught on every little surface and smarts like a fresh bee sting when it catches on a seam or a rough edge. It smarts like hell.

The next day a telephone call was made to the family of the 'goat guy' who had adopted Bernadette and Annie a year and a half before this time.

The phone was on speaker.

"I can't believe you're calling about your dog. Our old border collie died two weeks ago and my son is completely devastated. Sure, we'd love to have Feargus, and the goats will be delighted."

And that, indeed, was that.

His wife was out of town today, so he would talk to her about it and they would get some space prepared, get a new bed, and make arrangements to bring Feargus into their family. He suggested a date in about two days.

So it was that Feargus was to disappear from the palette of my life. It was so simply done. The remorse came later.

Sitting there with Ian I realized that I was cold, very cold. And I felt exhausted. He picked up a blanket and put it around my shoulders. He started a small fire in the woodstove. He sat by me without a word. I fell softly and quietly asleep against his shoulder.

15

Impediment

We had moderately high hopes for this, our second visit to the humane society. I was feeling a bit more relaxed about the whole idea. Of course we didn't have a crystal ball.

There was a sullen gray sky on that morning, with dense, heavy, settled-in clouds socking in close over the valley. The forecast called for light rain. We felt the moisture in the air, but we hadn't seen it yet.

We had agreed that this idea of getting a new dog was going to be an informed decision for both of us. Ian had dogs for most of his life, and I was determined to learn as much as I could from his experience.

I had also been reading a lot about dog behavior, but I was becoming just a little bit overwhelmed by how much there was to know, in order to be a responsible and informed owner. I was shocked at the depths of my ignorance, but I felt that I was making a real effort to be at least intellectually ready for canine parenthood.

Several of my friends, whom I consulted about my historical dog anxieties, casually brushed off my concerns with oversimplified trivialities.

Why are you so worried? It's just a dog. You'll have fun with it. Don't worry so much. You will love it. It will be your friend.

I could not shake the feeling that I would not be able to live up to the responsibility. I was feeling uncertain and inadequate, and I cannot think of another area of my life where those two descriptions might even slightly apply. I suppose down deep inside, we, even the most confident among us, all have our singular insecurities.

After we made a quick stop in the heady air of the Cattery, we were escorted back to the kennels.

The first dog we visited with was another really small dog. I couldn't even guess his lineage. I knew that a little dog was not what we wanted, but Ian sure liked playing with this little guy.

There was a Ridgeback/Retriever mix who looked promising. He was nine or ten years old. A Ridgeback has a life expectancy of about twelve years. Ian wanted a dog to be a friend and companion for the long haul. We agreed that this guy was not a good match for us for that reason.

I became distracted by a pretty female Shepherd mix playing with her five new pups in the second cage to the left. I had been leaning against the front of the first cage housing a very large dog about the size of a Great Dane, it seemed to me. This dog apparently did not like the color of my hair or maybe got a good whiff of the scent of the Applewood smoked bacon I had cooked for breakfast that morning which might have remained in my clothes, because he lunged toward me from the back of the cage. His bared teeth and excited eyes were at about the level of my left cheek when he rattled the metal just inches away from my face.

I let out an involuntary startled gasp of some sort, and of course the staffer raced over. She was oh so very, so dreadfully sorry. It happens sometimes, he's really not a ferocious dog, you just don't know, that was so unfortunate, hard to know why, etc., so sorry.

Ian knew from the blood-drained look on my face that this might not have been the very best thing to happen.

"I'm sorry, I didn't mean to scream. I just got startled." He took a perfunctory glance around the enclosure.

"Well, there don't seem to be any dogs here that we might be interested in this trip, so let's call it a day and try again."

"Okay."

It was a quiet ride home. I hated that this process was interrupted. I hated that it seem that there was always something to interfere.

At this point I think I was actually becoming eager to welcome a new creature into our life. But I had to confess that I still had some of the butterflies flapping around in my stomach.

The thing that bothered me more than anything else was that this situation, this issue, held the possibility of placing a giant wedge between Ian and me. How could I possibly let that happen? What was I going to do?

We had put our plans for the day on hold with the thought that we might be bringing home a new dog. Now, since we were apparently not getting a dog on this particular morning, we stopped by the garden center to look at some hardy plants for the large new glazed ceramic pots we had recently purchased for the front entry to the house.

The day was still cold and dreary. The close-in clouds had finally decided to relinquish some of their moisture, and a fine misty rain surrounded us.

Ian was quiet. We made our choices without issue, loaded the plants and the soil into the SUV and headed home.

Ian doesn't mind working outside in nasty weather if he's dressed appropriately, so he did some organization with the new plants and the bags of rich potting soil. We were supposed to have sun the next day and that would be a much nicer day for planting. I took a few minutes to straighten up inside the house.

I picked up the mug that he had left in the living room after breakfast, the one with the chip at the rim. There are four matching hand-thrown mugs, my favorites, and when he pours the coffee, which he usually does, he always takes the mug with the chip for himself and gives me one of the better ones.

Every time I pick up that chipped cup, from whatever remote or unusual corner of the house in which it happens to appear, I place it in the sink or in the dishwasher amidst a torrent of mini-thoughts about the interesting and sometimes peculiar nature of love.

What is he thinking when he makes that decision to give me the intact cup? Is it conscious, does he feel he is making a sacrifice, how much of love is just plain sacrifice?

I'm thinking this. Two people are choosing to see a movie.

One would like to see Movie A but the other would prefer to see Movie B, one agrees to see Movie B because it makes that person happy to make the other person happy. Now this sort of thing has to be done with an open heart and honest intention – one must purely wish to please the other – because otherwise, the recipient Jof the proposed affection will never truly feel comfortable with the decision, and always wonder if movie A might have been the better choice.

We talk. Ian and I talk. We'll go see both movies that day if we can arrange it. But we also have a kind of priority system which we use in case we can't make a choice. It is fair and equitable and we both win. I works out nicely.

I think, no I am certain, that Ian and I have equal affection for each other. I know that he treats me with enormous respect, that he always takes an active interest in my work, my friends, and in my opinions.

He is also a man who does not blush at passion, and I have felt that we both equally enjoy the ease and intensity of our shared feelings.

I descend into the silliness of a teenage girl in the throes of her first love when I take the time to just sit quietly and appreciate him.

Sometimes, when I am deeply engrossed in a project, legs tucked up under me in my chair, long hair held out of my face with a chop-stick through the thickest part of a casual knot, mountains of papers strewn about in seemingly incomprehensible piles, mumbling or grumbling to myself, that's when he appears, leaning against the doorway of the room, arms crossed, tall, reedy, relaxed, warm, smiling.

I might have no idea how long he had been standing there, except that I had a vague general sensation. His presence, my recognition of his presence, had changed everything in the room, the temperature, the color, the texture, the energy of the place.

Once, when I had been stalled in my work for a little while, sitting with my head in my hands contemplating how to proceed, I became suddenly aware that he'd placed his warm body against my side, and then his soft gentle lips touched the back of my neck.

"Need a break?"

I closed my eyes and smiled a sigh.

"A short one maybe."

Then he took my hand and led me to the big brown leather overstuffed sofa on the other side of the room in a gentle seduction. There is always time for this.

He is not just overtly affectionate, he is also wise, enormously intuitive, pragmatic, inventive, cultured and charming. My good fortune is unimaginable.

An intensely beautiful recollection, to be sure, but my immediate problem persists when I open my eyes. This longstanding deep-seated phobia leaves me riddled with angst, and uncertainty.

I have no real understandable adult justification for this extreme behavior, but phobias do not require legitimization in order to maim and to cripple. A phobia is a selfish thing. It requires that both the innocent and the afflicted conform to its regime as well. It prohibits an open heart and honest intention.

It is an albatross that strangles love and openness.

What was I to do? I was being senselessly and voluntarily handicapped.

I am not my mother, and I don't want her weirdness to affect me any longer. But I don't know how to end this.

Feargus

16
Intrigue

A heavy reinforced cardboard box, neatly wrapped in brown paper, sat mysterious and mute on the dark orange Mexican tile floor in the entry hall. The box had been carefully and efficiently delivered up the meandering flight of gray slate steps to the house's side entrance by a pleasant UPS driver, on a crisp cool misting Tuesday morning.

I knew in general what the box contained. I had been expecting it. My signature had been applied to the e-pad, the door behind the deliveryman had been closed, and the deadlock thrown. I sat down on the small sofa in the entry and stared at the box for a whole minute, maybe longer.

There was a newly poured cup of early morning coffee to be drunk, a fresh poppy seed bagel to be eaten with the last jar of the previous season's local blackberry jam.

I mused over the box for a bit longer as I sipped the coffee. The classical radio station was playing something by Shubert, perhaps, or Schumann. I have trouble with those two. I got up and walked around the box one more time, assessing, considering, absorbing its silent fertility. It wasn't a very large box, just heavy, but its contents would mean very much to me.

My agent had arranged for me to look over a prospectus for a new documentary project, a form that had been developing as my particular specialty over the previous few years.

The cardboard cube had every last iota of my cautious and wary attention at that moment. I would like to pretend to be casually indifferent to it, but my curiosity was just too great. Most likely it would contain a few books, scholarly papers, newspaper bits, bibliographies, historical timelines, perhaps some photographs or statistical reports, and other items of the grey literature, relating to this new project. It should also have a preliminary outline from the producers.

I would have to go over the material in depth in order to decide if this was a project which would hold some interest for me. It is a serious decision, not just from a financial point of view.

If I decide to accept the proposal, the project would become my entire life, requiring many, many hours of intense daily work, and months of diligent and serious study on my part in order to have sufficient understanding of the subject in order to proceed. I would essentially be married to the project until its completion which could easily run to two years or more.

It would also mean that I would probably not be able to take on any smaller projects during that entire period. I might be able to squeeze in something, like an edit or a revision of a chapter or two, but I may have to pass on some larger projects which might be close to my heart.

I could have done any number of things before finally making the kind of commitment that would require going to the next room to get the bright orange box cutters and stripping the recently delivered carton of its mystery. I knew that the project was complex and dog-related, so dawdling a bit longer seemed only right, given my recent forays into self-confession.

Maybe I will go outside and mow the lawn. Or, having all the ingredients on hand, I could make some fresh spinach fettuccini on my hand-cranked Italian pasta maker. Then I could chop a small mountain of baby veggies, and cook a large pot of the fresh pasta for primavera. Of course, then we would have to invite some neighbors over to share it.

Or, I could just go out and stare up at the clouds. Anything but tackle the information and the decision that would have to follow.

I rarely waffle like this, and my ambivalence speaks to my state of mind. Once I agree to the project there will be, must be, total commitment, no turning back, so I am always deliberately cautious and slow in my approach to that decision.

But this is getting silly.

Apparently I am not the only person who thinks this way because when I looked up, Ian was standing in the doorway, reaching out toward me, palm open, bright orange box-cutters in hand.

Feargus

17

Hunger

Hunger is the author of genius. Its ache calls out for brilliance and tenacity, for violence and cunning.

Hunger is vicious and persistent, like the thought that plays inside your head and never goes away. It is with you everywhere and always, until it is slaked.

Hunger is a parasite. Nothing steals vigor and quells fire and robs vitality like hunger.

Hunger is fierce. It eats at your soul. It devours your rationality. It feeds on your frailties.

It was an unusually chilly late August with overnight temperatures in the forties and fifties expected from then on.

Here at the weathered dark brown tool shed on the Slough side of the road, there were still parts of the concrete slab that stayed warm from the daytime into the night. The earth below it had not yet started to change to frigid to frozen and the slab was still able to refract even today's weak sun's rays for hours on end.

One eye twitched, and then the other, and in a few moments Jack was almost awake from his thick, dense rheumy sleep. What's the buzz? It was just before dawn and there was a small commotion in the pack. Cotton was running around in frenzied circles but she was managing to keep quiet.

Buster was sitting up and alert.

Bjorn was awake but still lying lazily on his side.

Nacho was gone. Her scent lingered, though, profoundly in the thick morning air. That was just the thing that agitated Cotton. Where's Nacho? She would say if she had a speaking voice, Where's Nacho, anybody seen Nacho? What do we do without Nacho? Tell me, what's next without Nacho? Please! I need to know. I need an answer. Anybody? Anybody know anything? Round and round.

Of course, none of the other dogs could give her an answer.

They were wondering as well. What happened to the bitch?

Then, like some crazy canine improvised incendiary device, Nacho dove up from the bank below the house and onto the concrete slab in a total frenzy, with her cheeky brown Pug face all indigo and dripping. C'mon, let's go, wake up. Come with me, follow me.

Can't you see? We've got berries, c'mon. This way. Let's go.

Follow me, come on.

Hungry and always excited for adventure, they followed. Just about an eighth of a mile south, there stood a spread of evergreen salal, leathery thick, finely toothed with reddish-blue and dark-purple fruits ripe for the browse. There'd been a frost a couple of nights ago and the berries were now at their tastiest. Come, run, come along. Follow me. It's just down here.

Not two hundred yards from where they slept, Nacho had discovered a thick, rich mother lode of fully ripe salal berries growing over the bank in the full warm sun. They could eat until their stomachs hurt and their hearts were full. Safe, no worries.

Munching, gnawing, slurping purple juice, oh this was heaven, plenty for all and tasty beyond belief. Good job, Nacho. We can take or leave salal berries normally, but when they're this sweet and this sun-warmed and this abundant, and we're this hungry, we're deliriously happy to have them.

Somewhere over the bank, through the dawn light, they heard a screen door slam. All ten ears perked up, attached to attentive cocked heads. In the distance there was some heated human altercation and the screen door slammed once again.

Berries, delicious berries. Mmmm, more warm sweet berries.

A minute or two later, the screen door squeaked again but did not slam closed this time. A few seconds after the expected slam, the shell of a Mauser type .243 Winchester bolt-action rifle, mounted with a Weaver K4 scope, whizzed with terrible speed and horrifying lack of precision past the perked up right ear of Buster.

A second shell whizzed with ferocious speed past Buster's left ear. Then a third, hitting the bank.

The altercation at the house resumed with both voices raised in a screaming argument. Again, the door was slammed and the shouting went indoors.

The pack waited, quiet, licking each other's dripping indigo muzzles. The door slammed closed once again and there was quiet.

On Nacho's cue they were back to the frenzy. Berries, berries, berries, delicious berries, a sea of berries. The entire world is berries. Abdomens were beginning to distend, gas pangs were felt, time to head back and sleep it off.

The lady of that screen-door slamming house had gotten up before dawn that day. Mason jars had already been boiled and were holding in a large pot of hot water on the stove. Jam-pot, bags of sugar, lids, tongs, towels, lemon juice, measuring devices and liquid Pectin were all carefully laid out in expectation of the perfect day for canning perfectly ripe berries.

Despite the patient cultivation of the bank, and the attempt at canine genocide, she will definitely not have salal berry jelly for this years' Christmas gifts.

Up and over the ridge, the pack trotted contentedly back toward the shed. One house away to the south, Buster caught the scent of a trashcan full of promise. He wasn't a great huge dog, but he was broad and strong and he chest-butted the can. In a lucky blow, it fell over, snapping the metal anti-varmint lock as it hit the concrete, spreading a variety of fairly recent refuse from a family who believed that fast food was a way of life and not an occasional option.

Stomachs were a little grumpy right now from the carnival of salal berries, so each dog in turn grabbed just a little something for later, cold greasy French fries were always delicious, buns enriched with the juice of the flame-broiled burger, bits of fried fish, wilted salad, quite an assortment.

Dogs on their own are opportunistic feeders with catholic tastes. So for these ferals, this was all good stuff for later and should not be left indiscriminately for the next hungry varmint.

Now it would be time to sleep off the berry jag with a lovely mid-morning snooze. All five were out in a blink, like a second rate has-been fighter decked by a young contender.

An hour later, there was a stir in the atmosphere. A group of four kids, teenage humans, out for mischief, were looking for a place to get high, then eat their homemade lunch and play violent video games. They stroll with confidence into the back yard of the house, vacant for over a year, and tied up in the foreclosure process. The first boy, who'd been here many times before, came laughing and tripping into the yard.

The newly formed family of five canines, sensing a threat right out of sleep, had instantly become a chorus of barking, shrieking growling animals protecting their space.

Bjorn, stood stiff on all fours out front, starring at the boy. He began a low deep, threatening internal surly growl that you would not want to hear if you were a young boy in the backyard of a foreclosed house with a stocky sixty-some-pound Norwegian elkhound staring you down with his canines bared.

The boy then caught a glimpse of the pit mix up close behind him with his teeth equally bared his and tail stuck straight out.

Then Cotton leaped from the lid of a trash can up toward the shoulder of the teenager, almost into the boy's face, startling him while his eyes were riveted with fear and uncertainly at the Elkhound and the Pit. Her body glanced off his shoulder, distracting him, landing on the thick roll of de-composing shag carpet.

His reaction to the little dog's attack was convulsive and startling. The can of heavily caffeinated soda flew up into the air and then burst on land-ing on the concrete. From the other hand fell the precious brown bag con-taining his lunch. It had been expelled from his hand and dropped on the ground at the feet of the little white dog.

The young boy, who, from this one experience, would instantly become more of a man, ran as fast as his feet would carry him back to his pals. He would have to cadge some food from one of the others, and they would need to find another haven for their goofing off, but not this place, at least not today.

In the meantime, Bjorn stared at the lunch bag that had burst open on landing. They all surveyed the contents: a lovely freshly made ham sandwich on white bread with mayonnaise, wilted lettuce, and a paper thin slice of tomato, and a couple of pieces of green-dyed sweet pickle, a luscious green tart apple, a zippered plastic bag full of crispy chips and some Skittles. All had been nestled inside the boy's crisp brown bag. Bjorn stared at it, his head cocked slightly to the side, like it was some unbelievable gift from the gods.

Together, in an unspoken, eyebrows raised look, Bjorn and Cotton and Buster stared at the unexpected spoils. And then they looked at each other. Cotton cocked her head to one side. Some sort of unexplainable canine understanding took place. Fellas, that was not hard. We did that together. We tag-teamed that kid and look what happened. Here is yet another way to get food, freshly made, reasonably uncontaminated food, not that we much care about that, food is food.

Here's how it goes down. You growl with bullying, Bjorn, with your big surly self, keeping them riveted, with the pit as backup, and I sneak up and surprise them from the side with ferocious yapping and we get whatever is in their hands because they are so scared they just drop it and take off like a greyhound out of the gate. She looked down at the bounty, looked back at Bjorn and Buster.

Bjorn, buddy, thought Cotton, we can do this. This could be fun. Let's try it again.

And they did try it again and again during the next week, with variations of success, at the nearby convenience store.

Happy people, fresh from purchasing a nice individually prepared deli sandwich or a fat old corn dog or a hot juicy oversized breast of flash broasted chicken from the deli side of the little store, became unhappy freaked-out people when they encountered a feral dog trio with teeth bared, and they reactively threw away their precious cargo.

These humans just weren't sufficiently alpha, or in control.

Perhaps they hadn't any kind of understanding of the laws of nature, and how those laws might help them to hold on to their property. Just ignorance.

Buster started to take the lead in this activity now and then, and the three became a real team. The owner of the convenience store was getting tired of customers' complaints and called the police, but the only dog that was able to be described to the authorities was the elkhound.

Just about this same time, somewhere in the immediate neighborhood was a young man with access to multiple sizes and styles of firearms who was pissed that he lost his lunch to a stinking dog. That stinking dog was going to have to pay the price. He would see to it.

All during this period of time, maybe a week, Nacho and Buster spent hours with their heads together, alert and on watch.

Buster had become a kind of canine counselor to Madame Nacho.

Their time was limited in this location, and they both knew it. They didn't factor in the pissed-off teenager with access to guns; they just knew that this was a very temporary location and that their stay here couldn't last much longer.

Then a combination of dark and meaningful events occurred that would convince the band that they needed to move right now.

It was Sunday night, a quiet night in general, until about two in the morning, when the big nasty noisy sanitation trucks came along to empty the dumpsters, transferring all the wonderful detritus of the town into even bigger portable cauldrons of filth to be hauled away to an unthinkably immense cesspit somewhere out in the county, away from the town and neatly tucked out of everyman's mind's eye.

What this meant was that there would be no dumpster diving, no trashcan foraging, no scavenging, no nothing much to eat for a couple of days until the humans re-created their refuse anew in this incessant cycle of waste.

There had been a torrential downpour during the night, blowing and swirling from the south.

The ground was saturated and the plastic corrugated roof continuously dripped loud plops of moisture off the eaves of the roof above it. Soaked and soggy, they knew they could be a couple of days without much food, except for what Bjorn and Cotton could scare away from the patrons of the convenience store. They were generally okay with that. Dogs don't really need to eat every day.

However, previously domesticated dogs like these, who have become accustomed to eating good food on a regular basis, sometimes find it harder to obey their natural needs, and so they go off looking for a mouthful of this or that to satisfy a kind of artificial hunger.

The remains of a fairly fresh kill of a young lamb that Jack discovered this morning a surprisingly short distance from their home shed was an opportunity not to be missed, and a gift he was happy to deliver. He loped, he never ran any more, and barked an odd C'mon guys, this way, kind of deep-throated bark that was unusual for him and which caught the attention of all the others.

It was a smallish ten- or eleven-week-old lamb that probably strayed from its home. It was most likely an early morning coyote kill, by the look of the neck lacerations. It lay just off the edge of a pasture fence a little to the west.

The coyote probably planned to return pretty soon, most likely with friends, so these dogs would have to make use of this carcass in a hurry to beat the coyotes and make sure that the crows and the other scavengers wouldn't take over first.

These hand-fed, home-bred dogs didn't know their way around a carcass very well, but, hey, offal was offal, off a dead lamb or out of a can, and they would figure it out.

First, they circled the barely-warm carcass and looked and sniffed. How hard could this be? Nacho tore away at the trapezius, her canines sinking deeper into the supraspinatus, her head flailing from side to side, ripping and tearing.

Next Bjorn went right for the abdomen, his big teeth tearing away the soft superficial fascia and then hitting the pay dirt of organ meats and intestines, liver, heart, and stomach – still filled with not quite soured milk and the little lamb's first bits of ingested sweet grasses.

Buster, after sating himself with muscle and fat from the haunch, moved over to the head and snapped off, with his massive jaws, a piece of the mandible with milk teeth still attached and planned to cart it home. He had his trophy for the night, his chew toy for a later time.

Jack and Cotton concentrated on the large muscle mass at the rear of the lamb, Cotton's sharp pointy teeth shredding and tearing at the flesh. There was plenty for everyone and they scarfed down as much as possible into their short and fast digestive systems.

No serious and sensible mastication was necessary, leading to the perfect bolus to slide effortlessly down the throat for this pack. Instead, huge chunks of viscera, bone, fat, connective tissue, all went down the gullet in a flash to let the stomach decide what to do with it. It might be a long, long time before another feast fell so innocently into their paths.

Bjorn made one slight move with a snarl to grab the morsel of jaw away from Buster who growled back, teeth bared hard against his cheeks but clenched just enough to hold on to their precious cargo. Growling call and response. Then in an instant, Nacho was on them with a fierce sharp maternal knock-it-off bark and they separated good-naturedly.

However, the tribe was not alone in its hunger on this otherwise nondescript gray day. In the midst of the pack's dietary rampage, a black Labrador, nothing but a thin coat of fur sagging in ripples over protruding bones, down on her haunches, tail tucked far under her body, desperate for a taste of the precious treat, but too afraid to take it on her own, came from behind the thicket of hemp nettle and purple pea vine, from the south, inching forward toward the target.

Cotton was the first to sense her, and yapped her little head off as the other dogs abruptly stopped what they were about and came to attention.

They raised their bloody faces and placed ten eyes keenly on the interloper whose size shrank under the intensity of their cold gaze.

Once upon a time she must have had a name, but she will stay nameless for this account. Her history was horrifying. She had her first litter of five pups at thirteen months of age. She then had subsequent litters about every six or seven months for the next three years with various Lab partners, always black. Those pups that were not absolutely black were removed after a day or two and never seen again. The remaining black pups were taken away from her and sold at about four weeks.

When her last litter produced only two sickly pups, she nursed them until they died. She was then left in her cage for several days with the dead pups. One morning her cage door was left open after the bodies of the two little pups were removed.

She tip-toed her way outside the kennel and past the enclosure to find fresh air and a semblance of freedom. That was a day or two before she caught the scent of the lamb and dared to face this feral juggernaut in the hope of a lick of fat.

Bjorn, who'd lost a pound or two since the availability of multiple solid meals per day at his previous home was abruptly ended, was feeling fit and covetous and was the first to growl at the intruder. Nacho backed him up, standing her tallest with two front feet on the now exposed rib cage of the baby lamb and yipping her short get out of here bark.

Even Jack, who was very happy sitting over to the side with a nice crunch of femur covered with smooth and fatty abductor femora, half growled her way, dark red meat still held solidly between his clenched teeth.

But Buster, he would have none of it.

Without a breath of hesitation, he sprang from his berth at the recently dead trough and attacked the poor undeserving interloping cur with the full force of his clamping lower jaw which became embedded in her bony unprotected trachea. The top jaw crunched down on the dorsal side of the spinal column.

Flailing and franticly smothered wailing from the interloper shocked the entire tribe, and there ensued a loud chaos of barking and whining and frenzied growling.

Nacho let out a shrill bark. Wait, wait, Buster! Yes, she needs to go away, but don't kill her! Then a horrible mixture of barking and whining rang out from the group.

Buster let go of her head and backed away. With her last few gasping breaths, she laboriously lurched a few paces away, stood for a second looking sightlessly west and away from the pack, and dropped heavily down to her knees.

A pair of resident crows began to squawk, pitching and yawing in her direction. Her legs had given out the last bit of their strength. She sprawled onto the ground, death rapidly overcoming her. She would provide a scrawny target to fill an ever-present gap in this, the latest cycle of predation and scavenging which dominates the wild world that lies just beyond our respective doorsteps.

Buster shook his head and began to trot back toward his place at the table, but he was met with a row of three glaring and furious dogs, tails out, stiff on all fours. He stopped. Nacho then walked slowly past him and circled the female who was obviously deader than dead. She stood for a second and stared at the bony still-warm carcass.

Nacho didn't like this, not one little bit. Buster had made light work of her, that's for sure, because she was already so weak. But, this was just too far. He went too far. And he didn't stop when the whole pack barked him to do so.

She walked right up to Buster and put her teeth into his neck and shook her head. She didn't draw blood and he didn't argue or fight back. He backed up a step or two, his tail pulled down, his big head low on his shoulders.

She'd made her statement then walked back to the others. They just stood for a moment and stared at him. Then Nacho gave some bobs and wags, and they all returned to the business at hand. Buster stood for a second, gave a snort, rejoined the group and resumed his repast. One by one, first being Bjorn, the others resumed their immediate business.

Interruptions to the feast will not be tolerated. Interlopers on this family would not be tolerated. Hunger would always win. The pack would stay in agreement to be sure.

Buster knew he would have to watch himself from now on over this. His impetuousness would not be tolerated. Nacho's actions let him know that he had gone just a bit too far, just a little too far – without her approval.

Hunger and entente were proving to be a complicated combination.

Short work, short grizzly, dark clotted blood-red work was over for now. Nacho signaled this segue with a small throaty noise and a tip of her head, and off they went, running down along the shoals to the edge of Coalbank Slough and straightaway into the cool incoming tidal stream.

Feargus

So much splashing, playing, and general frolicsome fun was being had. What a great morning. Fur was becoming free of blood, fat and grime, then shaken out like a series of mops. Soon it would be home to the shed with dark brown peeling paint, and a good long afternoon rest.

18
Counterblow

The coming night bored into the day, first with soft gray shadow, followed by darkness, chill and foreboding creeping in and eventually dismantling the last suggestion of light. For the ferals, the day's forage was over. As was exercise. Tonight, if possible, a good solid sleep was due.

Toward the deep of the night, he of the stolen sandwich, with one of his father's unlicensed hand guns, and with only the very merest understanding of the mechanics of combustion, walked up to the properties behind the convenience store, and came to the one lone vacant house that stood empty and in foreclosure.

Fifteen and mean and mad that he let a dog scare him into submission, he walked, alone, as quietly as a human can, around the back of the house, behind the garage, around toward the junked up patio. He held a Ruger 357 single action revolver cocked and ready, his hands shaking, sphincter clutched, heart racing. Gonna kill a stupid parasite dog tonight. Gonna kill something tonight.

He rounded the edge of the garage to stand alone in the center of the patio. As his eyes adjusted to the darkness, he realized he was encircled by five erect, up on all fours, nothing-to-lose dogs with straight-out tails, curled upper lips, bared teeth, intently staring eyes and low guttural angry sounds emitting from each of their chests.

Buster stepped forward, his growl intensified, unafraid, bold, a grrrrrr-rrr, emitting from bared pearly canines. Bjorn backed him up on the right. Nacho pulled her lips back from her teeth and Cotton stayed quiet and growled. Even Jack, off to the side, managed a guttural growl.

Back up to the street, sphincter still intact, but bladder evacuated all over the inside of his Levi 550s, the kid ran, with enough sense to put the safety back on the Ruger, up to the main road.

Ashamed again, and cold and angry, he sat down heavily on the bench in front of the closed convenience store and cursed the very god that put him on this most ungodly planet. Then he recocked the gun and sat with it hanging loose in his hand between his skinny wet legs. He was crying now, wet angry tears, clenched jaw tears, ugly frustrated teenage tears. He held a tight spasm of a fist on the handle of the gun, knuckles raised white. He was hungry, hungry for payback.

Some poor local family, following their familiar nightly habit, had just let their beloved ten-year-old domestic longhaired gray tabby cat out the kitchen door for his nighttime prowl. He stretched a good long indulgent full-bodied stretch and then walked leisurely up the driveway to the street, anointing a favorite bush or two along the way with his tail aquiver.

Then he crossed the road near the intersection toward the convenience store under the glaring street light and came to within the 100 foot range of the Ruger single action 357 revolver with 22 mag hollow point ammunition, and became target practice for our malevolent, angry teen.

Window and front door lights flipped on at the cracks of the gun, but too late, the angry boy slinked back into the darkness of the street.

There would be tears in the morning for the family, and for the unsuspecting little six-year-old girl, the first to encounter the remains of the cat, on her way to meet the school bus. The vision of the meager corpse at that moment, shattered and bloody, too shredded for the rigidity of rigor mortis, lay plastered against the curb.

For her there would be no breakfast for a month. Her early morning hunger was gone with the image of the splattered cat flattened on the roadway pressed indelibly into her young mind.

The gun that the young angry boy had taken was discovered to be missing by his father while the boy was out. The stern and violated father was waiting for him outside the front door when he returned.

19
Wonder

The stolid neatly packed brown box sat on the work table in front of me with its careful wrappings ripped off and lying in tatters on the floor. A book, one of the numerous works contained therein, lay open on my desk. My fingertips touched the page, attempting to hold onto the last thought emitting from the lines of the cold set type.

Here is the transcendent thought that rose up at that moment, in three-dimensional full color vapor in front of my face:

The mating ritual of the Emperor Penguin requires that the male hold, for extended periods of time, numerous sustained artistic poses to attract a female with similar sensibilities.

Before some other idea had cracked or bullied its way into my thought process to wipe this one out, I wanted to make the correct neural connections to keep this picture in my mind.

'Numerous sustained artistic poses held to attract a female with the same sensibilities.'

Roll that over in your mind for a bit. Would not the world be a whole lot simpler if humans employed a similar mating ritual? Certainly more men would be attending yoga classes in preparation for the event, and that would be a universally beneficial thing.

From what I have observed, those of us who are not penguins take very much in our lives for granted. Relationships, let's say, or family. Let's start a family we say glibly and amorously, after we have held our 'definingly attractive posture' for a sufficient enough time to lure a compatible mate. We have only the most superficial inkling of what it actually means - to start a family – and often, we have no real positive role models in our lives for the entity we imagine.

Nevertheless, we propel ourselves forward instinctively and bring a new life into the world. And then we blindly hope for the best, thereby answering a call, regardless of the ignorance or ineptitude or insouciance inherent in our nature, since the first frog sat croaking on a lily pad.

This is a mercurial, mutating business in which I find myself. Every documentary contract is different. At times I have been invited to spend considerable time exploring the site of the story, conducting interviews, filming survivors or witnesses. Other times I have been just one member of a creative and studious panel that develops an idea from a kernel, or from a series of historical facts. Other times I work independently with a great deal of guidance in an effort to write one consistent voice for the entire project.

This new proposal has come in yet another form, and I was told that somewhere in this box there would be a two-page summary of the pitch. I expect there will also be a contract awaiting my signature, should I decide to proceed, carefully folded into an envelope and sitting, crisp and unambiguous, atop the data. It falls to me to ingest and digest this disparate information that has arrived at my doorstep, ideas like that of a penguin holding an elegant pose for an extended period of time in a complex and sophisticated ritual.

My interest was definitely enlivened. What could the project be that involves elaborate penguin rituals? Was there some way that I could make that a metaphor for dog consciousness?

This may take a while to sort out.

20
Hope

The third time's a charm. All the stars aligned on our third visit to the humane society. We wanted more of a selection, so we decided that a Friday afternoon, which had been reportedly less busy, might be a good time to go look. We would get a jump on the weekend shoppers.

Ian had no classes on Fridays as a rule, so we got up early, went to the gym at the college, had breakfast at our favorite bagel shop, and headed off to the shelter.

On the whole, I was feeling pretty good about this trip. Ian was sure that we needed to be on the same page as far as training is concerned, so we had been spending quite a bit of time going over different theories and discussing what style would best suit us, our personalities and work schedules. Eventually, we knew that the personality of the animal itself would dictate some of the techniques we wanted to use.

There was one major issue. Which of us was to be the alpha? My schedule meant that I would be the stay at home parent with occasional meetings here in the house or downtown, and only an occasional out-of-town trip.

Ian was either teaching or travelling, so already we had a situation where the less experienced and less able person was to be the trainer and disciplinarian for a great period of the average day. This was going to be interesting.

We could come to only one conclusion: We would both have to act as the alpha parent. By that I mean that we would have to absolutely agree on every element of the training program, and then honestly live up to the promise, without slacking.

I like a calm and quiet life, so I realized that it would be in my best interest to give my full attention to the plan.

We arrived at the Humane Society about noon. The greeter told us that the staffer who had assisted us on our previous visits, and knew we were serious in our quest, was in the back and he would get her.

"Oh, I'm so glad you came in today. I was hoping you would.

There is somebody I want you to meet. I think you might like him. May I bring him out?"

In a couple of minutes, out she came with an adorable little liver and white Springer Spaniel walking nicely on a leash. He had been brought to the shelter three days previous and had just been cleared through their comprehensive and rigorous process. He had been up for adoption for less than one day.

"Here, you should take these. He responds well."

She handed me a little bag of dog treats along with the leash.

Of course he had a story, and it is a story that was neither new nor unusual. A woman who lived by herself was advised to get a dog as a companion. She heard that Springer Spaniels were loyal and good companions, and here she was not wrong. She should have done just a little more investigating.

When she saw him at the breeder, he was just so very adorable. He was a small soft puppy with a sad-eyed brown mask of Zorro. She thought he would make a perfect lap dog. She decided instantly to take him home.

She was right to a certain extent; eventually he might become the companion she imagined, but by the time he was well trained, he might also be about forty or fifty pounds and a little big for her lap.

He had been the runt of his litter and at that moment was still enjoying his original home with the breeder, even though he was already ten weeks old.

His ears were too short for him to be trained as a show dog, and his coloring was ever so slightly off of standard, so the breeder was anxious for this sale even though the conditions, selling him to an inexperienced dog handler who lived alone, were not optimal for the animal.

It was less than a week before it became apparent to the once hopeful new owner that the rigors and demands of puppy parenting – the necessary vigilant training, walking, grooming, playing, socialization, cleaning up, feeding, vet trips, asserting continued and unwavering alpha-ness, dog-proofing the home, instilling purpose, and of course the occasional encounter with drool, were just about ten obligations and responsibilities too many for the reward of the occasional twenty minutes of lap snuggling.

Poor sad exhausted woman. Poor confused and unloved dog. It was a sad story, but one that is unfortunately often told.

She was too embarrassed to return him to the breeder, who really wasn't anxious to have him back anyway. So her son brought the poor dog here to the Humane Society where he would have to take his chances. They hoped that he would find a new owner who was interested in the dog's personality and not just his breed.

The woman would have been far better off to seek out an older dog that had lost his home for some reason. That dog might have been able to train her about his needs, and give her the gratification that a mature dog can offer.

The staff person walked with us out to the sunny walkway. Ian asked me for the leash and the three of us spent about half an hour getting to know each other on the gravel path and lawn area behind the kennels.

I could actually start to feel a part of me unclench - the part of me that had been tied up in a tight ball, the part that was held in my psyche beneath a cloak of obfuscation and regret, the part of me that was drawn with a darker palette. They began to ease, to become lucent, pliable.

Cautiously, I started to think that this dog seemed perfect for us. Ian knew it instantly, and I, in the deepest part of my frightened and confused heart, knew it as well. I felt a little giddy and gently excited.

But, of course, we wanted to be absolutely sure, so we paraded around with him over the walkways and lawns. We had him meet and greet other dogs being walked by volunteers and other potential new parents. We saw that he was calm, gregarious, and not at all fussy about the leash. He was perfectly willing to socialize with other people and dogs. We also felt that he had the right energy for us.

I sat down next to him, stroked his head, and looked into his eyes before I took back the leash. I whispered under my breath.

"I hope we can understand each other, buddy."

We walked around for another ten or fifteen minutes, adjusting the leash, giving him some love, a couple of treats, and generally feeling his energy. Ian looked at me and smiled.

"What do you think?"

"Absolutely."

Feargus

At that moment we were ready, our house was ready and our minds were both excited and prepared.

21
Magic

There was to be a little bit of magic in Feargus' life, I am happy to say. And why not? Magic surrounds us. We just have to be brave and have the courage to bump into it.

We occasionally hear stories of couples who have been separated for impossibly long periods of time and are then quite suddenly brought together by some event of Karmic magnitude. We have heard these stories and we know them to be true. Perhaps we know these people firsthand. Nevertheless, these couples have become a part of our folklore, a part of the legends pressed indelibly into our minds.

Somehow these special couples manage to become reunited, by chance, by good fortune, by a stroke of the divine. They stare intently into each other's eyes and then they take careful, tentative baby steps across the impossible toward one another.

They will have to face and overcome a fresh assortment of obstacles, and sometimes they become blissfully rejoined and live happily ever after.

We call these stories fairy tales. We keep them shuttered away in our medley of myths and legends because they are beyond our world of acceptance, beyond what could be considered reasonable and normal. They are unreasonable, yes. Not impossible, but just unreasonable enough to make us uncomfortable believing them, and so we keep them at arm's length by using some childish sobriquet to describe their importance.

Feargus

These stories do not always end well. Often they twist around upon themselves, feasting upon themselves, like elements in an Escher lithograph, and lead to even greater misery and pain than the time spent in the purgatory of not knowing.

However, even for these latter individuals, these star-crossed, ill-fated, confounded and luckless few, maybe sometimes just that one fleeting touch, that spark of connectedness which is all they are to be allowed to have, like Michelangelo's fingertip touch from God to Adam, perhaps that one touch might be enough to infuse each of them with a joy so supreme, so intensely ravishing, so wickedly stunning, that the resulting paroxysm of pain becomes meaningless.

The rest of us, we unimaginative, we meek and humble onlookers, we will never know that kind of passion, that kind of love. We sit here in awe of it and we are dumb and empty and lifeless, because it happens only to the very, very few and we are not of that blessed and select tribe, and must remain merely eternal voyeurs.

———◆•◆———

Feargus, of the beautiful face and delicate pointed feet, still and always did not appreciate being a passenger in a motor vehicle of any kind. So it was with studied reluctance that he allowed himself to be tethered into the bed of Rob's little black truck for the trip to his new home. He squirmed and whimpered and felt slightly ill the whole time in expectation, even before the car moved an inch away from the newly poured stamped concrete driveway.

I wasn't given any warning that Rob was taking the dog away at this particular time, on this particular day. It disturbed me that I might not have been able to say goodbye. I was for some reason feeling that this whole thing was my fault. I knew that was not entirely true, maybe not true at all in any way, but I felt that was the commonly held belief.

A few bits of miscellany had been thrown into the back of the truck, a bag of dog food, the dog bed, a blanket, a couple of well-chewed toys.

When I realized what was happening I rushed out to the driveway, unprepared, in my yellow robe and slippers. I cried there, right there for everyone to see, big fat sobbing tears of confusion and regret.

I could see that Feargus felt unease at this and let out a thin high pitched whiny wail. We had a bond. He guarded and protected me, and did not like to see me in tears. He looked anxious and uncomfortable, unable to sit still and throwing his shoulders side to side. I stared into his eyes and held his face in my hands until he had to snort and shake his head and shoulders away from my gaze.

He stood there, quite exposed and vulnerable. He might have been feeling as if something was going all wrong, but he was unable to reach inside to identify just what it was.

My mind had been alive and active all the preceding night. I was discovering that this dog-human relationship is a very strong tie. My thoughts were wandering all over the place in an effort to square that idea up for myself, to put some kind of explanation on it.

He was just a dog. Come on.

Without a word, Rob started the engine and the truck backed up into the street and then headed down the steep hill to the highway for the twenty-minute ride. It was as if a plug had been popped out of my chest and I had been spewing heartbreak across the lawn. That was the last time I saw him.

I knew as I watched the vehicle dissolve into the traffic at the bottom of the hill that something was just then broken between Rob and me. Hope, trust, belief, perhaps even the relationship itself, they were now broken, but I couldn't bring Feargus back to fix it, to start all over and make it better. At that moment I did not believe that I had the capacity. I had so much to learn.

Feargus braced himself reluctantly and waited patiently for the ride to end. Freedom, joy, relief, appreciation, these were concepts which Feargus understood only at best on some abstract level. In fact, he might not recognize these ideas if they were placed neatly before him in some kind of canine illustration.

Anticipation might also join this group of emotional responses. He was, however, familiar with uneasiness so he just breathed a heavy sigh and rode in the hated automobile, steadying himself as best he could. The truck turned west on Shinglehouse Slough Road and then stopped abruptly after making a left turn into a driveway at the top of a hill.

Feargus did not have any experience with fairy tales. They were another concept several stages higher in consciousness above that which he could readily grasp. He would just have to be faithful and live for the moment, but he was not at all comfortable.

Rob had been to the spread once before when he brought the goats to live here almost two years ago, but even he who was not often impressed by anything stopped the vehicle abruptly at the top of the road to take in the spectacle.

A long freshly painted bright white four-rail paddock fence, punctuated with six inch square sturdy upright posts at eight foot intervals, paraded, proud in the bright sun, in a straight stately line seemingly forever along the high, right, side of the driveway and out of sight down and around the bend to the south.

This neighbor's property, dotted with matching crisply painted white out buildings, all with blue metal roofs, and home to five or six fine, well-kept horses, rose up from this point to extend for a great distance right, up and over the hill and into the pasture away to the south.

But to the front and slightly to the left was a piece of heaven, a property only dreamed about. The land fell off slightly to the north and flattened out in a pie shape with a crumpled ridge of alder, cedar and fir to the left. But the totally amazing thing about this property was that, to the east, out ahead and to the front of this flat stretch, just beyond the green meadow and the clutch of house, small barn and garage, the view was of the wide elbow of Isthmus Slough, which was broad and navigable and fishable at this point.

A slough is a place where a confluence of little rivers and streams gather in a broad flat body to head toward the ocean. On the tide, that fresh upstream water is mixed with the salt of the sea.

The wide part of the slough, or finger of the bay, came directly toward you as you stood at this spot. It then turned sharply to the north at a one hundred twenty-five degree angle, grinding its way against this bank in an effort to turn back to its mother tide.

From here, and down the quarter mile driveway to what would be his new home, the home where a new and equally anxious mistress and master stood waiting for his arrival, Feargus felt a strange new excitement, an odd feeling, an unknown sense of anticipation.

At a distance of about two hundred yards from the barn, Feargus became aware of a scent he had not detected for a very long time. It made him anxious, happy, and alive all at once. His wacky ears perked up, his snout was afire with memory scents and the hackles stood up on his elegant neck.

Rob removed his foot from the brake and began to coast down the slow motion course along the remaining fifteen hundred crunchy gravelly feet to the homestead. Feargus paced agitatedly in the back of the vehicle. Why is this taking so long?

Rob pulled the truck up in front of the waiting homeowners and sat there in the cab for an awkward half a minute.

Mark and Lisa looked at the dog. All three remained unmoving. Feargus looked back at them, his head slightly cocked, his senses on overload, his brain taking in their aspects, their emanations, their smells. Finally, Rob decided he was ready and exited the truck, unhitched the back door, took the tether off of Feargus' collar and motioned for him to jump down.

Feargus got warmly petted and stroked and patted. The two men shook hands and exchanged a few necessary bits of information. Bags of dog food, favorite blankets and toys were unloaded.

His canine olfactory senses were on overload, and he knew something. He knew something that was wonderful and his head was confused. His heart was beating hard against his ribcage and his throat was dry and when he tried to bark he emitted a silly strangled rasp that he didn't recognize.

The woman, Lisa, said something directly to him. Feargus looked up at her but of course did not understand her words, except that her tone was commanding, yet soft and gentle. Then she clipped her brand new leash to his collar, snapped her fingers and walked away and he followed her, perfectly naturally it seemed to them both, to the clean, tidy, three sided, double gated and roofed enclosure twenty yards behind the house.

And now Feargus was to be in possession of his very own fairy tale.

Bernadette and Annie had been agitated and bleating all morning. They had been disturbed and unquiet. Goats have an amazing sense of smell and hearing. Some goat owners say that all their senses are keen. But now, on this singular Sunday afternoon, those senses had gone into overdrive.

Lisa opened the front gate, and Feargus walked, no not walked, hopped, scampered, and sprung actually into the large goat yard. She went across to the pen, slipped the bolt, and unlocked the second gate and Bernadette and Annie were free.

Ah, such a moment of joy and blessed reunion.

This is that moment, the one in which the finger of God, incredible, wondrous, and astonishing, regardless of what god we believe in, touches the earth for one split second and enlightens everything, redeems, delivers, forgives all that has gone before - this is that moment.

Love, - the kind of love so completely faithful and unconditional that we sorry humans can never understand it, never experience it, because our elemental senses are so corrupted and disfigured – the kind of love embodied in that slightly downward pointed elegant finger of God, that was the love that allowed these three creatures to have this completely unbounded and unqualified moment.

There was a flash of brilliance in this cedar-smelling, straw-strewn goat shed. It was an unlikely, an absurd place for divine revelation perhaps, but there it was, nevertheless. The flash had a white and golden radiance on which the humans could merely look with shielded eyes and weakened knees, in awe, through heaving, sobbing, convulsive tears. Such joy.

Right before the eyes of the humans, there was this event that was not impossible, but just unreasonable enough to make them uneasy. Sometimes when we feel uneasy about something that we can't explain, we call it fantasy.

In the face of this remarkable display of honest feelings, Rob found it necessary to rub the back of his hand roughly across his eyes. Then he got back into the car without a word to anyone. He drove slowly back up the long, lovely, now lonely driveway to the road.

———◆◆———

Mark and Lisa had left pretty good lives in the Bay Area a couple of years ago to come up here to this place on the edge of human existence.

Two weeks before they made their decision, a fellow owner's dog attacked a boy at their condo and the homeowner's association placed a moratorium on dogs. It didn't matter that the dog in question had been confined to one room in the condo for a fairly common eleven hour workday, tripped on and spilled his water, was insanely hungry, had a full bladder and was just about blind from inactivity so that when the front door was opened, he shot out past his master and knocked over the first thing in his path which happened to be a seven-year-old boy who was visiting his grandparents for spring break. But none of these mitigating circumstances mattered.

One thing, one dark yet innocent thing can lead to another and another until they form a pattern that results in a string of eventualities. Now it seemed a good time for Mark and Lisa to reevaluate their living situation.

She was a statistical programmer and could do her work from a Wi-Fi coffee shop on Easter Island or Chang Tang, if she so chose. He did something complicated with hospitals and medical facilities and was away from home on consultations about a third of the time.

They had both grown up in suburban leaning to slightly rural environments, paid their dues to city life after five years in the Bay Area, and were ready for some space and maybe some chickens, a good home for their cat, running room for their border collie, maybe a pig, and definitely some goats.

They were both runners, so access to running trails and paths was also high on the list. Above all else, they wanted a place where Jeremy, their then-six-year-old boy, could play in safety and enjoy the free kind of life they had enjoyed as children.

The picture of home that remained in their minds, in its idealistic full-color representation, is what they wanted to recreate or re-imagine for themselves in this place. It would be their own early lives, directly from the childhood of their imaginations, only better.

Cheap land, relative quiet and obscurity, decent schools, fairly good land-line Internet connectivity, these were the things they needed and found on this far strand of the world.

He just wanted to make his wife content and would do anything necessary to do so, including battle the less-than-accommodating airline schedules in and out of the less than pretty town.

◆◆

By now the excited braying and nuzzling had lessened, and the raspy woofing and eccentric canine ballet had stabilized. Feargus made himself content with rolling on his back and being licked like a newborn pup by the two delighted goats.

He also allowed himself to be clucked at by a half dozen hens, squawked at by a large territorial goose, oinked at by a curious black pot-bellied pig, and regaled with a chorus, a cacophony if you will, of neighing from the well-kept horses in the paddock just slightly up the hill.

Their young boy, Jeremy, had been away at Saturday soccer practice.

Not long after Rob's truck had made the sharp right turn out of this picture forever, a shiny new green Dodge minivan stopped at the top of the drive, discharging the boy from his practice.

It was instant. He raced down the driveway and dropped to his knees, backpack and gear tossed aside along the way, threw his arms around the neck of the irrationally ecstatic dog, and cried unforeseen and equally improbable tears. Feargus licked and wagged and lifted his left paw onto the boy's shoulder.

Feargus

What makes a dog just know his boy? Feargus was so happy that he just knew this would be his boy, his very own brand new boy.

There was more sobbing, from the adults. The lady reached for the gentleman's hand. We are more of a family in the last five minutes than we have been for quite some time. He squeezed back.

There may be a few tears shed among the humans, but, like this lovely summer day, Feargus' life seemed to burst open with ripeness right before his eyes. What new wonders might there be to astonish him? And then he saw her.

She was a monster. She was a beautiful, huge, round, longhaired calico, owner of all she could see, an eleven-year-old sixteen-pound feline, and she was walking, with a deliberate and carefully measured step, one wary paw at a time, gingerly taken and dramatically placed, from the front door of the house on a fairly straight line toward the goat shed.

It was her path, a two-inch-wide mildly meandering, trail of matted grass which she used deliberately multiple times per day to go from the house to the barn, and which no amount of mowing and raking, seeding or sodding could erase.

Curious at last, after all the commotion which woke her one suspicious eye at a time from her precious summer sun-warmed window-sill afternoon nap, to find out What The Bloody Hell was going on in Her Yard, in Her Goat Shed, in Her World.

Mathilde, this is Feargus. Feargus, meet Mathilde. Feargus is our new dog.

I do have eyes, humans, to see that it is a dog, and a nose to smell that it is just that, a dirty dog. I will continue to swish my well-groomed side against your ankles to show that I'm just being my normal self. Then if that big brown goofy thing comes anywhere near me … and then that big brown goofy thing did just that, sniffing his way slowly closer, stopping at a respectful distance, and sitting, presenting himself to her, face to face.

Dogs, you see, are European and cats are Asian (no matter that in this instance her name is French – *il importe peu*), so some careful sniffing investigation, one species of the other, is necessary for the simplest most basic kind of communication.

Feargus, as a general rule, liked cats, so he inched closer to Mathilde as she swooned languidly against Lisa's ankles. Lisa was frozen in place, barely breathing, her only moving parts were her wildly moving eyeballs, rotating intently to observe the outcome of this full frontal encounter between species. Mark stood equally frozen at the other side of the structure, waiting, with Feargus' leash in hand.

Mathilde stood her ground, head up, eyes lowered. He sniffed at her, and at her rear end with that fabulous puffy tail windshield-wipering expressively side-to-side, thump-thumping in a vague attempt to be enticing and threatening and grand all at the same time. Have you seen this fabulous tail, you dirty dog, you? Have you taken in its majesty and voluptuous grandeur? Have you seen it swish?

Feargus was not threatened or cowed, by the tail or its owner. He was cautious, perhaps, and curious, as well he should be, considering his past generally mixed feline associations, but he was neither daunted nor fearful of this particular feline presence. She was awesome. And she was giving off some kind of vibe – he couldn't identify it, but it was imposing, formidable. And she had, after all is said and done, a particularly awesome and voluminous tail.

He edged to within a mere foot of the other creature. Suddenly, after a sufficient amount of sniffing and eyes-down-the-nose disdain, a cat's paw, with its claws retracted, tapped twice on the nose of the dog, the final tap staying in place with a determined touch.

The dog stared right at her and did not move, waiting there with her paw on his nose. The paw stayed. Her aloof gaze shifted off to the left and she appeared to be casually focused on some object in the middle distance, her head tilted to the side in superb hauteur. Both animals breathed. Not in sync, but in a kind of rhythm. They did not move for what seemed to be ages. His eyes slightly crossed as he tried to focus on the paw invested on the tip of his nose.

So, here it is once again, the pointed finger of the divine, stretching in to instruct and bind, to accept and respect, to tolerate and countenance, to welcome and affirm.

Big old Mathilde, if her truths were able to be voiced, missed the recently demised canine family friend of many years. This new one would do nicely, she thought. He seemed to be trainable. Then after a few more seconds of trust, the paw was removed.

A few final sniffs were made in each other's direction and then Feargus backed slowly away, one step at a time, as if from royalty, content with this first interview with the queen of the household. He'd learned his previous lessons well.

Détente.

Feargus

22
Hello

"His name is Amadeus. You can go ahead and change his name if you want to, but that is the name he got from the breeder, and the name his previous family member used."

We'd been 'auditioning' the dog for about ten or fifteen minutes. There was a tight little gathering of hyperactive butterflies hovering in my stomach. They were caused by that awful mixture of hope, trepidation and the unknown. I would have to calm my mind in order to control the flapping.

"I love the name. How about you, Ian?"

"Amadeus. I think it suits him."

We took another lap around the grassy lawn, away from the little groups of other hopeful new parents.

It was all fine. He was well behaved, and as cute as he could be. It seemed all fine. Then why were the butterflies flapping harder and harder?

The attendant was waiting for us.

"Well, folks?"

Ian nodded affirmatively and turned to me. The moment had arrived.

My heart was pounding and my ears were ringing but I couldn't respond. I opened my mouth and nothing came out. They both just stared at me. The seconds ticked. This was it, this was the moment. Oh lord, what am I going to do?

Finally, the silence became uncomfortable, and the staffer spoke.

"Here's an idea. We can put him on hold for two hours. That is our policy, so that is all I can give you. After two hours I will have to put him back out for general adoption. Do you think a couple of hours would help you make your decision?"

I tried to apologize, she said no worries. Ian said great idea, thanks. And off she went with him trotting at her side. Back into a cage, not understanding what had just happened, not knowing what was coming next. He heaved a giant sigh and down he sat.

"Isn't there a little Irish pub near here?"

I nodded.

We didn't say anything on the way. The place was just up the street a block or two. He asked for an iced tea and I ordered an IPA.

"We've talked so much about parenting and feeding and training issues. You've done a lot of studying, compared styles and philosophies. I thought you might be ready. He's a sharp, friendly, pretty adorable little dog. House trained, medium size, not a baby, everything we've discussed. I'd say he was ideal."

This was torture, absolute torture. I knew he was right. Right about everything. I had let him think I was ready and I failed him. I failed myself.

His tone could have been stern, but it wasn't, it was kind.

"Tracy, why don't you lay this burden down? Or if you can't let it go, then try to shift it to the side so that it doesn't tie you up and block your future, or your potential happiness. Why don't you try to change your truth? Be here, not in the past, be here in this moment."

I had no sensation of crying, except the observation that there were giant drops of salty water rolling down my face and landing on the table. They were tears that had been held back for so long that I could not stop them if my life depended on it.

Maybe in some ways my life did depend on it. This hole in my heart, this dark cloud, this disease of guilt, wasn't it time to put all of it aside, put it away? I could sense the dawn breaking over that miserable gray strangling horizon.

I couldn't let myself get this dog for Ian's sake alone. That would be a pretense, false and superficial. I would be giving him something to please him and for no other reason.

Instead, I needed this dog for me. That silly ball of fluff and bones was my hope, my chance at redemption.

Ian was right. It's been a heavy weight to carry, and I had carried it awkwardly. I let it pummel and suffocate me. I let the weight of it crush me.

As I sat there, my tears soaking the third pile of bar napkins through and through, I realized that we all have burdens, but it is about how you carry those burdens that matters. Regardless of whether they are made of bricks or grief or guilt, it is how you straighten your back, pick them up and keep your dignity.

"Let's go get him."

We finished our drinks and went back. In the front office we bought a proper sized collar and some little extras, signed the papers, and out we walked into our new life.

A week or so ago, while straightening up the house, I picked up that peripatetic chipped coffee mug, this time from the top of the pony wall outside the bath at the top of the stairs. As I was placing it in the dishwasher, my eyes looked out of the big double window over the sink.

Two back yards down the street, I could see that the young neighbor couple was tossing a Frisbee to their handsome young Boxer.

These young people were both nursing supervisors and often worked evening shifts at the hospital. Nights when they were both gone, you could sometimes hear the dog whining for his people.

Not loud, just a little lonely whimpering.

As I watched the three of them play and run, I think I saw them for the first time as a family.

I stood there for quite a while. I could hear their muffled voices in the relative distance and heard their laughter and an occasional happy bark, but I could only imagine their words. The dog was young, maybe a year old, and he was lopey on his still oversized feet.

Once, with the disk caught firmly in his teeth, he turned his head to the side and backed away, not allowing the woman to have it. The man had to distract him from the other direction and then he dropped it. They both laughed and the dog jumped around in a circle, gave a short bark, and then ran to his 'corner' of the playing field.

They were having so much fun.

Feargus

23
Insistence

Mark had been using loud exploding firearms since childhood. He shot in Scouts and again in high school, and he liked the feeling of having mastery over firearms. He liked being good at everything he tried.

He had spent some time teaching his young son some basic gun safety lessons. These were great father and son bonding times.

Jeremy was a serious and cautious student.

Lisa, on the other hand, detested guns with all her heart. First, she had a basic and far from irrational fear of detonating a loud incendiary device at the end of her fingertips for one thing. And then she also objected to the idea of such destructive devices being available to anybody at anytime and anywhere.

When she was pregnant with her child, a truce was reached between the husband and wife, and an eight-gun fire resistant forest green combination security safe was purchased for the three or four armaments they owned at that time. If Lisa didn't like guns, at least she knew they were lock up correctly.

After moving here, to this extension of civilization, where she and the boy might expect to be alone for protracted periods of time, she promised to learn to use the philosophically and intellectually detested devices to make Mark a little more comfortable. She at last could imagine the slightest glimmer of a need.

A day was determined, preparations were made, all else was put on hold, dinner was assembled early in the day, and the crock pot employed for its semi-annual usefulness. Jeremy was visiting a friend to explore the wonders of the other boy's new PlayStation2, so they were prepared to have a few hours at the shooting range.

The guns were laid out in ascending order of ability to do gross bodily harm and/or fatal injury.

Mark knew he had only this one opportunity to do a thorough job of communicating the entire science and philosophy of firearms to Lisa. He realized that her tolerance was limited and that the subject made her a little sick, but he had to give the training a try. A second chance might not be possible.

So, safety, trajectory, firepower, cartridge cases, ammunition, sizing and lubricating, cartridge reloading, hand loading ideas, open sights, and on and on and on, were all covered in the rapid fire first hour. There were so many points to be remembered, but the most important seemed to be: always treat any firearm as if it was loaded; always unload, always, and put away thoughtfully.

She would do her best to remember it all. Her mind was aflutter. She was a bright, mature woman, but this is something she never thought she would have to learn. I will, I will, of course I will. I will remember that, yes all that. Got it. Now am I ever going to hold a gun? Of course, right now.

"This is a simple Ruger 22 caliber compact auto-loading rifle."

Mark said this as he pulled his gun case out of the back of the forest green Subaru Outback and laid it on the floor of the hatchback.

"Just load some ammunition and we'll see how you do." She pushed a dozen shells into the chamber.

"Is this right?"

"Yes, just right."

Earplugs were placed and he situated the gun for her and she fired and missed her first target. Thank goodness dinner was a-simmer on the counter at home.

So much to know, so much to learn. Her head was just about exploding. It was cold at this informal 'neighborhood' range; here at the top of this wind swept hill with vast emptiness all around. The pop, pop and rat-a-tat sounds of the other hobbyists in the near distance seemed to come from all around. The sky was gray and it was getting cold as the winds started to come up.

Her first shot from the twenty-two-gauge rifle hit the next target, a nice straight hole in a six by six by six inch chunk of Douglas-fir. It would make a nice little souvenir. A few more hits and a few misses, but she was not doing badly for a first try. It was a smaller target this time, a soda can. She hit that a couple of times. Not bad at all.

"Good. You're doing great."

Now a bolt action Mauser style 243 rifle with an M8-4x scope. She hit one out of ten. Her thoughts were flying around in her head.

It was hard to see in the sight with glasses on. She was slightly off the placement of the gun on the first shot, and the kick hit the knob of the shoulder. Wham!

"That would be black and blue. Won't do that again."

"Try again. Place it right and lean into it, lean in!"

"Okay, okay, I'll lean in."

She found the right shoulder placement this time, but the sight was impossible to maneuver, she just couldn't see.

"I can't see anything. Don't use the sight? OK. Oh god, I'm hopeless."

Next, she had a go with the 357 Ruger single action revolver.

"Wow what a kick. Three out of ten. Not good. Two hands? One hand? Made no difference."

"Lean into it, don't squint, and take a breath! Try to squeeze the trigger on the exhale."

"Still not good. It's going to take a while to get used to the kick."

The last gun, the little Ruger SR22 felt like a toy compared to the 357. She liked the fixed white dot on the front site. She could see it. She hit the first target and the second target.

"It still has a kick, but it's manageable. Yes, I could use this little gun. Don't want to ever have to use it, but I'd probably grab this little guy first."

Lots of ammunition was used during this foray, brass casings still in good condition were recovered for refilling and the guns were emptied and packed carefully away for transport back to the big green combination security safe that sits next to the nightstand in the corner of the bedroom.

She knew she would never be very good at this, but at least the basics were now in place. She was cold. Her nose was red, her fingers were stiff and her brain was tired.

He was pleased, and happy that she at least tried. So he was satisfied for now.

Feargus

24
Revelation

My work was going well. A blustering, impressive early fall Pacific storm with high winds and pelting horizontal rain had taken a full ten days to snake its way across my little corner of world.

This day, at last, there was a sunny, fairly warm-for-autumn respite of a morning, and it felt like a true blessing.

I love those long, wild, unpredictable storms with spectacular high surf, but a break in the weather was definitely welcome.

For a few days, at least, I wouldn't have to dress Amadeus and myself from head to toe in slickers and boots in order to go outside for a walk.

I thought I might try to get some sun while doing a bit of work. I had just wrapped up the last loose ends of a short-term commission that I had just written, and it felt great to hit the send button and know that the final check would be in the mail.

Now I was able to devote all my energy to this new subject.

Ian and Amadeus had just come home from a hurried errand to campus. Ian was about ready to leave for a two-day conference in Seattle with a couple of colleagues. He was presenting a new paper, so he was looking forward to the active, rather than passive involvement at the annual event.

The silly rambunctious dog was obviously happy to see me and gamboled about, cocked his head to the side and looked long into my face, then licked my hand, stumbled all over my feet, gave out a happy little half of a bark which was just meant to get my attention. He was still very much a goofy gangly puppy, with feet that seemed perpetually too big to maneuver, but he was learning fast and seemed to be enjoying our puppy parenting classes.

As I looked at him I suddenly thought that he was like some small human of six or seven years of age of age, who bursts into a room with so many exciting stories to tell that he just can't contain himself.

Amadeus wanted to tell all about the new friends he just met, what other dogs had been there on campus on an early Friday morning, how Ian had let him stick his head out the back window of the car on the way home, just for a few minutes, that someone threw him a ball and he ran after it. So much to tell.

According to Ian, however, Amadeus did run after a ball which someone had thrown, but then he just dropped it and let it sit there on the ground. Retrieving, for this spaniel pup, may not naturally be a strong suit, not yet at least. We would definitely have to make fetching a priority when having play time and see how he develops.

My learning curve had been steep and there was a lot of work entailed with the adoption, but it was a lot of fun as well. I have gotten into the habit of keeping a couple of treats in nearby drawers and in pockets at all times.

Most of the emotional issues and dark memories that I have had over the years relating to dogs have been the result of ignorance, mine or others, bad training, or no training at all, so I am very happy that we three are getting an education and beginning to understand what is expected of each of us in this new configuration.

There is a young charcoal gray female Standard Poodle in the obedience class for whom Amadeus seems to have a special appreciation. He was spayed as part of the humane society contract, so he and his poodle lady-friend will remain just pals, I'm afraid. Our Amadeus definitely has good taste, because she is tall, beautiful, intelligent and most of all calm, which is a humorous offset to Amadeus' slightly gangly excitable gait and perpetually wagging tail.

We would have to arrange for a doggie play date with her owner at some point. She would have a good influence on him.

Ian came out onto the patio. He was ready to leave, just waiting for his ride.

"So, you're looking at the new project this weekend?"

"Yes, finally decided that I better get serious."

"Anything interesting?"

At that point I didn't yet have a lot of information about the concept.

So far I had seen three pages of heavily annotated notes of a newspaper expose' of puppy-farm abuse, a bunch of scholarly papers which will take some serious digestion, a copy of the Cambridge Declaration on Consciousness, numerous Xeroxed pages from Darwin's The Descent of Man, a color diagram of Maslow's 1970 enhanced Hierarchy of Needs, a NOVA DVD, plus the penguin book.

"This is all very Large Concept stuff. So what are you thinking?"

"That I better dig through this box right now and find the prospectus to see exactly what the client wants." We both laughed. He looked down at a text message.

"My ride's here, I have to go. I'll see you on Sunday night. Don't you two get into any serious trouble while I'm gone, hear me? Are you ready to be all alpha, all the time?"

He kissed me, looked right in my eyes and smiled that broad warm genuine, deliberate smile of his. His timing was perfect. It was a lovely one-two combination that always leaves me a little weak-kneed and keeps me longing for the next time. With Ian, a kiss is never an obligation or an afterthought, but is always offered consciously and completely.

He gave Amadeus a hearty chest scratch and he was out the door.

The weekend flew by and before I realized it, Ian was back. He was a few hours ahead of plan, so we had time for a lovely dinner out on the patio. I had decided to grill some fresh halibut and corn on the cob. He pulled the cork on a Willamette Valley Chardonnay and tossed a salad.

His new paper had gone over smashingly well. There was a ton of interest and several invitations to speak at other universities. He was very happy about the response and talked about it all through dinner.

"So? Come on, tell me, what is the theme of the project you've been buried in all weekend?"

I did my best to consolidate the ideas.

"It is about Canine Sentience."

"Excuse me?"

"The producer has asked me to fuse a ton of existing research and create an understandable scenario to make a case for Canine Sentience – for the general audience. He also wants me to include the curious relationship of animal abuse and the evolutionary possibility of canine consciousness."

"Hold on. Really? That's a . . ."

"A stretch, yes I know."

We think of pets as members of the family. We treat them very differently, often much better, than we treat other people. We choose. We adopt, rescue, cage, and we take for granted. We breed them, sell them, and treat them like commodities. We even kill them sometimes, if the animal does not suit our social life or does not blend into our color scheme. That's not an equal relationship and it's ripe for abuse.

"What is the essential question that you are going to try to answer?"

"Is human association accelerating canine consciousness? If so, how?"

"Where does that great penguin quote come in?"

"It's Maslow, we accept that some animals have achieved the three lower rungs of his development scheme, like physical needs, then safety needs, and even belongingness and love. But the fourth one is esteem needs, and that's where the mating ritual of the Emperor penguin comes in. Not only is this bird achieving an artistic pose, but he is holding it for hours to attract just the right female. That's one representation of self-esteem."

"It certainly seems to be. So what happens now?"

"I have been given six weeks to develop some clear ideas in a broad-brush approach. Then there will be a meeting with the producer for discussion of an outline and approval to proceed. He's not a scientist himself, he has a panel. But he has a feeling that there is something here that could be important."

"Tell me again in one sentence what is the objective? What's their angle?"

"Would canine abuse exist if we saw that the animal was on a path to consciousness?"

""Wow."

"Perhaps, but the whole thing is kind of a circular argument, though, because Darwin made a case for the potential for animal consciousness back in 1871."

We both laughed out loud. I was glad to have him home.

25
Folly

The assault by the angry teenage boy on the little feral pack's sanctuary made Nacho sleepless and ill at ease. She knew that the family had to find a different shelter. Next time they might not be able to scare off the intruders.

Right now, though, on this gray, sullen morning hunger had reemerged as the chief priority. Bjorn and Buster nudged around in corners for any scraps, but there was nothing.

Nacho gave a grunt and the group started their move south along the slough. Buster had a favorite spot to show them, an old feed shed with a discarded back seat of a mini-van for comfort. Nacho took a look and they all sniffed around for a few minutes, but Nacho had a bigger dream.

They all did her bidding, marching down along the slough, all five alert, calculating, assessing. Even Jack, the slowest and the most worn out, was still attentive and aware.

South, off of Coalbank Slough, slightly east of Red Dike Road, they came upon the pithead of an old coal mine near an outcrop where a seam of coal had broken through back in the day, almost a hundred years before. Here there remained just this rough indention in the hillside that served as the gangway to the old tunnel.

The immediate terrain, here southwest of the town, was riddled with subsidence dimples and sinkholes where insufficient support from below let the earth give way into the mine's under rooms. But this particular pithead had held up.

For a good twenty feet inside, to the first of the stoppings that blocked off the path to the deeper tunnels, you could navigate in relative safety above the seasonal waterline.

Rowdy, acne-cheeked, hormone-riddled teenagers had, for decades, loved this place and had brought old mattresses and blankets, coolers, flashlights, barbecues and all kinds of other now unrecognizable gear for crazy after-homecoming and after-prom and after-school parties.

First kisses had been exchanged here, first tokes of marijuana inhaled, first sips of alcohol had been tasted here, and babies, unknown numbers of babies were conceived here in awkward, ignorant, hurried, unsatisfying and sometimes tearful first-time maidenhead-rupturing copulations.

So it was just the right sort of place for a group of transient dogs looking for a temporary home.

They made an encampment of sorts, each dog sniffing out his own berth, and the hunt for food and entertainment was on. The neighborhood was scoured for the random unemptied garbage can and several were discovered. The occasional patio with barbecue remnants was another possibility, and they came upon one of those fairly quickly. Buster found a small cache of salal berries, a little overripe, but oh well. They whiled away most the first day in their new home, sniffing, pushing things about with their noses, nudging objects into corners, and making comfort out of the old rotting human rubble.

By the next day hunger was becoming a larger spectre. Hunger and boredom were always a troublesome combination.

It started as a bit of mischief to relieve the tedium during the morning walk-about. Nacho spied some motion near a cluster of sword fern under some alder trees about fifty yards from the pithead. Her ears perked up and her body tensed, bringing the others to immediate attention. They looked at her and followed the trajectory of her gaze. She trotted softly at first to get closer to the activity then slowed to a silent, slow deliberate stalk, stiff-legged, with nostrils and ears on fire.

Aha. There they were, nestled in a clearing of bunchgrasses and young wild rhododendron, a trio of ground-nested baby quail, their little speckled bodies agitated, awaiting their mother's return.

The other four ferals caught a glimpse of the action and followed, each with his or her own interpretation of first, an easy trot, then running at a stiff legged tails-down stalking pace. Jack came at the rear, an observer rather than a participant.

Nacho sprang from the downwind side and had the first little one's head in her mouth, shaking and shaking it and letting the body go flying headless through the air, blood spurting through humid air like tiny red fountains, landing just a few inches from Bjorn who saw it as manna from heaven and proceeded to gnaw into its crunchy left scapula and warm juicy breast.

Buster and Cotton chased the other two little things and brought them both down from their fevered, immature and unsuccessful attempt to fly away.

A forlorn mother quail would be unhappy soon.

Everybody in the family got a little something out of this adventure, some fun, some exercise, a few playthings, and a snack.

Thus might it be that dogs make rationality out of chaos.

Some rhythm and symmetry began to emerge, in this nascent autocracy. This new construct was defined to a large extent by the whim or caprice of humans, but also by the emptiness of dumpsters and by the availability of prey. Relationships were made, remade and blended with enviable behavioral plasticity.

Buster and Bjorn, in an at-times uneasy and tentative alliance, practiced and refined their double-teaming efforts, joined on occasion by Cotton. All humans were prey, including the elderly man, close to town off Libby Drive, getting out of his car late in the afternoon with a giant family-sized box of fried chicken with sides which was intended for his wife and visiting preteen grandchildren.

The two predators had been exploring the wonders of this particular household's exposed and overflowing trashcans when the car drove up with the smell of hot fried chicken reaching the dogs well before the tires reached the driveway. They looked at each other with some kind of canine Knowing, with nostrils flaring, then each placed one foot quietly and cautiously in front of the other and came to opposite ends of the old man's vehicle, enclosing the car like mangy commas.

Then, as the man placed one foot on the concrete outside the door of the car, seemingly out of nowhere, menacing simultaneous growls and toothy snarls from the front and the back of the car frightened and bewildered him and he tried to flee.

He had no choice but to drop the precious cargo and head for the doorstep and the broom handle he thought might shoo the dogs away, protect him, and retrieve his prize. But he barely made two steps toward that goal before Buster had snatched the box in his massive jaws and took off behind the neighbor's fence and into the brush and alders at the dead end of this little corner of civilization.

Bjorn stood a second or two more to give a low Don't Move an Inch growling jeer and a smart-assed smirk, then he took off after Buster.

Nacho and Cotton weren't far away and heard the commotion. There was plenty of food for all in this family-sized take-away package, so they joined the resident bullies for a lovely picnic out on the flats.

Cotton never ate very much, so it was surprising when she cached a significant whole, juicy, deep fried chicken tender from the KFC bonanza between her teeth and trotted off toward home. A couple of times she dropped the tasty morsel and Bjorn was suddenly right next to her, threatening to take it from her, but she held her ground, and growled her high-pitched, almost laughable yap and won back her prize.

Back at the old man's house, the disappointed family, hungry, unhappy, and perhaps a little frightened, got into the car, protected by the man with the broom handle and a grandson with a baseball bat, and they drove into town for pizza, their taste for chicken suppressed for the moment.

Jack was finding it harder and harder to run with the pack. He got up later and later in the morning, even though Nacho attempted to rouse him, nudging him with her paw or her muzzle.

Let's go. We're going now. Come on. We want you to come with us.

His strength was not there. By this time he was up a couple of times during the night to take himself a distance away from the camp to empty his overactive bladder, or to evacuate his urgent bowels, or to vomit up some bilious yellow fluid.

The other four were gone for a good portion of the day on their hunger and entertainment-driven excursions. Jack was grateful for the rains from the previous night that filled hollows in logs and deep gouged-out furrows just outside the pithead with fresh water. He didn't ever have much hunger any more, but he was insanely thirsty almost all the time.

Pop, pop, pop through the grasses. Jack's vision was surprisingly still pretty good in full sunlight, and he could see something white showing itself in a pattern across the high grown meadow grass. Pop, pop, pop on a trajectory directly toward him. It was the top of Cotton's puffy white head showing itself intermittently above the tall grasses and weeds as she hopped and sprang and raced her way back across the meadow to the pithead carrying the precious fried chicken tender in her mouth.

She laid the morsel, slightly worse for the wear but still juicy and crisp-coated, at the feet of the immobile dog. She was the first of his cronies to bring him food. She had carried this bit of nourishment across fields and around settlements, over roads and back to the little pit head homestead where she hoped to nurture her sick and infirm mate. She laid it at his feet and then paced excitedly, pranced really, back and forth in front of the gift, waiting for a response from the moribund spaniel.

The morsel sat there. He looked at it. She paced. He looked long at the little white benefactor with the black bulging eyes. He cocked his head at her, thought about the act of kindness, and then he sat. As he did so, he exhaled a long snorted sigh, his big chest heaving on the exhalation. He stared at her again. Then he took the delicacy into his mouth and started to crunch on its precious nourishment, its combination of spicy crunch coating and dead bird flesh pleasant to his less than healthy appetite.

Cotton skittered left and right, happy. She had no expectations, made no assumptions, and probably did not have any glimmer of the concept of gratitude, but she saw in Jack's tired rheumy eyes a kind of appreciation, a kind of awareness, a kind of understanding of her act of total selflessness and she felt warm and good. Who knows if the concept of 'happy' was possible for her, but this was a good feeling and she pranced and skittered in demonstration.

He hadn't eaten for about three days so Jack very slowly chewed the darn thing down to almost nothing, put his head over to the side in exhaustion from the effort, and drifted off into a lovely afternoon nap. Cotton cocked her head, pleased, then sat her little body down facing north, watching and waiting for the others to return, always on alert.

The rest of the family returned to the camp, some with tidbits that would be held in reserve for later. Others, seeming to know their limits, left such stuff behind. What a huge success. What full stomachs. What a good night's sleep there would be. What a wonderful, free, fabulous life these dogs were living.

But they all knew, even though it is said by some that dogs cannot think into the future, cannot plan for tomorrow, that the members of this pack all intrinsically knew or felt, that on the next morning or the one after that, the hunger would return and other schemes would have to be laid, other ploys plotted, other devices designed. But tonight there would be sleep, delicious sleep.

Mists often roll into this coastal valley in the early morning. Foggy mists that say one thing, that the temperature in the big valleys to the east will be very high today. But here on the coast it will stay gray and misty for the early morning. Some strange quirk of meteorological factors blankets the region in fog in this pattern. In the mist, creatures are slower than usual to wake.

Various tidbits from yesterday's bit of piracy were resurrected in the early morning mist. Buster's special morsel that he carefully stashed away in what he thought was a secret place, was stolen and consumed during the night by Bjorn who seemed to be always hungry, at least always greedy. So, after a nosing, sniffing, scratching investigation of his immediate environment, Buster was still without this dreamed-of morsel.

Where the heck is my breakfast?

Nacho had already been out on patrol and scouting. It was still very early. She liked to head down toward the slough. It became her ritual path, across the creek, through the weeded-over meadow, and up the hill.

She abruptly stopped when she reached Snedden Creek and came upon a stag Roosevelt elk followed by three females on a straight course from the forest to the water. The stag and Nacho stood in silence and stared at each other, but the stag, standing tall and grand, still in locked gaze with the dog, took one fluid graceful step to the side as the procession of females passed and came to a safe distance from the dog. The stag kept his eyes on the dog until Nacho altered her gaze and took a few steps away on her journey up the hill.

Best to be cautious, the big buck might have thought. Little sharp-toothed dogs can make a mess of the underside of a soft-bellied female in no time at all. Wise old heavy-racked stag elk.

A clamor of enticing smells whispered its way toward Nacho, here, near her favorite point at the crest, carried into the canyon and over the hill on the updrafts from the waxing and waning waterway. She was almost at her favorite spot when she stopped at Red Dike Road. As she sorted them out, she found a mixture of intriguing animal smells including the aroma of a chicken coop, all cedar chips and corn, and not surprisingly, chicken.

She was also aware of the strong slightly sweaty and straw odor of horses, and the moldy, metallic and fungusy smell of sundry nocturnal rodents.

She meandered closer to the east, the scent of the chicken coop calling to her. On her way, she nosed around the perimeter of the property, checking trashcans and sniffing at the trails of other predators who walked her exact walk during the night - possums, big feral cats, raccoons, a second generation feral hog, and she thought maybe a gray fox, but she wasn't quite sure, even though she had one very good and very reliable nose.

Buster and Cotton had slept in just a bit this morning, but they were now up and hot on the trail of Nacho. They raced down Coalbank Slough and across and down Shinglehouse Slough Road leaving Bjorn and Jack snoring away. They knew her habits and her scent was so familiar that it was easy to follow.

Buster would bolt ahead and crouch in the tall grass and wait for Cotton's stubby gait to get her closer, her white head popping up above the grasses in syncopation, then when she was near he would leap up and the chase would start again.

Nacho was in her usual spot. They could smell her before they saw her. Then, there she stood, poised, sniffing intently, all senses on alert. In an instant, she knew they were there. They stood slightly behind her, nostrils flaring, ears cupped and rotating to the sound, their eyes following the trajectory of her eyes. It was clear to them what she had in mind.

In a flash, on her nod, off they went, all three trotting cautiously down the slope in the direction of the unwary chicken coop. Then over the bush fence, into the broad yard, up to the front gate of the coop and over the top of the less than mighty fence, silent and cagey.

First to meet them at the entry was an unwary and unsuspecting gaggle of Rhode Island Reds ready for the picking, and pick they did, all three dogs, as fast as thunder, a chicken in each of their jaws, thrown, tossed about, pandemonium in the coop.

Next to be demolished were a half-dozen flighty and noisy Leghorns, tossing and heaving, squealing, squawking, bwaking, and then the four-week-old Plymouth Rock pullets being crunched and crackled, their bodies with heads, and then suddenly their heads disembodied, in a frenzy of flying feathers, wings and claws up and through the air, flying like strewn confetti. A big game of chase, and awful, horrific instant carnage ensued as the panic-stricken Leghorns and a few Cornish Bantams piled up in the northwest corner of the hen house in a desperate attempt at escape, smothering each other, body over body, in their frenzy for freedom.

And like lightning, it was over.

The three mayhem producers trotted victoriously away toward their camp with trophies of torn chicken breasts and heads, with feathers stuck to their mouths, clinging to their coats, adrenaline pumping, hearts racing.

The attack was swift, vicious and mindless, leaving the flock completely decimated in one minute and forty-five seconds of horrifying bedlam.

The devastated gentleman farmer would sadly round up the pieces of the dead chickens, most of whom had names and were considered pets, not just layers. He would carefully place them side-by-side as best he could, sorting the bloody bits out according to breed and color, on a ready pile of raked leaves and twigs and prunings.

He would stand there for a minute or two, all alone. Then he would strike one stiff wooden match and light the pyre, smoke stinging his already tear-sore smarting eyes. He stood for a very long time and he wondered at the lightning fast caprice of the universe.

26

Idyll

Feargus waited patiently every day until he heard the far distant sound of the big lumbering yellow school bus. He waited patiently until he heard it stop about an eighth of a mile up the road where it disgorged a half dozen elementary school students back into their miasma of life in semi-rural America.

Chatty noise erupted from the bus, setting off the local crow family in a territorial shouting match. Then slowly the noise diminished until the one last boy made the loop around the gatepost.

Jeremy pulled the day's paper out of its red plastic sleeve and turned down the long driveway to the house. Feargus had him timed, and was at the edge of the fence to meet and greet.

Now it was time for play. Jeremy needed a break in between school and homework, and it was the waiting dog that made him smile and get excited for the rest of his day. The true friend, the faithful pal, waiting at the top of the driveway. That was our Feargus.

Sticks were thrown and balls were tossed. Rolling in the grass or dirt, or on the living room carpet if the weather was uncooperative, was the order of the day. Trust and friendship were engendered, and love, fealty, confidence, amusement, wonder, all these sophisticated anthropomorphic attributes were ineradicably stamped on the relationship of this one particular boy and this one particular dog at this one particular moment in time.

Feargus

Here was a dog in his own private heaven. He had good people and his own door to his very own run. He had his own human boy to sleep alongside if he was so inclined, and if he wasn't, he had his own comfy bed to sleep in. And then there was a solid meal every day, and unbelievably delicious table scraps as long as he didn't beg, no, he would never beg, just wait and hope. Then there were his beloved goats, a cat and a pig. What else could he ever want?

This effervescent, happy life bubbled on for some time. The seasons came and went. The little pig which had become a very gigantic pig, was now the property of a neighbor who lived further up the river.

It was like playing the best part of a favorite movie on the VCR, over again and again.

Summer freedom was enchanting. The neat rows of blueberries down-slope that Lisa had planted a couple of years ago with many healthful intentions had produced an enormous crop.

Feargus sat by her side as she daily and deliberately picked at the treasured fruit. He loved blueberries, and she fed him just the right amount as she proceeded. There were too many blueberries for the family, so neighbors were invited to come by and pick as well. Feargus made many new friends, human and canine, at the blueberry patch.

By this time Jeremy was back in school, and the regularity of the fall season was starting to set in once more, with standard times for the bus, for the frantic race to get out to the bus in the morning, and for the frenzied drive to town in the car when the school bus was missed.

Feargus was happy, even when the boy was gone at school. He had a lady to give him attention, goats to nuzzle, and errant fowl to corral. The neighbor's horses had been gone for a few days. Now the horses had come back, daring Feargus to race them along the outside of the long paddock fence.

Today there was a substitute postman to greet, and a cat with whom to play interesting mind games. It was a life unhampered by worry or care.

On the special occasions when Mark was home for a few weeks at a time, an all-guy weekend camping trip would be planned. These excursions might take them to tall fresh frothing waterfalls, or down special hiking paths enlivened with foxglove and red clover, or out along the rocky salty trails at the ocean's shoreline. These jaunts were often extended, sometimes for several days.

In preparation for such an upcoming event, Feargus was driven to the kindly lady Vet where he was poked and prodded in some very questionable places, pricked with some little bee stings, and made to endure some smelly stuff on his neck and back. As hard as he shook his head, the stuff would not go away. He exhaled a long sigh when he got back into the car. These trips to the vet always make him tired, so he slept all the way home and a good part of the afternoon.

There was a three-day weekend coming up and a trip was planned at this most beautiful time of the year on the coast. Camping gear was brought out, and Mark made a shopping trip to buy propane and replace batteries and make sure the consumables were updated.

Feargus liked the change in routine offered by the camping trips but despised the necessary ride in the car, which still made him sickly and anxious and which always seemed painfully, queasily endless. At least sitting in the back seat and looking forward was a lot easier on his urge to throw up than those previous experiences facing unsteadily backwards in an open truck.

Often Mark and the boy would bring along one of his friends, Douglas, who would be accompanied by his ten-year-old son and another dog.

Now, this friend's dog was quite, well, quite special to Feargus. Quite special indeed, we must reiterate, because we wouldn't want the meaning to be lost. He became excited and a little silly when, early on this warm flawless late summer morning, they pulled up to the tan and white craftsman style house to pick up the others.

He realized that the drive in the car this time meant that he would be riding in the way-back seat, near the red Coleman cooler and next to the beautiful Tashi.

She was a lovely Tibetan terrier and she was sweet and thoughtful. She seemed calm and regal and female all at once. Oh my goodness was Feargus smitten, and with good reason. Tashi was perfection in a long silky white coat.

Her eyes were clear and black and only slightly shrouded by the heavy sensuous brows. She stood eighteen inches tall and her long sweet ears, a rich mocha color, drooped indifferently at the side of her faultless head. The rest of her was a solid pure white, and she had heavily furred front paws. She took a royal, broad, solid stance on the earth. Had he the ability to voice it Feargus would have said that she was unspeakably gorgeous.

There she stood, on the driveway, next to the second man. She stood in rigid attention to every one of his subtle hand commands, and then she obediently hopped into the back seat of the SUV with both boys and . . . Feargus.

She was as aware of him as he was of her. There was no mistaking it. These two dogs were fond of each other, if you will excuse the overlay of the human reference. They each created a feeling of calm and comfort in the other.

For Feargus it was a feeling pretty much like that distant but still warm and happy memory of his early life, nuzzled up against the big warm body of his mother, or napping with five other deeply breathing sleepy pups in a blue plastic laundry basket, all chins, paws, and backs piled on each other, ears against the heartbeats of the next one, breathing face to face, warm, full-tummied, happy.

That was it. That was the feeling. Tashi made him happy, and Feargus made Tashi smile a sweet, slightly glowing belly-warming knowing smile.

The drive this time, after the stop at the grocery store, did not seem so bad after all. In a couple of hours they were at their campsite, staked on their respective leads in a nice shady spot.

They were all ears and eyes, smelling and sniffing, alive to all the possibilities of this new place with new birds, new plants, a million kinds of ferns, fresh running water rippling over moss-covered rocks, and all kinds of new and wonderful sounds and sensations. He was slightly annoyed at the new tinkling little bell on his collar that jingled at every move, so close to his sensitive ears, but he adjusted to it and ultimately it was ignored.

Tents were erected and stakes were firmly placed. Cooking equipment would be needed soon, so it was laid out. All the housekeeping duties were assigned. Jeremy offered to keep the dogs fed and make sure their water dishes were filled. He placed water bowls both inside and outside the tents.

There was one lone power outlet at this campsite, located up at the rest room. The boys took the portable mattress up to the power source and inflated it, carrying it back overhead for the dad with the bad back.

All edible items were stowed in the bear-proof locker. Then there was just some fire starter to gather, and then they could explore the immediate environment. The dogs were kept on their leashes while in the confines of the park. They were pretty close to one another, so that was not such a hardship.

Soon they followed the rocky creek down to the ocean and back, a good little three-mile walk each way. They would save their energy for the next day and summiting the mountain. Their friend was a local general practitioner. He was a great hiker, climber, and general outdoorsman despite his occasional back spasms, so they usually got quite a workout when he was in the party.

On this particular day, they walked along the shoreline to a spot just beyond the north border of the park to a little hidden beach with a small stream running out to the sea where the dogs could run off-leash and free.

Feargus had not had much experience with the ocean, but he had immense curiosity about this strange and mysterious body of water that was there for a moment and then gone, then back again, this water that gushed and swirled and left its mark in swaths of greenish foaming bubbles on the sand.

He splashed and ran, caught thrown sticks in his teeth, paddled in the ebbing surf, dove head first into the incoming waves, and generally frolicked as the boys flew large box kites and the men played Frisbee with Tashi.

Tashi was ever so slightly in awe of the movement of the water, so she was content to stay on the dry sand while she very ably chased the plastic disk and caught it in her teeth.

Mark's friend noticed a large number of Razor clam holes, or shows, in the sand as the minus tide pulled out. Douglas had a shellfish license and he would remember to be here tomorrow prepared to dig some big fat clams for dinner.

Much time and patience was spent later that evening by multiple sets of hands, several brushes and a misting bottle, in the de-sanding and detangling of dear Tashi's fabulous soft woolly undercoat and her silky abundant topcoat. She closed her eyes and endured as Feargus looked on in jaw-dropping, drool-inducing awe.

Turkey and cheese sandwiches were prepared and devoured. The dogs were fed their cans of satisfaction. Later on, S'mores were roasted and the boys were bedded down. Feargus and Tashi made themselves comfortable at the feet of the men who talked well into the night, over a Northwest amber IPA or two or three.

They stretched out near the crackling, aromatic alder and cedar campfire, as they discussed the dismal and perplexing state, the decline in fact, of American medicine. This would be a topic discussed often during the weekend, in frustrating and elliptical dialogue that seemed to have no conclusion and no solution from either one of their perspectives. They'd made a pact before they left to avoid the subject of medical insurance for the weekend, but other topics were still legal.

"I don't understand what ever happened to personal responsibility. Do you see that fix-me attitude with your patients?"

"All the time. But what is worse is this Big Med algorithm based medicine which is turning humans into soulless data centers without nuance or humanity. Every day I feel pushed a little harder to just treat the averages off some print-out. I don't know why I went to medical school."

"I think our dogs get better, more personal care than your patients."

"True. The dog can't give verbal input so the vet has to examine – actually touch and listen, poke and prod, and then evaluate, to get an answer. Imagine."

They continued this kind of talk, but the only agreement was that the system showed all the signs of being broken beyond repair and a fix seemed overwhelming and out of reach for two mere mortals.

The next morning things were happening before the mist had completely lifted.

The divine and unmistakable aroma of sweet cinnamon pancakes flowered up in the moist salty air. Boys were playing, tossing stones across the stream, and a short time later, after the delicious breakfast, they all filled their water bottles, packed away some of the fruit and trail mix, and headed for the five and a half mile loop up the mountain, which had a seventeen hundred foot gain, and would be a pretty good hike, especially for the kids.

Tashi was stoic along the way, accustomed to hiking with her humans, and of course with the assistance of some genetic memory from her Tibetan ancestors. Feargus, however, was more of a sprinter than a miler. He wasn't used to this kind of activity and got tired about three-quarters of the way up the mountain. Too proud to let it show, he carried on bravely and made it to the top and over and down.

After a short rest and a couple of PB&Js, the group headed once again down to the beach at the north end of the park.

Mark's friend was prepared this time. He had gathered some improvised clamming equipment from the car - gloves, a mesh bag originally intended for dirty laundry, a small shovel kept in the trunk for emergencies and for the rare snow storm. Thus equipped, off they went.

Razor clams, the big ones, leave a telltale donut-shaped mark in the wet sand as they burrow away from the receding tide. Razor clam show is distinctive. This afternoon they were all over this beach in the receding tide.

Douglas was the only adult with a permit, so Mark could just help, while the kids gathered their few allowed to each. Soon they found a rhythm and before twenty minutes had passed, they had about seven or eight long skinny razor clams in the mesh bag. Plenty for a nice dinner.

Back at camp, Douglas washed the sand off the clams in the cold stream. He lightly steamed the clams in a big pot to open them up, then cleaned them and sliced them to quickly fry in butter and garlic and a splash of wine.

The boys got a big, hot fire going and filled their one big pot with water for fettuccini. Despite their initial reservations about the enormous clams, it was a delicious meal, with some sliced tomatoes and a chunk of olive bread.

It was a happy, memorable weekend, but Feargus experienced the first questioning moments of something akin to sadness when Tashi, along with her man and boy, was dropped off at her house. He wanted this time to go on and on. He probably didn't know it, not in any human sense, but she felt the same.

Everyone helped empty the car of the things that belonged to Mark. Goodbyes were yelled after the garage door was closed.

Tashi sat for a long while inside the closed front door of the house. She sat quite still on her haunches, listening with all her ears, and holding in her heart a little bit of hope and a little bit of longing for the return of the car which had carried Feargus away. Then she stood up, shook out her coat, greeted her other family members and resumed her life.

Feargus

27

Companions

Feargus had smaller, shorter excursions with Lisa as well. She also need-ed her change of scene and a bit of outdoor exercise on a regular basis. Feargus would go with her, running, on a lead of course, down the roads, and around the fences, and across the highway to the sandy shoals of the slough, where he would romp and cavort in the shallows, and chase the occasional mouse.

She always took a notebook, so that meant that he was free for a bit if she found a dry log that had escaped from the log rafts which were often penned in wide this turn in the slough, waiting to be loaded on board a ship.

Lisa couldn't stay down here too long, because there was no cell phone service there at that time. Her business depended a good deal on the phone so she liked to stay near their land line.

But for a while at least, Feargus was free to cavort and splash and chase imaginary water creatures, to dig holes in the sand and watch them fill up with the incoming tide. Then they would run back up the hill and Feargus would get a good hose-down in the goat shed, discharging the clinging sand and the salt and the dirt from the murky tidal waterway from his crisply efficient coat. He would have to submit to a nice warm but noisy dry-off with the hair dryer.

At last he would be free to sit in the sun and snooze for an hour or two, or chase the last of the season's Mourning Cloak or Monarch butterflies who winked at him on their circuitous, rambling pathways, always just a little bit out of his reach.

Three decorated pumpkins remained from All Hollows' Eve.

They stood sentinel on the silvering deck, waiting for the crows. Soon the raccoons would get to them and they would have to be tossed out over the fence and into the meadow to the north to be reclaimed by the rest of nature's chain of utility.

They had been carved in sundry quizzical styles - one dreamy glitter-covered angel, one robotic head with ear buds attached Borg-like, and one pretty scary fang-fronted, gape-mouthed ogre.

Fall was descending, relentless and inevitable. There had actually been a freakish dusting of snow last night over to the east on the highest nearby ridges. But it was gone in an hour or two.

On a particular drizzly day in early October, the school bus discharged its quarry with a lack of its usual noise and bluster. Something was up. The boy, uncharacteristically ignoring Feargus on his rapid run down the long driveway to the house, threw open the back door and shouted for his mother.

Feargus came loping along behind and skidded to a stop on the deck of the house where the screen door had just slammed in front of him, almost hitting him in his face, and where he let out one irritated yelp which begged entry.

The backpack was thrown off, the door opened for the dog with a pat on the head and a Sorry, pal. Milk was poured, and a fresh still-warm oatmeal, walnut and raisin cookie, aromatic with cinnamon and ginger, was eaten over a racket of quick-fire news of the day. Demonstrative arms were flailing, crumbs were flying.

The conflagration of disturbing news had shot around the school like a packet of insane roman candles. The neighbor in the house a quarter mile to the south, the retired engineer with the two llamas in the yard and the Airstream in the carport, lost all nineteen of his chickens in the gray light of this early morning!

All of them! This morning!

The house phone rang. It was the neighbor two stops to the north. Her daughter was in high school, and she heard the story as well.

Nineteen chickens, the beautiful Reds, Bantams, Leghorns, pullets, all gone. Devastation. Most likely dogs. Probably a pack of wild dogs. Was their dog at home last night?

"What? Our dog? Of course he was, sleeping on the boy's bed.
What are you saying?"

"Well I just thought . . . "

Another call was coming in. The phone was incessant. The parental network made sure every neighbor for miles knew what had happened. A lady down the road said she had seen some dogs the day before yesterday. One guy said he thought he saw what looked like a pure bred Elkhound in the group that was standing on the rise above the dike. But how could that be the case?

Other neighbors also reported seeing the pack. One woman thought she recognized an old Airedale mix who used to live off Libby Lane. The guy from the house at the bottom of the hill, what was his name? He also said he'd had seen two or three dogs foraging around his trash cans.

There were no cell towers out here in those days, but the landlines were on fire. The older lady down the Slough road saw the pack when they came and foraged on her precious salal berry patch. Her husband tried to shoot at them but missed. Other neighbors had seen the pack from a distance but thought they were pretty quiet and not behaving badly.

There was a man in the gray house over the hill to the south, who was retired from Fish and Wildlife and had some experience with trapping, offered to look at the grizzly scene at the neighbor's chicken coop.

The owner of the birds, who had named most of the animals, gathered up the remains of the carcasses of the dead chickens and pyred them in an early morning ceremony. The coop, though, was just as the owner had found it on his first inspection that morning.

The guy from Fish and Wildlife reminded the owner that dogs like to chase down their prey, they like to chase for fun. It's an almost magnetic, irresistible force, so the motion of the chickens in the yard, and their high-pitched squeals and lower-pitched frightened guttural bwawking probably triggered the attack and then there was no turning back. Dogs like to bite and shake their prey, and that seemed to be the case here from the remnants of feathers and blood.

Their motivation, if we can actually call it that, was to hunt and play, it appears, and not particularly hunger-driven.

There was clearly more than one dog, and it looked like there had been a variety of sizes judging from the tracks left out in the damp mud from a light rain the night before. Prominent nail marks, a more squarish imprint and broader rear tracks made it certain that this was unquestionably a dog attack, and not a coyote. No bloody drag trails, no hiding of prey, just mischief.

Dogs can be up to nothing but just plain mischief.

Some believe that, when a dog has lost the continuity of nurturing needed to keep him in the unnatural emotional state of human domestication, a state to which he has submitted for thousands upon thousands of years, when those bonds are burst, and when that dog meets with other ungoverned dogs, this kind of mindless primitive behavior happens with regularity. That kind of pack would probably not be allowed to continue in an otherwise civilized environment.

The attack and the outcome was explained in efficient and detached language by the local resident expert, but all of it was cold comfort and bleak reality for our unhappy hobby rancher.

28
Opportunity

Just a few miles from the feral pack's lair at the mouth of the coal mine, Mark's carefully constructed goat enclosure was about to be tested.

Annie, the imprudent goat, decided to go off on an adventure this particular afternoon. Phase of the moon perhaps, or just an itch. She was getting bored waiting for the school bus and the general noise and excitement that always occurred when the boy came home in the afternoon, so she started nosing around the wire fence.

She noodged her way out of that inner enclosure and started pushing away at the thin six-inch wide cedar plank fencing. A couple of boards were loose because several of their nails had been popped out from one of her previous attempts at escape.

She pushed, and butted, and pushed away again this time and found that about two-thirds of her bulgy body was through to the other side. She could smell the freshly mowed grass out there in the meadow.

She was excited and lunged forward just as the bent board, which she was holding away with her head, thwacked back to its accustomed position, catching her right pelvic ridge and clamping her rump and hind legs in the fence with a sickening sound and a wail of surprise and pain.

Feargus, amusing himself at the top of the drive, also in expectation of the bus containing his boy Jeremy, heard the wail and raced down across the field to the fence. Annie by this time was bleating in terror along with the discomfort of the pinch, flailing her hind legs, wishing them to be with her in the front of the fence.

He raced to her, licking her frantic face. He made a general assessment of the situation. Then he raced around to the front of the enclosure where he jumped onto the top of a storage bin and vaulted over the wire fence of the outer enclosure. His weight combined with the weight of the bin pulled a strip of the heavy gauge wire away from the fence on his way down.

He was unharmed, but the bin spilled over and the strip of heavy steel mesh remained stuck out in space at a peculiar jagged angle. Now what to do? He tried to get up over the bleating goat and push the boards out of the way, but they barely moved, and snapped back once again bringing a shrill shout from the helpless goat.

Feargus took a good run and cleared the jagged piece of wire fence, leaped back up onto a shelf, and raced out along the fence back around to the front and the face of the goat.

He reached his head into the space between the boards and Annie's hip and carefully inserted his powerful teeth into the board and pulled, pulled it toward him, bracing himself with both front paws against the intact fence. He pulled with all his might, his neck bulging with sinew and strain and out she leaped, bruised but intact as the board snapped back into its original position with a loud thwack, which caused goats, chickens and cat to skitter and squeal with shock.

Feargus was not happy with Annie and prodded her, with a growl and his nose, around toward the front of the enclosure. Her body hurt like crazy, but she was free in this big outer yard, and she just wanted to run, even with a badly bruised hip, just a little bit, out here in the big broad space.

He was right behind her as she gamboled up toward the road and stopped at the fence. Here she lingered for just a moment and relieved her urgent bladder, now overflowing from the excitement. She then turned her bruised body down toward the inevitable return to the enclosure.

Annie and Feargus had been so involved with their dramatic recovery efforts and had not noticed that Jeremy was running down the hill from the bus. Jeremy, who had been standing at the top of the drive witnessed the whole event. He now rushed to throw his arms around his trusty dog.

What a good, good boy you are Feargus!

Jeremy grabbed the errant goat, opening the inner gate to readmit her to the wrath of Bernadette and fifteen squawking chickens who were very disturbed by the fracas.

There would be no smooth, neat brown eggs in this roost for a day or two, and possibly no milk from the goats that night, but the family was whole again.

The next day, at a nearby property just a little to the south, on the other side of the white paddock fence, a family had a similar situation occur with their own porcine version of Houdini.

That family had been working to restrain two new three-month-old pink Landrace piglets, Felton and Frances. One of these little piggies had already shown signs of being a proficient escape artist and regaled herself in finding new ways out of the creative enclosures the humans diligently and routinely provided. Rooting was her specialty. She had a crowbar snout which could get under every and all obstacles.

On this next new fresh breezy morning, with the clouds flying presto to the north across a rapidly clearing sky, the piglet exercised just enough ingenuity in the use of her sensitive snout that she was able to root down six inches underneath the four by four partially buried fencing, wiggling and squeezing.

She finally found herself outside the perimeter wall of the compound. Such a very clever girl.

Hobbling her awkward piggy run up around the bend in the road, she cavorted over the pasture and up toward the rise, her big floppy pink ears fluttering on every bounce, her head up, her heart racing with the exhilaration of freedom, freedom, freedom, higher and higher, Look at me, climbing up the rise, joyous unbounded freedom, up, up, up toward the crest, just a little more to the top.

At last the ground was no longer so steep and started to round off. Five more piggy gallops on her little piggy legs and at last she was there.

'There,' unfortunately for Frances, meant coming face to face with Nacho, on sentry at the top of her particular hill this morning, nostrils aflare, tail straight out. Just beside and a little behind her, Buster, Bjorn and Cotton, spread out and waiting, just over the crest of the rise, wide eyed, muzzles on fire, chests heaving with expectation and anticipation, watching Nacho for direction.

Damn!! Back, back, back get your stupid piggy bottom back down the hill!! Oh for the safety of pasture and gates and fences and straw bales and slop troughs, and a roof that doesn't leak, and my dear brother Felton, and companionship, and oh my god, faster, faster, tripping, falling over herself, rolling down the hill, trying to regain her little legs, squealing, falling again, rolling again, faster! Nooooo!

The dogs held their positions, excited, watching, waiting, and confident. As the piglet neared the flat of the pasture, Nacho tilted her head once to the left and met the eyes of Buster, and once to the right, meeting the excited eyes of Cotton, and then she pulled up her chin in the direction of the piglet and the two took off and raced downhill with fury after the little pink flopping thing. Nacho and Bjorn watched for a second or two and then followed, at a trot, a more casual, less frenzied pace. This one was bagged. No need to hurry.

Buster, three or four times the size of the piglet and on a furious run, overcame her easily and chomped down with this massive jaws on her right rear haunch and hung on, squeezing, severing the right lateral cutaneous femoral nerve which dropped her to the ground like a stone. They tumbled over each other, her other three legs still furiously chasing the air, his jaws clamped tight.

Cotton, excited that at last she had prey that was more aligned to her diminutive size, placed her pointy little teeth on the right side of the throat of the squealing, frantic piglet and clamped down, her head thrashing left and right, ripping at the piglet's neck. The piglet's squeals reduced to stifled gurgles as Cotton tore through the neck and a fountain of bright red blood from the left carotid artery spewed with awesome pulsating symmetry over the scene.

Bjorn trotted closer and then moved in to do his usual abdominal handiwork, ripping and tearing at the midsection with his strong mouth, slashing across the belly and exposing the vitals with determination and avarice. The eviscerated piglet, who had just recently received her name Frances, cast her final dazed and feeble gaze into the eyes of Cotton as she gasped another breath, her tortured, furrowed brow seeming to ask the only real question – but she already knew the answer. The dogs must have felt exposed in this open location, so they created a bloody drag trail across this end of the pasture. They deposited their capture closer to a thicket of Alder saplings and blackberry brambles on the perimeter of the parcel. Here they portioned out her plump young fresh meaty body, with more than plenty for all.

There was something to be taken back for now, and each had a greasy, crunchy trophy for the night. Soon, sated, they would be off again, adrenaline stoked, racing down along the banks and into the slough in their excited post-chase victory to bathe in the cool tidal flush.

This unhappy event occurred on a day when there was no school. It was an in-service day for teachers, so there was no classroom chit chat, no rapid-fire emanation of information texted on the phone of the one lucky avant-garde fifth-grader with his own brand new cell phone, able to call the land lines of some rural parents. But none of that happened on this particular day.

As a result of the lack of the normal in-school hot line, this new situation was understood slowly – it was doled out in pieces. The male owner of the lost piglet chose not to share the gruesome particulars of his flash-light-assisted discovery with his family. He just said that this time it seemed the piglet had escaped for good.

It was very late in the day when the horrified family discovered the truth and realized they had lost one of their very newest members to the often cruel, inimical, and always-unforgiving world that dwelt right outside their door. A new electric piggy-controlling fence was indicated.

Next morning Jeremy had a stomachache and a low grade temperature. He was deemed less than able to spend a whole day at the old school grind. Instead, he got the opportunity to sleep in late with Feargus at his feet and drive with his mom up to the airport and watch his dad take off for regions south on his next consulting mission.

He'd be the man of the house for the next week. He got to watch "X-Men" on the VCR for the fifth time, and have bake-at-home spinach and cheese calzone, less the sausage because of his tummy, with Feargus always nearby and on the alert for the wayward trifle of cheese, or crust. And so the afternoon and evening went along without event.

Feeling better on the following morning, off he went to school and the day progressed as expected, with nothing new to report that afternoon over his milk and leftover pizza. Extra homework from the missed day put a crimp in the boy's play time after school, but Feargus was there, anyway, willing to have any time at all with the idolized boy.

Lisa had recently acquired a new client from somewhere in the UK and was hard at work well into the evening in preparation for an early morning phone meeting planned for two days' time. For tonight, all was quiet and it would be a sleepy night for both of them.

Such lovely, confoundable hopes.

Feargus

29
Grace

Nacho had done remarkably well. She had kept this errant pack of mangy cast-offs alive, and she managed to stay the alpha in the group by wits, dominance and maturity.

She had done this with virtually no deep sleep in a couple of months now. She ensured the social relationships of the members, creating a culture in the pack, and won unquestioned trust, respect and loyalty.

Because of her, this pack had been able to achieve its basic hierarchy of needs. Because of her this pack was able to form a fairly complicated interactive network which plotted out, to all intents and purposes, like a recognizable permanent social group.

Of course the ferals didn't understand life exactly in these terms, but they were instinctively able to achieve a variety of goals for the good of the group as well as the individuals, and this offered them all a bit of contented watchfulness. Quite a feat.

Nacho hadn't planned to perform a complicated contemporary sociological experiment, but she had done so nevertheless, and without coaching. It was the role of a lifetime for the little maestro.

At this moment, however, as hard as she may be gritting her teeth and holding on, this story slips and falls out of her capable hands. Here, the story's threads begin to unravel from the quixotic Ribbon of Fate, to which we are all at least occasionally in some ways subservient.

Right now there was an event facing her that was out of her control. As if through a window, she must now watch the slow and unforgiving path to nirvana for our old friend Jack.

Already the angels were surrounding him. Already one could sense the aura of the great beyond calling him, waiting for him. Already his sweet, humping, kindly canine self knows it is needed elsewhere and that he is being called away to a place that we'll just call home.

Yet, Jack was a smart sensitive dog, and he still felt a strong bond of fealty, of kinship, of sharing and community with his roadside partners. The last few months had given him a glimpse into the possibilities of trust and friendship, and he was feeling gratitude as well as some other undefined emotions.

Some other hastily configured feral assembly might have made a very different and very ugly choice regarding a sick and debilitated dog which came along asking to become a member.

But this pack chose to nurture and support their sickly brother. This may speak to Nacho's leadership, or it may also simply be a blind coincidence. We will never know.

The pack could feel his call. In acts of sheer, sweet and unchallenged loyalty and faithfulness, every foraging expedition embarked upon these last few weeks had brought home some morsel, some precious nugget of nutrition for Jack.

He had been prodded and poked and encouraged to join in a romp, to move, to get up, to exercise, to eat, but his strength was limited to his brief excursions to empty his sad tired bladder, to choke up the last bit of bile from his stomach, or to empty his spastic and angry bowels.

His gums and eyes were now quite yellow, his urine was dark brown, his energy was all but gone, his abdomen was distended and uncomfortable and his heart was fighting, pounding fast and hard against his chest.

Any semblance of his former self was gone. He gasped as his need for breath increased. Almost anything would be preferable to this harrowing, wasting, slow march toward death.

Just a short distance south of the entrance to the derelict coal mine which the pack had called home these last few months, there was a south-facing bank above the slough, just to the north of the dike. This was the vicinity, away from the camp, to which our friend often came to ease his incessant and demanding bodily functions, intentionally away from the group's lair.

Further along this small stretch of sunny slope there was a plant which always pleased him, made him feel that his pain and suffering were not so bad, just another part of normal. This plant, which befriended him in his pain, was called Lonicera, and this summer-blooming climber had stayed sweet and fragrant on this warm sunny, wind- and freeze-protected slope well past its normal span, perhaps just to give our boy Jack some minimum of comfort in his final days.

This particular day had been unseasonably warm for early October. The last bit of afternoon sun had lingered in a cloudless cornflower blue sky and its declining rays hung on to that impossibly beautiful sky with obstinate abandon, like the tentacles of some desperate celestial arachnid, sliding slowly away down a filament.

The family could sleep outside on this lovely, rare, clear, star dappled night.

Accustomed to the hourly needs of his bodily functions, the pack thought nothing of Jack's slow uneasy trudge off toward the south. Bjorn, who was sleeping closest to him, simply shrugged, snorted and went back to sleep.

Nacho, in a rare moment of physical release, was snoring softly next to Cotton, whose days were so filled with angst and activity that her nights were dense and dreamless. Buster always liked to make his berth alone, a little distance away from the group, curled up on a mat of Siberian candy-flower encircled with sedge and deer vetch.

Jack, his sweet brown eyes now perpetually weeping and engulfed in a yellowed sclera, his black and copper coat matted and manged, his nose dry and dull, made his way to his favorite patch of bankside shrubbery.

He inhaled the sweet, honey-scented enveloping aroma, nestled his poor beleaguered body to an almost comfortable curl and felt his heart, so often pounding almost out of his chest, now able to slowly begin to release its heavy burden. His eyes were closing, and his fading heart was happy in the smell of honeysuckle.

Buster had been awakened by Jack's move and got up to follow. For some reason, he was just a little curious this time. In a move more kindly than his pit side might admit, and showing more faithfulness and fidelity than anyone would expect, Buster sat right at Jack's head and stayed with him until, in the slow-moving hours past midnight the breath halted, the organs released what was left of their remaining vital energy, and he was gone.

Such a good boy. To the end.

Buster was still sitting in this vigilant position at Jack's head, unable to remove himself from this now pointless watch, when Nacho came down the decline into the small alcove where Jack lay. She was followed by Cotton and then by Bjorn who had noticed that Buster was gone from his spot, and thought he'd better check out what was going on.

Nacho observed the situation, gave a gentle push against Jack's sweet big old head and then sat down on her back legs with a sigh, very close to him, just staring at him.

They all, each of them, knew what death looked like and smelled like. This was not a new experience.

Cotton was nervous and paced back and forth in blessed quiet. Bjorn stood quite close to the body, just barely touching, but with his back turned on the scene. He looked to the east instead, throwing his gaze down and away and onto the steely gray moon-lit waterway, as far into the distance as his misted-over eyes could see. His mouth seemed suddenly full of saliva and he smacked his lips and swallowed a time or two.

Buster got up at last and began to push and roll the body of the dead dog a little deeper into the crevice with the overhanging sweet vine. He found a few fallen Alder branches with grayish shriveling leaves still attached, grasped them in his teeth and pushed them toward the dog. The others followed his lead and gathered other fallen debris to give the body just a bit of cover.

This little bit of shelter wouldn't be sufficient to offer much protection, but they knew that by morning, their friend would become food for any number of the other wild inhabitants of the land they shared, and they hoped that their small efforts might offer him at least a few hours of dignity.

Before long a murder of crows would shout out the location, like a cacophony from hell, and then there would be coyotes, raccoons, vultures, gulls, cougars, bobcats, owls, snakes and eventually worms and insects, all wanting their own piece of this relentless and immutable chain of being.

Jack had ventured to achieve entente with this group and he had not been disappointed. This motley pack of truants had been his first constant and true family.

A storm had moved in overnight, chasing away the clarity of the star-smattered sky and casting an added pall of grayness over the already subdued pack. There wasn't much action in the group this morning.

They hit up the garbage cans of a nearby upwind house, where they found a bonanza of pork ribs from a recent barbecue. They each got something they liked, and the gnawing and crunching went on well into the late evening, each dog quiet with his or her own thoughts.

Long before the yellow and lavender of the very next new dawn spread its mystical presence over the land, Nacho was up and trotting off on what had become the established route to her favorite rise. Her curious questioning senses were alive to all possibilities. She nosed around along the now familiar path, but today she decided to go on a little distance from normal.

In another quarter of a mile she stopped and gave the land a survey from a perch atop a lean-to, just outside the south end of a freshly painted white paddock fence encircling some neat outbuildings with tidy blue metal roofs. She was taking a million mental notes from her sensory antennae, but she was not in the mood for adventure this morning, not in the mood for sport, or for excitement. She felt a little angry perhaps, restless definitely, unhungry surely, and generally off her game.

The others had not followed her this morning, which was also a strange exhibition of their dis-ease. She sat down on some soft grass and simply stared off into the distance for quite a while.

Soon she stretched, stood and then trotted back to the lair. She would take perhaps one more days' time to recover from Jack's departure. Enough for today. This will be a good day to rest.

Tomorrow would be here soon enough.

Feargus

30
Ojai

Mark had planned a business trip down to Ojai for a week, and he was set to leave the next morning. He thought a few extra precautions might be in order.

While Lisa enjoyed a quiet bath, father and son would have a few bonding moments on this night with a bright almost-full moon.

"You know how much I think about you when I'm away on business. Your safety and your mother's safety are the most important things in the world to me. So listen carefully. If anything odd should happen, don't be a hero. Do what you're told. Follow your mother's lead. Trust her, support her, and don't argue with her."

"'Nuf said, dad."

He put the lad to bed, poured a couple of fingers of Glenlivet into a heavy-bottomed glass, added a couple of cubes of ice, and went back outside.

He stood alone on the east-facing deck on this crisp fall night. The moon was four-fifths full, lighting the elbow of river with silver, like tinsel on a Christmas tree. The air was gently moist.

He tapped on the outdoor barometer. There would most likely be some serious rain in the next day or two. The air was heady with the essence of balsam and salt. Also on the light breeze there came the scent of a variety of mosses, and that dry pervasive, delicious smell of decaying leaves, specific to the fall. A memorable smell, dense and primal.

Feargus

She'll think I'm being silly and overprotective, but I'll check the placement of the ammunition in the safe and move the laundry basket so that there's nothing blocking the access door.

This is a long trip. Better to be prepared.

31
Process

Ian knew what he was doing, so I was comfortable taking his cues on our decisions on behavior and training options regarding our latest family addition.

Amadeus had ben crated at night and occasionally during the day when he was still with the breeder. So, we decided to crate him at night for his first few months, and to keep him as close as a short leash in and around the house for a while, maybe even until his first birthday.

I noticed immediately the first time he was not attached to me. A deliveryman came to the front door and Amadeus' protecting and herding instincts came out and there was quite a to-do.

When he is attached to me and the doorbell rings, it is a whole different story. He trots along with me. He is polite and watchful, but quiet and not frantic. I was unsure about this philosophy at first, but by now I'm observing and liking the outcome.

When he gets a little more mature we will begin to relax those restrictions, but this was the training path we chose and it is working. The dog was starting to learn what was expected of him, and he was also learning to communicate his simple needs without a fuss.

My two males started going off together for short runs and walks. Now, they frequently take half-day bicycle jaunts. Amadeus has his very own brand new bicycle doggie trailer and he seems to like it very much indeed, judging by the eagerness with which he hops through its little zippered screen door.

The Amadeus who we were getting to know seemed to be a very affable fellow, and that gregarious energy was very much appreciated by us both. He was fast becoming our friend.

I was learning a ton about canine husbandry, and I have not had any trouble switching into the role of alpha when needed. I am comfortable taking over when necessary.

We swore to this dog that, as long as he lives, we will do everything in our power to insure that he will never have to eat from a dumpster, or find shelter in the wild, or face a lonely, unnecessary or painful death.

32
Nature on This Night

The night is starless and overcast with a high haze, allowing only the soft light of a four-fifths moon to lift the gloom.

Moisture is collecting on the leaves and blades of grass. It is cool, fifty-one degrees. The barometer has been holding steady for the last few hours, but it was able to shift in a second in this unstable coastal microenvironment.

It is now very late at night or very early in the morning, maybe four a.m. Nacho has not slept well. She had been anxious and hungry, which is an uncommon sensation for her, even though it had been two days since their last meal.

She can sense the day's arrival and is itching to get started, so she goads and nudges the others into semi-awakeness and then takes off in the darkness on her accustomed path up to the crest of the hill. She's in a mood. She wants to try something different, something challenging.

The pack is slow to wake at this early hour, but they slowly rouse themselves in the darkness and follow her nevertheless. They come upon her again on the top of the lean-to on the south side of the white paddock fence, nostrils aquiver, muscles flexed in tension.

They gather here, behind her, at the top of the hill. She moves away and they watch her go over the fence and into the meadow where she stops and sniffs at the spot where Annie carelessly deposited her frantic runaway pee.

Nacho circled the deposit, sniffing around and under the brambles. The others hop over the fence and also sniff around the deposit of urine.

They look at Nacho. She has eyed the target, and then she offers her jutting chin-up command. They start to creep silently, stalking down toward the goat shed, slowly, on bent legs, tails straight out, on a breathless bead toward the other compelling scents.

Mathilde, who had been asleep most of the previous day and much of this earlier night, has pushed her impressive feline head through the pet flap and is roaming freely on the outskirts of the property. She checks on the livestock, hisses at a raccoon, shooing him away.

It is very quiet.

She then saunters slowly around the perimeter of the fence where she catches the scent on a sudden downdraft and encounters four truculent dogs, intent on mischief. They were upwind of her and her aging senses did not give her the grace of warning.

The dogs see the cat and instantly forget their primary target. She becomes the new toy. Buster is the first to see and challenge her. They roll into a fierce inter-species battle and Buster is the worse for it, with deep bleeding scratches to his eyebrow and nose. Nacho barks shortly, a deep-throated hushed growl that insists that they stop the commotion.

Mathilde pulls away and springs to the top of the tall paddock fence where the dogs can only bark and growl at her and throw themselves against the hard unweilding boards in frustration.

Inside the house, Feargus hears, smells, senses something and becomes restless. The sleepy boy thinks the dog has to go outside and motions for him to use the doggie door. This has happened a dozen other times, so the boy rolls over and goes back to sleep. About five minutes later, there is a definite stir outside.

This time Feargus shoots out the doggie door like a lightning bolt.

Always a light sleeper when her husband is away, Lisa hears some kind of commotion and gets up. At that very moment she meets the boy who is running into her room announcing that something is up outside. She races to the northwest side of the house to see if she can get some idea of what was happening. She opens the window and then it hits her, slams her in the face, the cacophony of dogs growling, snarling and grunting, cat wailing and hissing, the strident bleating of goats, chickens squawking and bwawking, the dry coarse frenzied neighing of the horses up the hill, all heard over the outrageously loud and incessantly high-pitched one-note screaming of her very own voice inside her very own head, and the boy's shrill cries of Mom! Mom!!

She runs back down the hall to the master bedroom where in the corner of the room sits the big green combination lock gun cabinet. She tries to remember the combination, what the hell is my birth date?? She tries to remember the instructions. Stay calm. Make the screaming stop. Stay calm.

She picks up the Ruger 22 rifle. The noise outside increases to cacophony! What is going on out there?? Make the screaming stop!

Horses neighing, kicking against their stalls in the distance, goats braying, such noise! She knows she can't go out without a gun. Could be a coyote, or a cougar or a bear. This 22 rifle won't take down a bear. She knows that. She isn't that good a shot. But she's got to have something and she is afraid of the larger guns. The rifle will have to do.

She grabs the box of ammunition placed directly under the gun for quick loading; trembling fingers manage to load three. Two fall on the floor, three more in the chamber, four more on the floor, eleven cartridges in all into the little vault. That will have to do. She snaps the chamber closed, walks over to the northwest windows, flips on the switch for the outside lights that illuminate that side of the property, revealing a gruesome sight.

Feargus shoots out the doggie door and skids to a stop on the deck. Some of the bleating and squawking abates as all eyes turn to him at this moment. What in the world is this? He tries to steady his gaze and make some sense of what he sees. Some small yapping thing is perched on top of the first perimeter barrier to the compound, yapping and screaming at the goats.

The pit mix, in an effort to take the easy way to get at the goats, has tried to bolt the fence. He has caught his right rear foot, with a sickening twist, in a loosened, gaping jagged section of the heavy steel fence wire which solidly snares the foot. His body weight thrust him forward as his leg is caught, snapping the fibular tarsa clear off the tibia in a pitchy loud crack and a muffled whimper. His body is now draped in a bizarre corkscrew down the side of the fence, his head ending on the dirt in a dazed moan.

The other brown pug-faced thing stays off a bit, watching as always, but here, in the clearing just under the roof extension of the shelter, standing confused and bewildered is a gorgeous, lazy, out of shape, good for nothing silver elkhound intent on having fresh goat for breakfast, while making the least effort to get it. He is acting only as muscle, as backup for the instigators.

Feargus' eyes narrow on the hound. This is my target. If I take this one out, then the others will not be so confident.

Off the deck, in a moment of total courage and resolve, Feargus races toward the hound. With his tail held up stiffly, chest puffed out, ears up and forward, lips pulled tight against his teeth, eyes on fire, he flies at the unprepared elkhound.

He grabs the muzzle in his teeth, twisting him over, pinning him to the ground and in a fierce moment of frightening anger, sinks his teeth into the throat of the interloper, twisting, shaking, pounding with fury - my land, my home, my people, my goats, my family, you will not live, you big lazy fool.

Bjorn takes too long to recover from the initial shock of the attack and makes only a feeble attempt to dig away at ears and nose and eyes with his teeth and front paws. He can manage to do only ugly superficial damage to Feargus' beautiful face. His rear claws rip at Feargus' underbelly. There is total confusion, fierce snarling, growling, fur flying, and spit-hurling bedlam.

Bjorn, using his powerful chest, pushes his attacker off and to the side.

They right themselves and stand for a second or two, muscles taught, eyes on fire, and then Feargus attacks again. They are writhing in a growling fearsome jaw lock. Bjorn is thrown off balance as he tries to use his front feet to inflict more damage on the underbelly.

Feargus, furiously fast, takes advantage of the shift in weight, releases the muzzle lock, and plants his teeth firmly into the neck. He hits pay dirt in a thumping, spurting carotid artery. Bjorn is pinned and shocked, flailing wildly. Feargus releases his jaws for a second and grabs again under the neck, blood is everywhere, this time the crunch is audible and the windpipe is breached. Bjorn's eyes are bulging in terror.

In two final gasping, wide-eyed, thrashing, jerking gurgling breaths, we can say only a moderately fond goodbye to Bjorn.

Feargus stands over him, panting.

The pit mix, at this moment, in an act of evil determination, pushes up against the rough wood floor, grabs the corner of an overturned tub and re-twists the limp and now useless ankle out of the fence. He swings around on the three good legs, and in a moment of unspeakable pain fueled with adrenaline, clears the fence in two excruciatingly hobbled bounds, lands upon the left rear flank of our Feargus, digging his pit-bull jaws into the flesh, ripping and tearing the muscle.

Feargus' front legs give out, reeling from this new shock and pain, and he drops his upper body onto the chest of the expired elkhound, throwing his head in thrashing agony around to his left side. This is the moment the other two move cautiously in.

Lisa looks out the glass slider. In the silver brightness of the four-fifths moon she identifies the four intruders and her beloved Feargus. There is a big gray one bloody and apparently dead. A brown one has moved in on Feargus' upended shoulder, and its teeth have clamped onto the tensor fascia latae all the way down onto the crunch of the femur.

The white thing looks about to attack his neck.

She screams at the boy to stay inside.

Oh my god, oh my god, oh my god, oh my god. Get those filthy teeth off my dog. At the edge of the deck she lifts the rifle.

Lean in; take your position. Lean in. Focus. Lean in.

Being outside of herself, acting beyond herself, she puts the gun to the notch just inside the knob of her shoulder, leans in and fires. Miss. The dogs don't move, don't hear anything, consumed with the fierceness of their deadly fight. The next bullet - blam! - into the left exposed ribcage of the pit, and then one more shot - grazing again somewhere in the hindquarter. The body relaxes into death, but the jaws and teeth remain imbedded in Feargus' hindquarter.

The next three shots miss any hoped-for target.

Cotton, too small to be a decent target, races off into the night. But she does not go away unseen. A pair of keen, watchful big Barred owls drops down in silent synchronicity and utter stealth, from the middle of an old-growth Douglas-fir on the near perimeter of the property, sensing fear, an easy chase, and sweet success.

Gun raised, she sights directly into the eyes of Nacho, who looks up and turns her head to the woman, and in a sublime operatic duet of two angry women, soprano and alto, in the same key, in the same tempo, they scream at each other, eyes locked, in exactly the same language and the same words, separated only by species - You mangy she devil, you will not take my life, you will not take my loyalty, you will not take my dedication and unbounded devotion to this family. I made this family and I will stand here alone and above it all, and I will win. Both voices ring with truth.

Lisa shifts her aim, grateful for the arrogant profiled stance of the target who is trying to seem larger and more threatening than she is.

Feargus

She pulls the trigger and watches Nacho fly off her legs, like a tin dog in a carnival shooting gallery, her black eyes still glaring, intent and on fire. She lands six feet away in a slump on the tattered and bloody grass. She continues to breathe. It seems endless, her front legs twitching, her mouth drooling dense heavy red blood. She lingers still longer, coughing, wheezing, gurgling. Then, finally, the legs stop their spasms and the coughing slows.

Lisa falls forward as well, her knees buckling, the rifle flies off to the side as she collapses onto the earth. Her face is now covered with the early morning wetness of the grass and red angry streaks from the scrape of pea gravel that place a red highlight across her nose and chin. Green stains of the fresh grass streak the front of her pale pink pajamas as she impacts the ground, lunging uncontrollably forward.

Her left hand and wrist slam down hard on the earth, taking the full weight of her off-balance body.

Jeremy is calling from the deck. Mom, Mom! She shakes her head to him. She's OK. She comes to her knees, grabs the deck railing with her right hand to help her up, rights herself on the earth, hugs her son tight to her chest, and they walk quickly toward their dog, their Feargus.

There is a ghostly quiet now.

The caged animals are once again learning to breathe and have shied to the farthest corners of their respective enclosures, watching, weeping, and waiting.

It is so awful, so gruesome, so sudden, and so very final. Feargus is grievously injured. He lies with his head yet upon the dead silver gray hulk. She and the boy pry the teeth of the pit mix apart, their fingers showing the effort with canine lacerations on their ventral pads. They push the body, bloodied and limp, but for the locked jaw, away from the shredded hindquarter of our Feargus.

She tries to staunch the blood from his neck laceration, touches the rent shoulder with the white knob of the humeral head exposed. Feargus shudders.

She stifles a high-pitched wail that she hears pounding loudly inside her head. Our dog's nose is red with lacerations, his abdomen ripped open. Those would have to be her best observations. She couldn't look any closer. It was horrific.

My Feargus, my boy, my sweet boy.

He is breathing a labored breath that tells of pain, suffering and pride in its elemental sounds. Hs goats were safe.

It is raining. It started as a fine mist at first, now it falls in light drops that plunk and plop on the dog's eyes and face, then run in red streams down his cheeks. The goat pens and chicken coops are now absolutely silent.

Stay with him, she tells the boy. Stay with him, talk softly to him, look in his eyes, and comfort him. I will be right back. And you know how to use the rifle, but don't pick it up unless that little white dog or some other dog comes back.

She returns to the house, to the green gun cabinet in the corner of the bedroom. She reopens the door and looks at the pistols. She picks up the 22 revolver and turns it over. Her hands are shaking violently. Then she opens the barrel.

There have been so many stories, over cocktails, over fences, over children's birthday cakes, over the years, from the intrepid, manly pet owner who has had to 'put down' his own animal. Stories about the towel wrapped ceremonially around the head. Tales about the gross and disgusting and unexpected smell of spent, burnt brains, overpowering and revolting, which rises in the steam after the deed.

Turn your head away from that if you don't want to throw up, that was the warning.

If you just remember right ear to left eye, it isn't rocket science.

These stories are told with a certain amount of stance and swagger by those in this social group. These folks are emphatically comfortable with their own 22 caliber pistols and other objects of unquestioned mayhem.

But right this minute her very own dog, the best dog she has ever known, is dying and in so much pain. What recourse is there?

It is not quite five in the morning. The answering service at the vet won't pick up until seven at the earliest. It is clear that Feargus' wounds are many and deep, the worst is the gaping spewing gash at his neck.

She heaves a loud, strangled sigh and loads the little gun with two bullets, just two. She hopes that will be one more than enough.

Be a man, she says aloud, be a man. She reaches around the corner to the linen closet and grabs an old blue and white wide-stripped beach towel and walks toward the door.

Her footsteps feel odd. They make a kind of hollow galumph on the floor and on the deck, as if there was an unexplained space between her feet and the floor. She seems to have some kind of thick hard-soled shoes on her feet but she knows that is ridiculous.

Her knees and hip movements are stiff and awkward as if they belong to another being who has forgotten how to walk, or has not been able to walk for a very long time.

She feels strange and otherworldly. She has no feeling in her body except for an odd increasing sensation in her wrist that seems both serious and muffled and far away at the same time.

There was no time or thought to place ear plugs, so her ears, unprotected during the shooting, are hearing things oddly, muffled, as if she was under water. Everything seems in slow motion.

She is acting on instinct and adrenaline and would not know her name if asked.

Morning is starting to break, and the sky is becoming a mauve mix of mist and cloud and soft falling rain.

She looks up at the sky, takes a large inhale, then walks to Feargus, gun wrapped in the towel. She asks the boy to go up to the house and find one particular blanket Feargus always liked. The boy is crying, doesn't want to go. She pulls him gently away, holds his head against her heart for a moment, looks into his eyes and points him toward the house.

"Please go, darling."

The blanket, she knows very well, is in the dryer, and the boy will not think to look there for quite some time. He doesn't want to go, but she insists.

"And call the vet," she shouts after him, "leave a message and tell him what's happened, what you saw."

She decides that there must be a slight detour and walks up to the perimeter gate and opens it. She takes the few more steps to the goat's enclosure, pops the bolt out of the second gate and returns to the yard.

Bernadette and Annie follow her slowly and stand, leaning against one another, still shaken and shaking, fat bellies touching, long necks almost intertwined, at the entrance to the perimeter fence.

She goes back a step and leads them beyond that fence, encouraging them, out toward Feargus. Her voice is deep and rough. She feels and hears this croakiness and tries to keep her words soft and gentle. The goats breathe shallowly, inaudibly, reluctantly, and take slow measured steps toward the beloved dog.

Sweet Saanen Bernadette comes to her knees. She looks long into Feargus' eyes. She licks the blood from his nose, from the rest of his face. Annie kneels as well but is unable to look at Feargus. She leans her head away, at an angle, against the elongated neck of Bernadette, emitting a throaty sob, but her body contacts his fading warmth along the spine. The sound she emits is heartbreaking and indefinable.

After a minute or two, Lisa gently leads the distraught goats back behind the first barricade, closes the door and slips the bolt.

She takes the towel and wraps it around the gasping suffering dog's head. She gives the two ends a gentle twist under his chin. Her left hand is almost useless. She can still move her fingers a little, but the hand looks odd, is slightly angled, and has started to report shooting shocks of pain that almost bring her to her knees, but she has to go forward.

She cocks the little gun in her now oddly calm, otherworldly right hand and holds it to the base of the skull near the right ear. Every move she makes is in slow motion.

Right ear to left eye. She looks into his sad tearing eyes.

"Thank You."

She hears the hoarseness of her voice, surprising herself.

Thank you, Feargus. You are fierce and bold and loving and protective. You have my utmost respect and esteem. But you are hurt and I cannot fix you, no one can fix you, and your life is slipping away in pain and suffering. I see the hurt and the pride in your eyes.

You are my dog. You are a good dog. You are a great dog.

Unstoppable tears are streaming down her face. A deep breath, in, then out . . . Her forefinger touches the trigger. All time and space are suspended; rationality is pushed down into a place of suffering and pain, and just wanting to end it for this true and faithful friend.

Faithful friend. To what are we truly faithful?

Is this the place that her faithfulness, her personal fidelity has taken her? Can she ever repay in kind the love and loyalty it took for such a sacrifice as this dog has made for his family, their family, for people and goats and dogs and cats? Is this the way to repay that sacrifice? What is her truth? Is this her way of showing love and fidelity?

She fires the gun.

But at the very last second she has straightened her elbow and lifted her aim away from Feargus' head. She fires instead at the still-rasping Nacho just ten feet away. The pug-faced rales stop and the scrappy body ceases to spasm and goes limp at last.

In anger and frustration she points the gun at a forty-five degree angle to the sky and discharges the second bullet out into the grayness of the morning light as a fearsome wail is wrenched from her throat. Her hand relinquishes the gun and it falls onto the wet gravel and grass.

She removes the towel from Feargus. She leans down and kisses his bloody face. She crawls around on three limbs to his head and sits cross-legged, lifts the head gently onto her thigh, her good hand stroking his forehead. The slow gentle but relentless mists of rain mix with her tears as she raises her head to the sky with her eyes tightly shut against the cruel incursion of reality and the coming dawn.

"Mom, Mom." The boy has found the blanket and has carefully and lovingly covered the poor dog. He comes around to his mother, crawling in the now-soaked grass and dirt.

"Mom."

She does not respond.

"Mom! He's gone. Feargus is dead. Look."

The dog's eyes are glass, his breathing still. The boy throws his arms around his mother and they sit, arms entwined, for a minute, Feargus' head still resting on her thigh.

She tells the boy to go get the telephone and call his dad and he heads for the house.

She lays the dog's head on the folded towel and touches her elbow to the earth to stabilize her body. With effort, she points her frame to the right, to the fence post at the end of the deck, not walking, not crawling, but thrusting and stumbling on her good hand and her knees, hair and thin pajamas dripping with rain, clinging to her body. She presses forward with every ounce of being, until she stops, shoulder and hand supporting her, and throws up, her stomach heaving four, five, six times.

At first there is some foaming bilious liquid and then dry, dry, empty, retching heaves. Finally she spits and swallows the acid out of her mouth and is able to take a breath, compose herself to some degree, and returns to the body.

The eyes of her beloved dog no longer reveal emotion, no longer register the mystery, the love, the kindness, the unbounded devotion, the contained and focused ferocity, the childlike curiosity and playfulness, the inherent quiet faithfulness, the until-death-do-us-part loyalty, which were all part of Feargus' persona.

Some would say that those traits are complex and unknowable constructs too far beyond an animal's understanding. Too human, too humane to attribute to a canine we say, in our infinite conceit.

And yet, those attributes are displayed, again and again, throughout the lifetime of devotion of this one particular and sweetly remarkable dog.

The moon, which has until now lit this gruesome scene with horrific ease, has now turned itself away from view. The low sitting wisps of mist have disappeared.

Feargus

33
Fealty

The attempt to tell this story of Feargus' demise has wrung out my soul, and yet I know I must press on. I have been coming back to my scribbled bits of notes whenever there has been a little bit of time in between my major projects. As I reflect on the story of Feargus, I find that this catharsis has left me with many major questions, but there is one question that invades every facet of this story and stretches out above the others. I am not sure if I can answer it, but it must be asked.

To what are we ever truly faithful?

What is our capacity for commitment? Does a little voice in our head shriek out some kind of red-flag warning when it suspects the potential for an escalation of promise?

Is the word 'always' ever used in any serious or meaningful way? What does it mean, I will 'always' love you? If you beat me I will love you still? Then what a fool am I.

Perhaps 'always' is just a comfortable old shoe that never barks at our feet, never questions our trajectory, or squeezes our toes, but simply warms, and to some degree protects, making it easy to thoughtlessly sort out decisions in the early morning twilight.

And what about that silliness - until death us do part? Why do we find it necessary to swear to something that we would, under normal circumstances, consider prohibitively intimidating and dangerously arbitrary for any kind of serious obligation or commitment? We would give more thought to a handshake on the sale of a dog.

We hate the idea of obligation, with its necessary requirements of trust, debt, burden or liability? We want to have free choice. Free as long as it suits.

Take a part of your life and give it to me. Give it to me now. Like Shylock's pound of flesh, give it me, this chunk, this section, this quadrant of your life. Trust me with it. Let me handle it, manipulate it, re-create it. You won't be sorry. Wait and see. Trust me.

What kind of devilish fun is this? In what state of idiocy would one have to reside to make this kind of commitment, and then to add the manacle 'to death do us part' to the end of it? Nonsense! It's all utter drivel and indecipherable stupidity. All of it, fidelity, devotion, trust. I take my life and offer it up to you. I will take a bullet for you. Here is my pound of flesh.

Touch it, feel it, love it, reshape it. I am yours.

Devilish good fun! Why? Because, for every iota of fidelity, of trust or truth, there is an equal and opposite iota of treachery and disloyalty and shame and betrayal, and pain, and I know this to be the case, because I have experienced it, all of it.

Do we feel accountable to any sort of commitment at all? Do we make serial vows? Do we believe in vows? Or have we become accepting of ourselves as a serially contracting, a serially monogamous people? I think this is perfectly all right, actually, given the temporary, disposable, drive-up, wash and wear, in-and-out nature of our society. But will we as a society survive this duality?

Trust and distrust, loyalty and disloyalty, these are yin and yang, and the two must balance to be complete in the end. Nothing can ever be all white or all black. Ancient wisdom, from many quarters, tells us that there must be that kernel of the opposite within the thing itself in order to achieve a true and lasting balance.

So there is no perfect ever after, there will always be the kernel of the imperfect hovering within. Does any higher power expect something else? How could they, when they themselves must each contain that same kernel of imperfection in order to exist?

Until death do us part . . . really?

What then, is loyalty or fealty, or constancy, or fixedness, or just simple trust, for that matter? Can you exist with constancy on more than one level at one time? Can you stay eternally true, yes I said eternally true and yet 'relatively' true to another entity at one time?

Of course you can. Humans are capable of much greater dualities. Duality seems to be a part of our nature. Depending on your particular surroundings, however, it might not always be socially acceptable.

What does this question of fidelity mean, and how does it translate to any sort of human activity or human character? I am confused and searching. I really don't know.

For some time I had been at some sort of existential crossroad, observing some manufactured and unproven cardboard image of commitment, unadorned and wanting, and wondering what in the world it all means! Because this story is nothing, if not about loyalty and trust.

A dog, you see, has a very different level of trust, a different level of truth. A dog simply believes.

I was beginning to truly understand and to identify more with that idea of simple canine belief than with the human explanation of belief which demands trust and fidelity, but which is so overstuffed with guile and principle and self-preservation that any semblance of true and honest belief is lost to it.

To what are we ever truly faithful? What is our capacity for commitment? I give you this pound of flesh. Do with it what you will.

I am and always will be . . . yours.

Feargus

34
Subsidence

White streaks run down Jeremy's dirty, stunned and speechless face. He's just a boy, after all, just a ten-year-old boy.

Lisa places her good hand, on his shoulder and leads him several steps away from the horrific scene. Then they both collapse onto the ground in the rain, hugging one another once again, sobbing.

She's freezing now, shaking with chills that come from deep inside, from some central core of ice-cold sickness and revulsion. The left wrist is starting to scream with pain sending shocks up to the elbow and shoulder and into her neck and head.

The hand is limp, slightly askew and must be gingerly supported.

She can't make it all the way into the house, so she lurches forward toward the bench that sits under the eaves and out of the rain. Every movement is propelled by adrenaline and nothing else.

Jeremy gets the cordless phone, a bottle of water, a towel for a splint, and as many blankets as he can carry out the door in one enormous armful. He takes the comforter from his own bed and places it gingerly across his mother's shoulders. Who should we call first?

Nine-one-one should probably be first. That will set things in motion. Then the neighbor up the hill in the green house, but first we'll try to reach your father on his cell phone.

She utters a small startled gasp at his surprised Hello.

"I'm all right. We're both all right."

"Lisa, it's five-thirty in the morning. Oh my god, tell me what happened."

So she did. She is crying now, as hard as she is trying to stay strong. Her voice is high and thin and she can't bring it down to its normal range. She is grateful for the comfort of his voice. She does her best to tell as much of the story as calmly and unsensationally as possible.

"I'll be home as soon as I can get there, Lisa."

I Love Yous are traded with stifled sobs and she hands the phone to Jeremy who says a few brave dry-eyed words to his dad and puts the phone down on the bench.

She and the boy stare blankly at the now dumb cordless phone as if they are expecting it to suddenly animate or to transform into some other magical device or perform some function that would offer them any kind of additional comfort or support. But no, it sits there cold, inanimate and mute.

The pain in the wrist is obscene and she has to squeeze her eyes almost shut to block out even a small portion of it.

They do not speak. She shudders from the cold.

There is still no normal sound from the animal enclosures. There are no birds, no chirping. Even the annoying caws of the crows are silent.

They hear the faint sound of a siren, then another. They do not move. The noise of the first siren chirps off at the top of the road.

First is a sheriff's car, then a state police vehicle and then an ambulance.

The cub reporter from the local newspaper was awake enough to hear the squawker box in his apartment and shot down the road in his beater of a car.

In another thirty minutes or so there will come the animal control van, driven by an earnest but still sleepy volunteer.

She is still in her bloodied and rain-drenched pink pajamas, wrapped in a brown plaid comforter. I must look mad, she thinks for a second. She has lacerations, contusions and, of course, the wrist thing. She's feeling light-headed and dehydrated and wishing she could throw up again.

The scene speaks for itself, but there were many questions nevertheless. Were there more dogs than these? Did that other dog get away? Were any other animals killed? Is anyone else on the property injured? Had you seen these dogs previously? Do you know of anything that might have sparked the attack?

No, no, no, no, no! She does her best to answer the questions as best she can while the officers and the newspaper reporter competently note her answers. She declines photographs.

The deputy picks up the guns and asks if any more firearms were involved. He empties the remaining ammunition from the chambers of the pistol and the rifle, and props both guns open out of the rain on the deck next to the door to the house.

He asks permission to enter the house. She stops to think about that for a minute, scrunching her brow together in the effort to think. Her judgment is cloudy.

"Just routine, ma'am. Just need to take a look around." She weakly nods in agreement. Any strength for objection or inquiry is not to be found. He enters cautiously through the screen door and makes a quick survey of the interior, looking for whatever he is trained to spot in these kinds of circumstances. He locates the gun cabinet in the bedroom and looks inside and takes a picture with a small camera from his shirt pocket. All seems in order.

The Stater walks over to the fight scene, looks over the carcasses of the dogs, takes a few pictures and bends down to Feargus, examining his multiple wounds.

"This one was your dog, ma'am? He took quite a beating." She nods.

"Goats are safe, though, and the other animals, too. Brave dog."

She nods again.

"And you folks, you're safe now and you'll be well."

Indeed.

She tries to make a smile appear on her face, but instead, she feels her face contort as a little creep of a smirk which runs across her eyes and down into her chin. She thinks, but does not say, that she is not quite ready to be cheered up. The family's best friend just lost his life to make sure that they were safe, and he did this only because of his ferocious loyalty and his willingness to preserve and protect what he loved.

The officer is just being kind. The items that he just listed, in that great calmly defined canon of good and hopeful outcomes, are facts only because of him, because of Feargus.

The big dense gray angry clouds in her head are getting thicker and moving faster and faster swirling out to the horizon.

"I know this dog," pipes up the Stater, looking at Bjorn's lifeless body. "Those folks live on my road out in the county.

This one went missing a while ago."

The EMTs are taking her blood pressure and pulse now, looking into her eyes with a bright little light, asking her how old she is and what day it is, what year the Phillies won the World Series or something like that, some sports analogy which went right over her throbbing cloud-muddled head.

The nearest neighbor to the north, up and dressed for her every morning rain-or-shine five mile run, races down the driveway to the house and takes one look at the grizzly scene.

Rigor mortis has just now set in on Nacho and she looks strange and bloody, like some macabre eviscerated stiff-legged piñata less the actual candy treats and the sense of joyful expectation. The other two strange dogs lie in grotesquely angled death lumps in the yard.

The neighbor gets to work in an effort to remain efficient and prevent the picture of the carnage from taking any kind of hold in her mind. She'll take the boy to her house with her, keep him home this day, call the school, feed the animals, she's done that before. She grabs some clothes and toiletries from the house and packs a quick bag for Lisa. She'll see to anything else that's needed. No problem. Don't worry. It's all taken care of. Don't worry.

The EMT is checking the lacerations on the boy's hands and gives the neighbor woman instructions for cleaning and covering, and the signs to look for if it should become a problem. Are the boy's shots up to date? Of course they are. Lisa is feeling testy about the obvious. Pain does that.

Jeremy bids a tearful goodbye to his mother with a long and meaningful hug. She gently slides the thick long hair back out of his face. He goes obediently off with the kindly Good Samaritan neighbor. The efficient lady has called her husband and his silver SUV is on the way down the driveway at this moment. She whisks the lad into the back seat and they are off. Thank god for special friends like this.

The car halts after it makes its U-turn to head back up the driveway. The back window rolls down and Jeremy looks at his mother for a long moment. He is choking back boy tears.

"You're awesome, mom, you gotta know that."

He says this with vehemence, his voice cracking at the end.

That was enough to start her waterworks again with sobbing and fat plopping tears. She reaches her good hand out toward him and does the best she can to smile between her tearing eyes. The window is rolled up and the car departs back up the hill.

It will take Mark ten or twelve exasperating hours to get home with a three hour wait for the next flight, multiple stops and layovers and a delay taking off from the fogged-in Santa Barbara airport resulting in a missed connection that caused yet another layover. Maddening as well as wildly frustrating. He is sick with worry and sadness that he wasn't there to protect his beloved family.

The deputy has called in his preliminary report. The newspaperman has asked a few final questions, mostly about Feargus. Animal Control has loaded the bodies of Nacho, Buster and big bulky Bjorn onto the van.

As she is strapped down to the gurney and trundled into the ambulance, she asks the animal control volunteer to have Fergus placed in the bolted feed locker behind the goat enclosure. She wants Mark to decide how to handle Feargus, to handle Feargus' body that is. She must start to think in those terms.

The ride to the hospital seems loud, grossly uncomfortable and endless. An IV line has been quickly and painlessly inserted, and Demerol added to the IV saline solution. Her head is becoming heavy and the wrist pain seems slightly more distant, like a familiar but obnoxious voice that keeps repeating your name from far away.

She is trying to hold on to a thought about the EMT, but it is starting to drift away. They are the last of the true doctors in America, or something like that. They use their senses, they touch, they listen, look, smell. Doctors don't do much of that any more. She is trying to hold that thought to share with Mark. Hold on, hold on, but it slips away and is overtaken by the remnants of other more savage images.

She still sees in her mind's eye the picture of the ferocious and lightning-fast onset of the violence and death, like a horror movie on fast-forward, mixed with the picture of the sweet unambiguous black eyes of a knowing Feargus. Good drugs.

The break in the wrist involves the distal radius and it is slightly displaced. The ER doc calls in a colleague to attempt a reduction.

There will be a hard cast for the next six weeks, and a cautious and painfully slow return to some kind of normal for this small family that will be simultaneously healing from numerous injuries.

But there will be no Feargus there to greet them on their return. No Feargus pacing excitedly at the gate with his customary joyous camaraderie, fidelity and gentle, quiet strength.

The next morning, after surveying the horrific blood-spattered scene at his home, Mark would dig a deep oblong hole along the west fence of the property. He will wrap Feargus' body in his favorite blanket, and place the remains in the heavy black plastic bag left by the animal control driver.

Then he will seal the bag and deposit it into the wheel barrow, roll it up the hill to the fence and then carefully lower it into the deep hole, packing the soil back down ever so tightly, tamping after every few inches of dirt. He will then top this small rectangle with pea gravel from the shed, and add some larger, heavier stones on top of that.

Finally, he will stand back, sweaty, tired and sad, but satisfied. He will observe his work, as pleased as it is possible to be at the outcome.

The goats, Bernadette and Annie, whose lives are owed to Feargus, will be nurtured and lovingly cared for and hand-fed during their period of grief at the loss of their dear old friend. In a few weeks they will begin to return to normal, but it will take them many more weeks after that to rest, comfortable and at ease, during the remaining long dark winter nights.

In the spring, three humans and two goats, overseen by a multicolor cat with a large fluffy tail who seems to be in full charge of the activity, will all help to plant a small Pacific Dogwood sapling right next to the neat grave.

From this spot, the little tree's leaves and precious creamy white blooms will be seen from the deck, the kitchen window, the boy's bedroom, and from the goat shed.

The tree will be hardy and do extremely well in its well-drained and wind-protected location, facing east and south, in front of a tribe of ancient Douglas-fir. It will bloom its sweet, simple, white, joyous blossoms profusely in its second year and every year thereafter.

This was not the way this family saw the fairy tale playing out, the young couple and the boy, on that magical afternoon that they first welcomed Feargus into their lives. They imagined something quite different for their future with this dog.

Instead of a fairy tale, their story of Feargus is now a local legend. That will have to do.

The body of Cotton, the last to be seen on these pages of that other circumstantially yet serially bonded, faithful, loving, unlucky, unlikely and mischievous feral family, was never found. She became a gift to the endless cycle of natural predation occurring out there just beyond our front doors.

Her confreres, our feral friends Buster, Nacho and Bjorn, were incinerated without ritual or liturgy later that morning at the county animal control office.

35
Cold

"Tracy, I don't understand how you found out that Feargus had died."

Ian and I had been preparing dinner together. A Panang curry with lots of green beans and other vegetables. Lots to cut and chop. There had been a little Chopin playing on the sound system and I had been endeavoring to tell him everything I had learned about that event.

"It wasn't right away."

"What happened?"

About a month after Feargus died, I received a phone call from Lisa. She was hoping that I would know how to locate Rob.

She wanted to tell him that something had happened to Feargus.

Lisa and Mark had owned the dog for more than three years and they and Jeremy had become very attached to him. Lisa wanted us, me at least, if Rob could not be reached, to know the story and what a brave and wonderful dog he was. To her and her family he was a real hero. He single-handedly saved the goats and the rest of the animals.

Lisa also wanted us to know about the dogwood tree and the proper burial. Seemed important to her that we knew about that, and I was so very grateful for it, but I felt an overwhelming sense of loss. I took some quiet time, thinking about all she told me, and then there were some tears, and a few days of walking around with his big beautiful face in the forefront of my mind, and the idea of his incredible fealty in my heart.

Feargus

I lost Feargus twice. Even though it had been years since he was given away, I still felt the sting of that first loss.

I wished it could have been different, that the dog I neglected and helped to abuse had been some awful mangy disagreeable cur and not Feargus, but then, why should that matter? Abuse is abuse - habitual, casual, or unintentional. I guess I'm still working through that guilt.

Ian apologized for the interruption. He had to leave for a meeting at seven o'clock and I had been taking my time telling this story over dinner. When he left, I poured myself another glass of Riesling, went into the living room and stood watching the town's lights come on at the tall windows out to the deck.

I was thinking that, in the whole time that Rob and I were together, he only met my best friend Maggie on two occasions, once when she came to the coast to consult with the School District about a potential art curriculum, and another time when we stopped by as we were passing through town. So it is probably not surprising that Ian never met Rob. Ian and Maggie were my old 'out of town' friends, and they were not easily welcomed into my life with Rob.

Rob simply did not like Maggie. He made no effort to conceal it. He said she was pretentious and affected. For some reason, he felt small or left out, or something else when she was around and the two of us were enjoying a good laugh with our free-ranging conversations. We tried to involve him, but those efforts mostly failed.

He didn't seem to like any of my friends, as a matter of fact, for one reason or another, and he made no effort to try.

Though I have told Ian so much of my very personal history regarding family and dogs, I haven't told him much about the uncomfortable story of the end of my relationship with Rob.

I liked the idea that I was not polluting our lovely young relationship with some putrid and warty scenario which did not really need sharing, in the greater scheme of things.

The relationship devolved with a speed which spun my head for a time, but I remember with clarity every minute of the painful break down.

The act of giving away Feargus, I feel, was the penultimate blow to the relationship. But the undisputed ultimate blow occurred after that, in early December of that same year.

This is the part of my story that I really did not want to share with Ian, at least for the foreseeable future. Nevertheless, the memories of the end are deep and indelible, drawn with a dark, disturbing palette. So with a sigh I will let it go.

It had been an odd gray day, on the hill above the not very pretty town. It was by now a couple of years after Rob had surrendered Feargus to the new family.

It was a day with a suffocating sky, heavy and pregnant with itself, a kind of sky that causes people to move slowly, quietly, with their heads down, making only furtive eye contact.

We don't have days like this very often, here on the edge of the world, where it would still be possible, given the right circumstances, to once again imagine that the world was flat.

In this place we have wet in winter. That's a given, accepting of very little nuance or variation. We are always guaranteed our winter wet. We plan for it. We expect it. We understand it.

People stomp in the rain; they splash through puddles, their voices are raised in the rain to match the sound level of the dripping drumbeats on cars and concrete and metal roofs. Rain is all noise and pattern and percussion. Rarely do we need to brace for rain.

But in this muffled-up quiet, we know there will be snow.

Like our pagan ancestors, this great gravid sky gives us pause.

We don't have days like this here.

I couldn't allow these musings on the weather, even with this rare and mysterious forecast, to interfere.

Rob had gone out for dinner with a manufacturer's rep and later they were joined by a local contractor at the bar at the Holiday Inn. I got a text from him about eight o'clock. Don't wait up.

I put on a pair of heavy socks under my Uggs, not so much because I was cold, but because there was the potential for cold. I got up and opened the door to the deck to quickly look around the jamb at the thermometer. Thirty-one. It was thirty-three an hour ago. Tap-tap-tap on the barometer. Thirty and falling.

I felt an even deeper chill, one that warm wooly socks could not quiet.

Unquestionably, the relationship was in deep trouble, had been for some time. I don't know exactly how long.

Gradually the initial blush had worn off. I think this took at least a couple of years. There were sudden unexplained absences and weird gotcha moments. I am not a game player, and since I couldn't compete, I had started to feel that the ground was no longer solid under my feet.

There were odd occasions when parts of a puzzle, as an example, or the instructions for a new device, or some other necessary item, were deliberately left out or misplaced. I am perfectly capable of reading directions for just about anything, but this meant that I had to ask for help or assistance.

So I was at once was made to feel stupid, incompetent and dependent. It always created a profound squeeze in the middle of my chest when I came across the 'missing' bit of instruction neatly folded up on a corner of his desk, or in a shirt pocket ready for the laundry.

And then there were the feelings of abandonment. He would just walk out the back door if we were preparing for some function. She doesn't want to do it my way, so let's see how she gets herself out of it without me.

I always did get myself out of whatever predicament that came my way. I managed to compensate for the other half of the chore left undone, or figured a solution to being stranded without a key, or ad-libing what I could remember of his speech to the board. I always managed, but those moments left scars, red, angry, ugly scars.

There had to be some mammoth demons that were causing some of this behavior, demons that controlled so much of how Rob thought and what he did or how he treated people. They must have been great scabby foul-breathed monsters.

I suddenly realized I was very cold. Then a stern lecture to myself. Stop it. Get back to work! I breathed a very large sigh. I was still desperately looking for distraction, and the snow came to my rescue.

Big white determined flakes were now falling softly with regularity and persistence. The streets had been dry for about twelve hours before this time, so it looked like the snow would stick this time.

Why do we say 'stick' about crystalline bits of moisture that land, more than stick, on a given surface? Do they have a choice? Could they unstick and bounce away to stick another place?

The flakes were mesmerizing. There was not a car on the street. It was so very quiet.

My Earl Grey tea was almost gone; the ceramic cup no longer held its warmth. I had accomplished a great deal of the work I swore to do that night, but I was still going to have to push myself to finish.

It was dark now, and from this hillside you could see that the lights of town had come on across the gully. White, yellow and orange orbs infused and refracted the constant snow, like the giant halos of the gilded saints in an iconographer's Last Supper, reflecting off the thick white illuminated sky. It was magical and beautiful.

I stood there and drifted into those halos like the flakes of falling snow.

By this time in the relationship, there was fear, uncertainty, and the constant undercurrent of violence.

He loved knives.

There were freshly sharpened knives in all kinds of places, in a briefcase, behind the visor in the car.

I was completely willing to care for, to do my best for the big wounded bear of a man, but I had become very aware of the demons, and had seen far too many glimpses of the Mister Hyde and his friends Smith and Jones.

My life was spent tiptoeing on eggshells around their various personas. That's how I explained it to our couples therapist. She told me that I had to choose whether or not tiptoeing on eggshells was an acceptable way to spend the rest of my life, because the behavior would more than likely not appreciably change.

I splashed some hot water on my face and looked into the bathroom mirror. My somewhat sad, definitely tired eyes looked back at me. I was ready for it to be over.

Someone in a Jeep with big-ass studded tires was coming up the driveway into the cul-de-sac. The tires crunched that special new snow chomp as each fluffy aerated flake became compressed by the metal stud. He pulled into a driveway just below me and shut off the motor. It was crazily quiet once again.

It was well after midnight now, and the cold, silent white curtain still came, oh so slowly and relentlessly down. There were about three inches of new snow already 'stuck.' I looked at my phone. Nothing.

During the long quiet and slowly precipitating night, the temperature rose a degree or two, and a heavy dense wet fog rolled down through the county, as if from the atomizer of some insanely giant fine French perfume bottle.

And then, at 4:52 AM, the coldest time of night, SLAM! Down came the temperature just three teensy tiny degrees to coat one thin half inch of crystalline ice over the totality of roadbeds, driveways, bridge surfaces, hand rails, secondary roads, hillsides, and sidewalks, all of it.

It was a lovely crackle crisp coating like the frozen chocolate topping on a Good Humor bar, slick, crunchy, treacherous underfoot and completely and unremittingly ferocious in every other way.

Airplane tires skidded almost off the runway, police cars careened into drifts and became buried. Brakes on cars in fresh snow were as useless as brakes on a skiff in the bay.

Vans careened into the backs of other cars. Power poles, already heavy with snow, snapped with the sudden extra weight of the ice and then, the one remaining sound in my private world, the drone of the refrigerator motor, abruptly ended.

No one in their right mind would be out on the road on a night like this. The phone startled me.

The contractor's girlfriend had just picked up him and Rob at the police station. She took them in her Jeep with studded tires to her house to dry out. Another DUII, driving under the influence in sub-optimal weather conditions. He'd slid across the street and plowed his Lexus into a stone fence. They weren't hurt. And nobody died.

These thoughts of snow and ice, these indelible metaphors – they represent my realities - the frozen wasteland of my marriage.

There would be an intervention. My family members would beg and implore me to be gone from this insanity, to be safely away from the constantly sharpened knives, the not very veiled threats which even the dog could sense, and the surly, sullen and overt aggression toward my family and closest friends.

And there would be a divorce soon after this time, this ugly, chilly early December time, with much very painful and avoidable heartbreak.

He would soon take off for parts unknown, leaving behind a trail of lies and deceits.

All love had turned to animosity; all understanding had turned to obfuscation and confusion; all warmth had turned to icy cold.

It was now after seven in the morning. The kitchen faucet had been on dribble to keep the pipes from freezing. I had been writing with a gel pen on a lined yellow legal pad by candlelight and the brightness of the snowy sky, which had the whole apartment bathed in a bright gray ethereal film noir light.

I got into bed, pulled both of my heaviest down comforters up to my chin, and tried to sleep for a few hours. I would need some rest to face all the unknowns of this coming day.

For me there would be no anger, no bargaining, just acceptance.

Ultimately the demons and monsters became too much and demanded their day.

Just one year and a few days after this time, the demons hovered all around Rob in the driver's seat of his white 2000 Isuzu Trooper, in the parking lot of the Piggly Wiggly off Route 79 just south of Pine Bluff, Arkansas, where he blew his brains out with the Glock 19 that he kept, loaded, under the front seat of the car in a black and yellow DeWalt drill case.

And that was that.

Feargus

36
A Choice

Ian awoke the next morning enthusiastic and rested. He was still filled with new ideas, and the general flush of accomplishment that came from presenting his new research at the conference. He was pleased with the positive response, and that made me smile. From what he said, there were a number of colleagues who would like to hear more about the ideas. In fact, he had already been asked to do a couple of university lectures around the country.

After breakfast we talked a little bit more about my project.

We had a great discussion about the basic ideas of the piece, and how I might go about attacking such a gigantic subject. He mentioned an author I might like to reference from a psychology point of view. And that's where we left the subject.

The following weekend we were off for a hike up the mountain next to the arboretum with our new four-legged friend. There is a little café near campus with a nice brick outdoor patio, and this is fast becoming our go-to place for a weekend breakfast. Amadeus is remarkably well-behaved and he has made quite a few friends at this spot in the last few visits.

A quick stop at the hardware store for some insulation for the doggie door, and we were on the way to our little mountain.

Amadeus was trotting along happily right beside us, managing to do the climb without encouragement or assistance. He seemed excited to be out with both of us. The hill was about a thousand feet in elevation over about a mile and half. As we neared the summit, he was doing just fine. We felt like proud new parents. He even managed to trot a bit with us near the top. I found it amazing that a little bit of education and training was making this so easy and pleasant for me, with the help of a good-natured, responsive puppy.

The vista from the top was beautiful as always, regardless of the weather. There is a 360 degree view of the city from this spot and it is amazing to see into the distance on a clear day such as this, as the jagged urban edges morph into exurbs then into lush green farmland in the distance. Ultimately you can see forestland with the nearest mountains tall and sharp in the backdrop. It never ceases to be breathtakingly beautiful.

My favorite kind of chunky bulbous clouds were hanging here and there in the sky.

We stopped for some water all around, just enjoyed the view for a few minutes, and then started back down the trail.

"I've made a decision about the big project."

"Oh? What's up? Tell me"

"I'm sending the proposal back to the client. I'm going to decline the commission."

"What?"

Ian had stopped abruptly on the 'what?' and a couple of downhill hikers behind us, who were power-walking at a similar pace, almost slammed into him. We were all on this downward march with gravity keeping us in lockstep and abrupt stops could often be problematic. We apologized and moved off the path.

"Really? Why?"

"I told them that they could have all my notes and that I would consult on the structure if they want me to, as the project continues, but . . . "

"But why? I'm very surprised, Trace. I thought you were so interested. You've been keeping this to yourself. Please talk to me."

"I knew you were busy with the conference, and I just didn't find the moment."

"You seemed pretty excited. What happened? I'd like to understand."

We walked a little down the trail to a little turn-out spot with a north view, and leaned against the rough rock retaining wall. My white puffy clouds had dispersed on this side of the hill. I took another sip of water. I was hoping to make this explanation lucid.

I told him that it had been fairly exhausting working my way through all the complex feelings regarding Feargus, and all the other associated difficult issues wrapped around my phobia. I felt like I was making enormous progress thanks to Ian's patience, and to the amiable and intelligent Mr. Amadeus, but I needed a little more time.

This project was immense. I would have to throw myself onto it with totality. I would need some new software and perhaps some other equipment, and I definitely would have to hire staff. Neither of these things is really problematic, the real issue is that I just don't feel like I would have the gravitas, or the confidence that I would need to do justice to the project at this time. Not as the primary writer, at least.

"But you put some ideas together already, no?

"Yes. I already had an approach sketched out in my mind and I'm sure that I could turn that mass of data into something very interesting and gripping. But on the emotional front, I just didn't know."

"Ian, I have my own story to tell, a story that is very important to me. I've had the epiphany of a lifetime, and I want to put it down on paper. But its a much smaller, more personal story, and I need to tell it in order to let it go.

"You've thought it through pretty thoroughly. I should have expected that you would. I'm just so surprised."

"I don't want you to be worried, Ian, I have plenty of other work coming in. I was going to have to say no to a couple of smaller projects that I was very interested in, but now I'll be able to take them on with a light heart."

Ian scrunched his eyes closed and spread his hand across his forehead in thought for just for a moment. I could sense that he was weighing how to respond, always careful of my feelings while being direct and honest. I put my hand on his raised arm and smiled.

"Ian, somebody else will get the Emmy for this one, and that's fine with me. I already have one."

I took his face in my hands.

"For the memory of Feargus, for the love of Feargus, I'd like to try to make a difference in my own way, one dog at a time."

We stood there in absolute quiet for a minute or two.

"That's my girl."

That was all he said.

Then off our little trio went, now on the modest decline, down the gravel path, his arm now around my shoulder, a liver and white Springer Spaniel loping along, happy on his leash, at my side. There was not much more I could ask. We were a family.

We love Amadeus. I love Amadeus. How about that? He is becoming my little friend, and I am happy with the relationship.

I feel it developing day by day.

But I still often think about Feargus, absolutely. I still miss him. Letting go of the guilt does not mean forgetting it happened.

His picture remains on the bookshelf behind my desk. I have no choice but to see it on a daily basis, but I am happy to say that glancing at it no longer shoves a cold stiletto of guilt through my heart as it once did.

I am very glad that in the end, I didn't say no to the idea of a new dog. Amadeus definitely makes Ian happy. It is so much fun to watch. And I am happy to say that I am no longer awash in debilitating regret about my part in Feargus' cyclic mistreatment. As Ian would say, "facing so many unaddressed childhood traumas" has been a true and difficult journey. I didn't realize how much my life, my beliefs, my outlooks, were being affected by these early traumas. I also did not know how deep I would have to delve in order to shake free of them.

The one remaining twinge of regret that I continue to hang on to is that, during the years of my acquaintance with Feargus, my mind was so totally closed to all of his possibilities. Perhaps telling his story will be enough to salve that nagging culpability.

I plan to keep his picture in a place of prominence in my office. Perhaps someday new pictures of Amadeus will begin to overcrowd it. But that time is not just yet. Not just yet.

213

An established playwright, McDonald turns her abundant imagination
to a story of haunted memories and sublime transformation.
Raised in Philadelphia, she has lived in Oregon for many years.
Feargus is McDonald's debut novel.

Feargus

Return of King Arthur
&
The Wisdom Keepers

(Sample Chapter)

Chapter 1

The Otherworld

Isle of Avalon, Between Time

Accolon navigated the glass ship with ease through the rough Atlantic waters. The vessel was almost transparent as it glided across cerulean waves. Morgen stood in the hull beneath the massive white sails, occasionally diving overboard for a swim and watching the life of the fish. Under the sea she called to the blue whales to accompany them. Soon the largest mammal ever known to exist appeared as a magnificent pair, and their songs guided the ship toward Avalon. A blue circle appeared in the water, crackling with energy, and they sailed through the star portal into a parallel world.

Morgen, sensing that she was close to her true home, walked to the bow of the ship, and then she raised her arms. The mist parted and an island rose up. She could see the light of the crystal that hovered like a full moon above the mystical island. A sky temple stood at the top of a rocky peak from which flowed a crystal-clear waterfall. The water from the fall streamed down to the lower ocean temple, which was surrounded by trees and a secret village. During her last visit,

Morgen had brought her wounded brother Arthur with her. This time she had come to see him, and request his return.

Morgen steered the ship with her magic to a long, narrow pier, where they docked. Stepping onto the pier, she was immediately flooded with the scent of lilacs and other blossoming flowers. Apple blossoms drifted through the air like snowflakes. Morgen breathed in and smiled. Accolon joined her and took her hand. Together they went to greet the Avalonians.

A woman so silvery white she was almost translucent greeted them farther down on the pier.

"Argante." Morgen embraced the priestess gently.

The two women stepped back, gazing at each other with true affection. Then they turned their focus to the knight amongst them.

"Accolon." Argante gave him a nod of respect. "Welcome to our fair isle."

They stepped from the pier into a smaller magic boat in the shape of a slender grey dragon holding a lantern in its jaws. The boat sailed through the rivers that curved into the heart of Avalon, the paradisical Isle of Apples.

Soon they approached the steps to the main ocean-level temple. There, in the courtyard, nine enchanted women were waiting for them, each wearing a different brightly colored cloak.

"The nine witches of Ystawingun," Accolon muttered, seeming concerned.

"Nonsense," Morgen snapped. "They are my sisters."

Moronoe, wearing a silver cloak, stepped forward with a silver bell, which she handed to Accolon.

"You may pass through the isle of women, but you may not stay for long lest you lose your way," she told Accolon.

Accolon shook the bell and listened to the lovely sound. It was like the sweet voice of a nightingale.

Gliten, wearing a richly colored violet cape with gold embroidered trim, handed Morgen a golden apple, and then she offered Accolon a silver pear. With grateful nods, they accepted small gifts from some of her other sisters. Morgen brought colorful ribbons for her sisters. After the friendly gift exchange, Thitis began playing the strings of her cittern. Feeling dazed by the music, Accolon staggered.

"The magic is overwhelming you," Morgen told him. "Come with me."

Morgen nodded to the priestesses in the courtyard, then took Accolon's hand. Together they ascended a long, winding staircase made of intricately cut stones that led up to the inner chamber of the main temple. The interior was decorated with luxuriant tapestries and finely woven area rugs. Morgen slipped her shoes off and Accolon followed, and then he felt the miraculous warmth of the stone floors. Accolon noticed that wherever they went, the weather was perfect, and his body responded by feeling increasingly vigorous.

They followed the winding staircase until, at last, they arrived at the upper temple that they had seen on the rocky peak as they had approached the island. Luxurious beds with colorful floral throws lined the west side of the main circular building. A gentle breeze wrapped around them like an embrace.

"There are healing spirits here," Morgan explained. "Rest now and let them get to know you. Whatever needs to be restored within you will be cured now. This is where I brought Arthur after the Battle of Camlann."

"And his nephew Mordred?" Accolon asked.

"We also restored him."

They gazed out across the sea. Off in the distance, they could see the whales departing.

"Are you happy to be home?"

"Immensely," Morgen replied.

www.ingramcontent.com/pod-product-compliance
Lightning Source LLC
Chambersburg PA
CBHW060601310726
48982CB00008B/1194/J